SURGEON'S MATE

SURGEON'S MATE

by

Linda Collison

Fireship Press
www.FireshipPress.com

ISBN-13: 978-1-61179-142-6

BISAC Subject Headings:
    FIC014000   FICTION / Historical
    FIC032000   FICTION / War & Military
    FIC047000   FICTION / Sea Stories

Address all correspondence to:
Fireship Press, LLC
P.O. Box 68412
Tucson, AZ 85737

Or visit our website at:
www.FireshipPress.com

Introduction
October 19, 1762

So much depends on a name.

My father named me Patricia, called me *his little Patra*, but didn't give me his last name, the name, and the legitimacy I wanted. I was born a Kelley, as was my mother, an indentured servant from Ireland, who kept my father's plantation house in Barbados. I have few memories of the woman who gave birth to me, for she died of a tropical fever when I was five.

After she died my father shipped me off to England to be raised in a remote boarding school—The Wiltshire School for Young Ladies, a repository for inconvenient daughters such as I. There I grew up—aloof, awkward, lonely—loving horses and the out-of-doors, loathing needlework, French lessons and small talk, waiting impatiently for my father to send for me, to bring me back to Barbados. I had not yet come to terms with the fact that I was merely the product of his desire for my young mother. (I would eventually find out my father had many salacious desires, which he ardently pursued without qualm, yet kept a proper wife and issue in London.) Yet he was not a bad man, just a man, and had he not gambled his money away I'm certain my father would not have left me to fend for myself.

Holding tight to the rare letter he sent, I survived my institutionalized childhood, and at sixteen was endowed with neither beauty nor patience. I was too brash and fiery-tempered, I'm told, and had no prospects for marriage. My horse was my best friend, I lived for the day my father would send for me, and I would return to Barbados to be mistress of the plantation. All naught but childish dreams. My father had never paid a penny toward my tuition, and upon his death when no payment came from his estate, I was dismissed from the school.

A tall, ungainly orphan, I stowed away on a merchantman bound for Barbados with a desperate and ill-thought-out scheme to claim the sugar plantation, still not knowing my father had lost it, had gambled it away before his death.

England was at war with France, in what would later be referred to as the Seven Years War, a rather prosaic name to distinguish it from the various other struggles for land and sea power we engaged in throughout the century. At the time I knew little of our political struggles and even less about the seafaring world, and I had no idea the tubby bark I chose to board was carrying ordinance to the West Indian forts. For me, it was a means to my own ends, and while the course of events that followed were not at all what I had hoped for, my life was forever changed by my impetuous decision to board the merchantman that chill November night in Portsmouth.

At seventeen, I married Aeneas MacPherson, ship surgeon, and became Mrs. MacPherson, loosing my former name and identity in the process. When my husband died of yellow fever less than a year later, his name was important to my survival, along with the name MacPherson, the skills he taught me, and the instruments of his trade.

And so I shed *Patricia* like an inconvenient skin, becoming *Patrick MacPherson*, surgeon's mate, of His Majesty's frigate, *Richmond,* on its undercover mission to Havana to take part in a pivotal siege that would cripple the Spanish who had recently joined the war against Great Britain.

One man aboard knew my secret, but even he didn't call me Patricia. The gunner called me *Princess*, the somewhat mocking title he gave me in jest when he discovered me, two years ago, hidden away in the bosun's locker of another ship, which is another story altogether. Now the gunner called me that teasing endearment in a whisper, when we were alone, which aboard a crowded frigate was too seldom, and most risky.

Chapter One

"This leg must be amputated," Charles Brantigan announced, his voice gritty as a holystone. "And you, Mr. MacPherson, will conduct the operation."

The surgeon looked at me, his blue eyes cloudy, nearly blind, yet still shrewd. Still as intimidating as the day I signed ship's articles. I nodded, my face a mask. At least I hoped it was.

"Mr. Freeman, you and I shall assist," Brantigan continued.

We stood between the hammocks and hanging cots, our feet apart for balance. The wind had risen and backed, the water was rough. The hammocks shivered and swayed erratically with the new motion. My stomach churned.

"No, please!" The patient's protest sounded more like the squeak of a rodent than that of a soldier.

Ignoring him, Brantigan untied the strips of muslin that held the thick pad of dressing, revealing the injury for our inspection. The kneecap, shattered by the recoil of a cannon a fortnight ago, looked like an overripe plum. The calf and foot were beginning to mottle as the discoloration spread distally from the swollen patella, a seeping wine colored stain. Leaning over for a better look in the dim light below decks, I caught a faint but unmistakable whiff of mortifying flesh.

I was becoming accustomed to the stench of illness. Such vile smells no longer made me retch. As Aeneas MacPherson might have said, were he still alive, *a discerning nose is one of the many tools in a ship surgeon's kit*. Indeed, my sense of smell was becoming keener and at the same time, my emotional response to repugnant odors was becoming dulled.

Brantigan cleared his raspy throat and fixed me in his fading field of view. "You are up to the task, Mr. MacPherson?"

I glanced at the young man's face, gone pasty white and causing his ginger colored freckles to stand out more than ever. So difficult to meet their questioning eyes when you had so little to offer them and so much easier to look at the injury or diseased part itself, rather than a man's face. Yet he caught my glance and held my eyes with his, asking me wordlessly if this were all a bad joke, a dream from which he might awaken. I forced myself not to look away, yet my own eyes surely gave me away. I was powerless to change his fate. All I could offer was a sharp knife and a well-meaning but not entirely qualified hand.

"Perhaps if I blister it again?" I said, glad for the excuse to tear my eyes away from the patient's awful gaze.

Now Dudley Freeman's glance was a dart in my side. "Why waste time blistering a rotting leg when a scalpel and bone saw will do the job in a wink? I'll do it, MacPherson, if you haven't the stomach for it."

Brantigan removed his spectacles and wiped his eyes with his fingers. "Please be so kind as to hold your tongue, Mr. Freeman. Now then, Mr. MacPherson, you can save the limb or you can save the man, but I'll wager you cannot save both. Unless a miracle occurs by eight bells tomorrow morning the

leg must come off else the poison spreads through his body
and kills him."

The stifled sob that escaped from the young soldier's
throat brought tears close to my eyes, yet it was Brantigan
who placed his palsied hand on the soldier's arm. I believe he
meant it to be a compassionate gesture, but the boy flinched
at the touch.

"Easy, lad. Easy. How old are you?" Brantigan asked.

"Sixteen, sir."

"Lee is your name?"

The young man nodded, his eyes brimming.

"What is your given name? What name does your mother
call you?"

"Everett."

"And where is your home, lad?"

A slight shrug. "Rhode Island."

"I am heartily sorry Everett," Brantigan said in a low and
gravelly voice. "But it must be done, you know. The gangrene
will kill you if we linger. You did not survive the siege of Havana to die of gangrene on your way back to Rhode Island.
You will go on to live a productive life, many a man has after
loosing a limb."

We all fell silent. A man's sigh from a nearby hammock
brought a slovenly girl out of the shadows to attend him.

Out on the spar deck the men called out in unison as they
hauled on the lines, bracing the yards, their voices carrying
across the decks and down the wooden hull, ringing
throughout the vessel. Masculine voices, powerful and purposeful. The frigate responded, creaked under the demand of
the sails, and dug her shoulder deeper into the sea. The
sounds made me long for the invigorating air aloft, the fresh,
wet wind in my face. I would surely rather climb to the tops
in a gale than have to amputate Private Everett Lee's leg.

"Mr. MacPherson, a word with you in my cabin," the surgeon said. "Mr. Freeman, carry on with today's sick call on the foredeck."

"Aye, sir." Freeman threw me a victorious smirk before clattering up the companionway. My heart lurched like the ship itself, for I was afraid I was to be reprimanded for some breech of military etiquette, or worse, that my superior officer had discovered the truth about me. Reluctantly I followed the old man down to the orlop deck to a crowded little room that served him as both berth and office.

Brantigan closed the door behind us and fumbled to light a glim. Though it was broad daylight on deck, deep in the belly of the ship it was as dark as a coal cellar. He eased himself into his chair, wincing as his knees bent, and bade me sit down in the other chair, opposite his cluttered desk. The cabin air was oppressive. My sense of entrapment soared and I fought the familiar rising panic that enclosed spaces bring upon me.

"Now then Mr. MacPherson, I must ask you to take over the bulk of the record keeping for me. My eyes, they're worsening by the day." He rifled through the logbook with shaking hands. His tremors too, were getting more pronounced; yet he said nothing about them and we all pretended not to notice.

"Aye, sir." I waited as he found the page for which he was searching. So that was it? He just wanted some help keeping the ship's medical log? I took courage and said what was on my mind.

"Mr. Brantigan, about the amputation..."

Brantigan looked up with the swiftness of a harrier intent on a field mouse. "Are you challenging my judgment? My eyes might be failing me but there's nothing wrong with my nose. That wound is gangrenous."

"No sir, of course not. I mean, I'm not challenging your judgment." I swallowed hard. "But don't you think Mr. Freeman should do the cutting?"

"Why?" He fixed me in his gaze. Though his vision was poor, I knew his perception was keen.

I felt my face and neck redden although I willed them not to. My coloring was always giving me away.

"Mr. Freeman is the more experienced."

"Precisely," he growled. "High time you had more practice, wouldn't you say?"

Reluctantly I nodded, aware of the fens forming in my armpits, dampening my clean shirt.

In truth, I was an imposter, not a bona fide surgeon's mate. Though trained by a man who was both surgeon and medical doctor, the finest in either profession, I had never sat for my exam. I had some knowledge, yes, and some experience, but my identity and credentials were shams.

Brantigan's expression softened. "I'm keen to see how well you perform, though I'm certain you'll do well or I never would have hazarded the young man's life on it. A little experience, a little confidence, that's all you're lacking Patrick."

Out of Brantigan's mouth, that was praise indeed. Yet it only made me squirm.

"And have a talk with our young Yankee foot soldier," Brantigan said. "Prepare him for his ordeal tomorrow. Help him find his courage and make peace with his Maker, perhaps call in the chaplain. Mr. Freeman and I shall assist you, but you'll call the shots, you'll do the cutting and ligation, you'll do the closing as well. Feel free to consult my surgical text." He pulled a book from the shelf behind him and handed it to me. *The Sea Surgeon, or the Guinea Man's Vade Mecum*, written by T. Aubrey. I was familiar with this work, for Aeneas had made me study it when I was apprenticed to him.

"Yes, sir," I managed to say, clutching the ragged manual in my hands like a talisman.

Shipboard operations were not new to me. I had assisted Freeman in sawing off more than one shattered limb during the grisly Havana campaign this summer past, but I had never taken charge. I had been an automaton those many weeks, merely doing what I was told, handing over tourniquets, bone saws, ladles of hot pitch. I couldn't recall a single name or face, just the chorus of their cries, the smell of warm blood and hot tar on flesh. The sight of severed legs and arms, livid and lifeless, covered with maggots, was a living nightmare. However, Havana was beyond the horizon, in the past, and I had tried to drop the memories overboard in the wake.

It was bad enough he must lose his leg; I didn't want to be the one to do the cutting. What if I wasn't strong enough? Surely, I wouldn't be quick enough. What if I froze? What if I failed? I thumbed through the pages of Aubrey's manual not seeing a single word or drawing.

Brantigan seemed oblivious to my anxiety. Rummaging about in the clutter of his desktop, he found a quill and an inkwell and with palsied hands pushed it toward me.

"Now then, Mr. MacPherson, if you'll write while I dictate we'll have our treatment book up to date in no time."

Chapter Two

I had signed on the frigate *Richmond* nearly ten months ago, taking the identity of a dead man, my late husband's nephew who had served as surgeon's mate aboard a warship that went down in the Indian Ocean, all souls lost. Patrick MacPherson had been his name in life; and now it was mine. I chose it because it was close enough to my real name that I felt easy with it. In return, I did not want to disgrace the name but to uphold its honor through my actions. It was the least I could do for my dear Aeneas who had loved both his young nephew and his young wife.

The *Richmond* was sent along with a fleet of two hundred ships, commanded by Sir George Pocock, who had recently done so well against the French in India, to take Cuba, a fabulously wealthy city and the stronghold of the Spaniards. The Earl of Albemarle led the fourteen thousand soldiers we carried on our transports. It was a daring plan, some would say mad, to approach Havana from the east via the Old Bahama Channel. It was a treacherous strait of water that had sunk many a galleon, and was avoided by ships of our day. Our combined attack, by sea and land, and the subsequent siege was eventually successful, but at a great price. Many of our sailors were sent ashore to assist the army; Freeman and I were sent to run a field hospital. So many of our men died in the weeks that followed. In fact, many more men died from tropical disease than from enemy fire, and men were still dying. I myself, had fallen ill to the dreaded fever, but was one of the fortune ones to recover.

Some weeks after our victory at Havana the frigate Richmond was bound for New York bearing 36 colonial soldiers suffering from fevers, fluxes and war wounds. In our wake sailed *Aeolus*, a transport carrying hundreds more casualties. We were returning them home, the most of them hailing from New York, Connecticut and Rhode Island, their transport having been sunk off the coast of Cuba. Where we would be sent from New York was anyone's guess, for the war between Great Britain and France and Spain had spread around the globe, even to the Philippine Islands in the far Pacific.

With any luck at all, *Richmond* would be sent back to England and paid off, though it was rumored there wasn't enough money in the treasure to pay us. We would be kept fighting or patrolling some predicted, until the money was raised. In any case, we'd be sent somewhere for His Majesty's frigates don't remain long in one place, you can bet a month's back wages on that.

Yet I was growing accustomed to navy life and in many ways I liked it. I was accumulating my two-and-seventy shillings a month on the books and thus far had no opportunity to squander it, nor was I in the red with the purser or any man. As a petty officer, I had the privilege of three meals a day, my allowance of beer and spirits, a deck over my head— and I felt I had earned the respect of my fellow shipmates. We had forged an extraordinary bond, we *Richmond* men, in the long and grisly siege of Havana, and although there were occasional disagreements, we were as close and loyal as brothers.

* * * * *

It was not as difficult to carry out my deceit as one might think. I was handily androgynous, a big-boned girl with one of those faces that, at nineteen years of age, was neither girl-ish nor boyish but a perfect blend of both. Had I a choice in the matter, I believe I would have chosen to be born male, though a man's life is no easy thing either, I've come to learn.

I wore a man's breeches and I flattened my not-very-significant breasts with a swath of muslin wrapped around my body beneath my shirt. A cambric stock disguised my feminine throat. My complexion had suffered from exposure to the sun and a ridiculous mass of freckles hid the fact that I had no need of shaving my face. (Even so, I performed the ritual every morning along with the other men. I could strop a blade and run it over my skin without nicking my lip or cut-ting my throat, even on a tossing ship.)

My new identity served me well, but I constantly worried that I would be found out and stripped of my rank. I would be reduced to becoming one of the invisible females, robbed of my livelihood, and forever dependent on the goodwill of others, the protection of men.

Presenting myself as a young man and living in close proximity to so many other men was fraught with the chance of exposure, but I was becoming quite adept at it. I found it was far more natural to straddle a chair, to yawn and stretch when the need arose, to laugh or sneeze wholeheartedly in-stead of daintily holding back.

In fact, except for the worry of being found out I was quite enjoying my life as a male. I thrilled to the free-dom—the physical freedom of climbing the mast if I felt like it, just for the challenge and exhilaration; the sovereignty of earning my own money and squandering or saving it as I saw fit; the liberty of expressing my own opinion on any matter that struck my fancy, and assuming the accompanying risk. I had also learned that a man must be willing to defend his words or have them figuratively—and sometimes quite literally—stuffed down his throat.

Good riddance to bone corsets and voluminous skirts! I preferred dressing as a man for the comfort breeches, men's shirts, and sturdy shoes gave me. Truthfully, I probably looked better in men's clothing than I did in a fashionable gown and bonnet; tall, broad of shoulder and slight of bosom as I was. I had learned to walk like a man, to stride confidently rather than to daintily mince. I had no ample hips to conceal, though I wore my breeches a bit more loose than was the fashion, so as not to call attention to the part of my anatomy that might have appeared lacking to a prying eye.

As surgeon's mates Mr. Freeman and I had access to the officer's privy, a rude but private place to relieve oneself (and for me to take care of my feminine affairs) instead of having to squat on the sailors' seats of ease at the bow of the frigate, in full view of anyone who cared to look. Rank has its privilege, even a middling rank such as surgeon's mate. And aboard a crowded vessel men respected one another's privacy, for privacy was dear.

For many months now, my ruse had worked, even ashore at the field hospital where we worked in our shirtsleeves, sweating like mules. No one had ever challenged my identity. But as I left the surgeon's office that morning, still glowing from Mr. Brantigan's praise, I worried that I would somehow be found out and this hazardous yet thrilling way of life, this sole means of my livelihood would come to an end. Then what would I do?

* * * * *

Upon leaving the cabin I nearly bowled over one of our loblolly boys, his little red ear pressed against the door.

"Henry Hollister! Were you spying on me?"

The young lad dropped his head. "Mr. Freeman bade me to find you," he mumbled, studying the tops of his bare feet, speckled with tar. "He requires your assistance on the fore-deck."

"You were eves-dropping, weren't you? And did you learn anything you didn't know before?"

He looked up at me with his guileless face, hoping for absolution. "Actually, I couldn't hear a word, sir. Nothing. At least, not very clearly."

"Henry, if I ever again catch you listening at doors I'll give you a thrashing you won't forget. I'll take away your plum duff for a month and I'll eat it myself in front of you, I swear it!"

The boy looked down again, his eyelashes fluttered, pale as corn silk. He tried hard to keep a straight face.

"Look at me, Henry Hollister." I took hold of his chin, my face growing hot. "Do you think this is a laughing matter?"

The lad shook his head, but dared not speak, his mouth contorted with suppressed laughter.

"Tell me: What's so funny?"

Unable to hold back his glee any longer, his face cracked open in a jack-o-lantern grin. "But I'm Frank, Mr. MacPherson, not Henry. No one can ever keep us straight!"

My anger was instantly dispelled and I couldn't help but smile at my mistake. "Frank, Henry, whatever! I'll have you both keel-hauled, the pair of you." I tugged his tangled yellow locks, sticky with salt, wanting to take a comb to them and to wash his impish, tar-streaked face.

"You may go. Go on with you, get back to your duties," I said as sternly as I could. "And in the future if Mr. Freeman wants to know what I'm about, he can come ask me himself."

* * * * *

The Hollister twins had been born on the gun deck shortly before the war began, nearly eight years ago, each earning the salty title of "son of a gun," given to those born aboard His Majesty's warships. Sadly, their mother had died soon after delivering them, and their father, the bosun, was killed during a subsequent engagement. Having no relatives on land willing to take the babies, the bosun's twin sons were looked after by the fo'c'sle wives until they were old enough to be of some use. They might have become officers' servants, as many young boys did, but because Mr. Brantigan was in need of a loblolly boy to help feed the men in the sick berth, Frank and Henry were assigned to the surgeon when they were six years of age. Because they were inseparable, he got the both of them in the bargain.

Although they were orphans, the twins had more brothers, uncles, and cousins than any child born on land. And a stern grandfather in Mr. Brantigan, who was quick to reprimand and stern with his punishments, but who cared for the boys as if they were his own grandsons, seeing to it that they were not only fed, clothed, and educated, but given the occasional shilling or extra serving of plum duff when they deserved it. It was strange to think that Frank and Henry had never known any home but the frigate. They held no memories, good or bad, of life on land. We were their family.

A floating family in service of the King is, as I was discovering, as imperfect as any other, but it is a family in the truest sense. We depended on one another for our very survival, for our isolation from the rest of the world was absolute, once land dropped below the horizon.

Chapter Three

Up on the spar deck Goodwillie was varnishing the larboard bow-chaser when a commotion above his head gave him pause. Gallivanting like squirrels in the foremast rigging, the Hollister twins dropped down onto the foredeck accidentally upsetting a bucket of water onto the gunner's mate's bare feet in their glee. Goodwillie, scarcely more than a boy himself, immediately picked up a wet sheepskin sponge and threw it, hitting Frank (or perhaps it was Henry?) square in the back as they scampered away, leaping over coiled halyards and dodging men at work. Having a clubfoot, the gunner's mate couldn't run as fast, but he had the advantage of a good aim, and a dog for an ally.

"Go at 'em, Neptune," Goodwillie shouted. A wiry little canine leaped up from its hiding place behind the foremast bits, glad for the opportunity to nip at a fresh set of heels. The boys shrieked with feigned terror and scurried back up the mast, away from the dog's reach.

Dalton came forward from the waist of the ship where he was at work inspecting one of the 12-pounders, holding a gunner's worm like a pike in his blackened hand.

"What's the rumpus?" We stood eye-to-eye, the gunner and I. The sleeves of his canvas work smock were rolled back exposing his competent forearms. He wore no hat this fine morning and the fresh wind had played havoc with his hair.

"Do ye think this is a lubber's holiday?" He scolded with mock severity. "Mr. Macpherson, please see to it that your boys are kept better employed." His back to Freeman, the gunner winked at me. A smile pulled at his lips, that ironic, asymmetric twist of his mouth that never failed to turn my legs to marmalade.

"Don't be so hard on them, Mr. Dalton." I was glad for any excuse to speak with the gunner. "They're just having a bit of fun on such a fine morning as this. I like to climb the rigging myself, as a matter of fact. Good for the constitution, better than any physic in the ship's dispensary."

"Is that so?" Dalton inched closer, close enough that I could see the nick on his chin where he had cut himself shaving this morning. Now the light in his eyes was unmistakably flirtatious. "Ye like to skylark, do ye?"

"No harm in that, is there?" I persisted, wanting to prolong our brief encounter.

He looked aloft, pretended to study the rigging, stalling. "Nae. I love to skylark myself. Just a boy at heart, like ye are." His best and broadest smile broke forth lighting up his face and warming me entirely; and then, in an instant he was gone, back to his cannon.

It was back to work for all of us and the foredeck fell quiet but for the squeak of block, the thump of rope being coiled upon the deck, the soft grunts of men at work. Work, always work, when one task is finished it's time to begin another. At the mast, a cluster of ailing sailors and marines waited to voice their sundry complaints and subject themselves to our cures. So warm was I from bantering with the gunner, I wondered if my own glowing face wouldn't give me away.

* * * * *

Many boys served on His Majesty's warships. Like our own Hollister twins, striplings as young as seven oft times made their way in the world by working aboard as servants to the officers, or apprentices to the tradesmen. Some young gentlemen were midshipmen, the navy's future officers. Many aboard were too young to shave.

Because boys and young men were so common aboard a ship, my ruse was possible. No one thought my voice peculiar; the frigate was filled with epicene voices and if we could have been induced to sing a hymn or put on an Italian opera, we'd have our full complement of sopranos, I'm certain.

A frigate was not so large as a ship of the line or a transport but she was faster and more maneuverable than those great floating beasts. Ours originally carried 220 officers, men and boys, though we had lost so many at Havana. In command of our vessel was John Elphinstone, as good a captain as we could ever hope for.

Just beneath the captain were officers, commissioned and warranted, and beneath them the petty officers such as I. Beneath us were the men, called ordinary and able, according to their experience. And finally, there were the servants and apprentices, just as on land, though the servant of an officer could grow up to be an officer himself, if he had the right connections. Though ours was a highly structured society, a freeborn Englishman's options were not entirely limited, I had discovered, and the floating world offered numerous opportunities, as well as risks.

I had learned the basics of my profession from my late husband, and had served as his assistant on a hospital ship for some months before he died. During the siege of Havana I had been baptized by fire, so to speak, and under Freeman's mentorship had became a better surgeon for it. Not all of our work was exciting. As surgeon's mates, Freeman and I were tasked with keeping the sick berth fumigated, the bed linens

and hammocks aired, the patients fed, bathed, shaved, medi-
cated—and bled when necessary. We had to sharpen and polish our instruments daily to keep them from corroding in the
damp and salty air. Chamber pots constantly needed empty-
ing, dressings had to be replenished and sometimes impro-
vised, dying men needed last letters written, and dead men
needed to be prepared for burial.

The *Richmond* carried no nurses, as might be found
ashore or on a hospital ship in port. Such nurses were said
to be culled from the dregs, sometimes taken from poor-
houses and prisons to tend to the patients.

Because we had no nurses, the lowliest of tasks fell to the
surgeon's mates, and whenever possible we foisted them off
on the loblolly boys, the Hollister twins. Freeman was a good
one for getting out of disagreeable work. He considered himself above such menial tasks and worthy only of jobs that involved a scalpel, lancet, or sharp tool of some sort. Piercing,
cutting and sewing was his forte and he didn't fancy stooping
to what he considered servile duties.

We carried an array of animals on board and at times
Richmond, like all frigates, seemed more like an ark than a
war ship. Officers bought livestock to supplement the plenti-
ful but boring navy fare of salt beef and pork, hard cheese
and ship's biscuit. Sometimes a consortium of sailors pooled
their resources and bought a goat or a calf for their table.
During the siege those men healthy enough had made forays
into unguarded yards and taken every animal worth eating
they could find. Now, such delicacies were few. Our manger
was presently occupied by six crates of cackling fowl, half a
dozen goats, and one lanky, miserable cow pillaged from Havana.

In addition to the animals intended for table, there were a
few monkeys, parrots, and other exotic creatures that had
been snatched as war booty. Terrapins, lizards, and snakes
were housed in sea trunks, to be sold at home or, in a pinch,
eaten. These curiosities were generally tolerated, though

many of the poor creatures died at sea. Dogs, however, were forbidden on our frigate, as they were prone to barking and howling.

Goodwillie, the gunner's mate, had illicitly shipped aboard Neptune, a dog rescued from a sinking ship in Havana Harbor. The little mongrel was quite clever. Smart enough not to bark, to recognize the captain's footfall, and to stay out of his sight. During inspections the dog burrowed into its owner's sea trunk as if hunting a gopher, completely hiding himself in Goodwillie's effects. He dined at our mess, ate meat off his rescuer's knife, and slivers of gristle the rest of us slipped him under the table. At night, he slept in his master's hammock or snuggled alongside one of the loblolly boys.

Cats, on the other hand, were not only tolerated aboard ship, they were practically given commissions. Because of their rat-catching abilities *Richmond's* felines were granted all the privileges of rank, and strolled, the quarterdeck at will, aloof as admirals, occasionally commandeering the most comfortable spot on deck to sun themselves.

Also aboard ship were women, fourteen of them, whose status was about equal to that of the pets, and certainly below that of the livestock and the cats. A few had permission to live aboard, for instance the wives of the warrant officers, but most of the females had been smuggled aboard and were maintained at the owner's expense. They were little niceties—something warm for Jack to snuggle with in the darkness. These women lived in the fo'c'sle or below decks, sharing their sponsor's hammock, his food, and quite often his fate.

The women, and the babies that inevitably came along, led a marginal existence. Even the men who brought them aboard had little time for them. There was little privacy for intimacy. Sometimes a makeshift canvas curtain, but more often only the curtain of darkness secluded them during their fast, furtive love-making which usually took place on the deck itself or in a hammock, one of more than a hundred strung side by side across the deck.

Out of sheer boredom, the women sometimes picked oakum or braided reef points together; or they made a little money on the side, laundering and mending the officers' clothes. During battle, these same women, along with the youngest boys aboard, became powder monkeys, carrying cartridges and shot from the magazine to the gun deck. In addition, they served as temporary battle nurses, assisting the surgeon and mates in their bloody work. During these times, we were grateful for their presence.

Our captain, like most captains I'm told, turned his head to the women of the fo'c'sle and the lower decks—as long as they kept out of the way, didn't use too much fresh water, and made themselves invisible in his presence. Unless one was needed to sew on a button, staunch a wound, or fetch a cannonball, they were ignored.

* * * * *

It was with this pepper pot of living cargo that His Majesty's frigate *Richmond* slowly made her way through the gray Atlantic waters, up the coast of the North American continent, toward New York. There some looked forward to a homecoming and some to a much-deserved liberty on a welcoming shore. Then, after replenishing our supplies, with any luck the frigate would be sent back to England where we would at last be paid and those who had loved ones there would be reunited. While there was no one in all of England waiting for me, I was eager to receive my well-deserved pay.

Chapter Four

"Drop your breeches," I said, preparing to lance a boil in the crack of able seaman Troy's buttocks. Like salt sores, boils were a common occurrence aboard a ship. I had lanced a many a boil on many a backside—white, black, brown, hairy, pimply, smooth—and every pair of cheeks quivered, anticipating the stick.

"Hold still, what ever you do, hold still or my trusty scalpel might miss its mark."

There was a burst of nervous laughter from the others waiting their turn to be seen.

Able seaman Troy did as he was told. He froze, still as a marble statue, his salty, tar-stained canvas work slops crumpled in a heap around his ankles. Hercules in shackles came to mind. Timing my lance with the roll of the ship, I pressed the edge of the blade against the base of the abscess, releasing a stream of yellow matter that narrowly missed my face. Wiping the scalpel on my apron, I used my thumb and forefinger to squeeze the remaining purulent humor onto a pledget of muslin, and then smeared a generous dab of salve over the small incision.

"There you are. In a few days you'll be good as new."

The marble god came to life. "That wasn't as bad as I feared," he said, gingerly touching his backside, as if greatly relieved to find it still there.

"See me again tomorrow morning. Until then, avoid the sitting position."

"That'll be nigh impossible," sniped one of his peers. "Sitting on his arse is what Troy does best." Another weak burst of sniggers from the other men waiting their turn.

"You may haul up your trousers now, Mr. Troy," I said. "The shine from your white bum must be blinding the helmsman."

This time the patient laughed too, laughed with relief, and I dismissed him back to his duties. A dose of lightheartedness was often beneficial to recovery.

"Who is next?"

Some two-dozen men had shown up for this morning's foremast sick call, a definite improvement over the past few months. An arm's length away Freeman had his own queue of men, waiting for his attentions. He had just finished bleeding one of the marines, who was slowly recovering from a tropical ague, and sent him back to his station.

"If you have any worries about the amputation tomorrow, MacPherson, just say the word and I'll step in," Freeman patronized.

"Thanks, but Brantigan wants me to do it."

A staged sigh. "Well I hope you are quick enough. I once saw a green surgeon's mate make a mess of an amputation because he hesitated. Oh, it was ugly ordeal, very ugly, and the patient bled to death right there on the table."

The men next in line blanched at overhearing this, for many had lost friends to the surgeon's saw; but Freeman was callous to such subtleties. Sensitivity is for sweethearts and chaplains, was his motto.

"Thank you Mr. Freeman, for your vote of confidence." I tried to sound dry, off-hand, and bantering. "I shall be quick and fast, I assure you."

"Oh you'll do well enough, I suppose. After all, I've tried to teach you everything I know."

Dudley Freeman was a born surgeon while I had come to trade reluctantly, and out of necessity. Had my father not died at an early age, or had I been his legitimate son instead of his illegitimate daughter, my life would be quite different, I can assure you. Fast horses and fine saddles were my first love; not sailing ships, and certainly not bleeding bowls and bone saws. Yet circumstances had placed a bone saw in my hand.

I admired Freeman his certainty, his brash confidence and I was fairly certain he didn't suspect my true identity. Or perhaps it would be more true to say he did not suspect my former identity and my underlying anatomy. For I was masculine in some ways and feminine in others, an amalgam of both sexes, the male and the female aspects of my personality becoming entwined like a vine grafted to the root of another. Perhaps, like a fanciful character of Jonathan Swift's imagination, I would wake up one day to find myself not man nor woman but some new creature entirely.

Mr. Freeman didn't really know me, and could not see past the façade I presented, as he was always more concerned and enamored with himself. On the other hand, I felt I knew *him* quite well. We slept touching elbows, our hammocks strung side by side in seaman-like fashion, bumped lightly as we swayed in rhythm with the ship's motion.

I was all too familiar by now with the rank of Freeman's feet, his farts, and the pharyngeal snuffle of his snores. By day, I knew his bray of a laugh that exposed an impressive array of teeth—big teeth that he continually caressed with his tongue, as if polishing them. I tolerated his piquing ways and was often at the brunt of his little jokes; but that was just Freeman's way of fraternizing. Though he lorded his seniority over me, it was entirely without malice. He looked upon me as a younger, less gifted brother.

He sometimes spoke of his biological brothers back home, a pack of them by the sound of it with Dudley somewhere near the bottom of the ruck. Having too many brothers ahead of him for Dudley to receive much of a portion, he learned early on he'd have to make his own way in the world. His haberdasher father already had a protégée in the first-born son so the others were naturally apprenticed out, Dudley to Charles Brantigan, his mother's second cousin. At eighteen years of age, he passed his examinations and when Brantigan was assigned to the newly built *Richmond,* Freeman was brought on as surgeon's mate. He was a competent petty officer and had seen a lot of action, but Dudley coveted a surgeon's warrant and the slight improvement in accommodation and pay that accompanied it. I believe he expected to move into Brantigan's position as soon as his kinsman retired or died.

Though Dudley Freeman could be insufferable at times, he was my mentor and my messmate. I considered him my friend, and although I didn't particularly enjoy his company, I had learned much from him. Like how not to faint or turn away at the sight of body fluids and broken bones, but to roll up my sleeves and dive in, bloodying my arms up to the elbows trying to save someone's life. He taught me to wag my tongue at fear even when my knees felt like clotted cream. A surgeon must have a tough hide and Freeman's was one of the toughest.

He was, in part, my cover. As long as Dudley had his way and because he wasn't threatened by me, I had been safe in his shadow. He saw me as his protégé; a supporting actor, a Jack-come-lately with less battle experience, less ambition, less skill. He never questioned me about my past. I don't believe it ever occurred to him that I might have an interesting story, or a secret to share. In Dudley's mind, I had been put into his world to look up to him, to assist him, and for the past ten months, I had been content to play that role.

Now his needling sparked something in me. If someone had to amputate Private Lee's leg, why not I? Mr. Brantigan had faith in my abilities, as did Everett Lee, whose leg it was. If only I could be sure of doing it correctly. Swiftly. Expeditiously, as Freeman said. Inflicting the least amount of pain possible on the poor young soldier.

A new feeling of ambition was spawning inside me, a desire to meet the challenge instead of avoiding it. I might actually have it in me to *be* a good surgeon, not just pass myself off as one.

Chapter Five

"And how fare the people's health? Mr. Frick called out from the windward cathead. It was the chaplain's habit to stroll the entire deck every morning.

I excused myself from my station to have a brief word with him "Improving, I'm happy to say. For the most part."

"And you, Mr. MacPherson? Are you fully recovered from the yellow fever?"

His concern for me was apparent and I gave him my best smile to reassure him. "I grow stronger everyday, thank you. And you, sir?"

"Never better, especially now that we're heading north. Everyone's spirits seem much improved."

"Largely, yes. However, tomorrow morning Private Lee will lose his leg. He's in anguish and I don't know what to say or do to help him. Perhaps you could pay him a call?"

"I would be happy to, if he requests it. I've noticed some don't take kindly to unsolicited visitations from a man of the cloth, especially at sea." The chaplain was well aware of his tenuous position aboard ship. Many ships didn't even carry a chaplain. Frick was on the payroll, not so much by the virtue of his good works but by the ties of friendship and the influence his family held.

The word was that Frick's father and Elphinstone's father were good friends and Frick's berth aboard *Richmond* was said to be credited to that bond. Rumor had it that handsome young Benjamin, the third son of a wealthy family, had been ordained and given a parish, but some scandal involving a woman had sunk his career before it had begun. Luckily for him, Captain Elphinstone felt obligated to do his old friend a favor by taking his dishonored son on board. Yet I had nothing against the chaplain, quite the contrary.

Benjamin Frick had proven himself to me during the siege of Havana. He might have stayed relatively safe below decks in his well-appointed cabin. Instead, he had gone along with our gun crews, sent ashore to help Albemarle's floundering army—and we surgeons mates who followed, to set up a field hospital. The sweltering, disease ridden trenches of Havana were hell itself, yet Frick had taken off his coat and rolled up his sleeves, working alongside us as nurse, messenger, and loblolly boy. I liked him for that.

"I'm sure Mr. Lee will be most receptive to any words of courage you might have for him, and for me," I added, thinking a good word from the chaplain on my behalf couldn't hurt.

"Oh, watch out," I warned, too late. A splash of seawater came over the rail and doused the chaplain, much to the delight of those watching.

Frick laughed right along with them. "You'd think I'd learn not to turn my back to the sea. Well no matter, it'll dry soon enough in this sun." He took his hat off and shook the water from it. "I shall be happy to pay you both a visit this evening," He said, his blue eyes meeting mine with a look of expectancy. Then, as if pulled by gravity, his gaze slid from my eyes down my freckled face and neck, and coming to rest on my breasts. I felt my breath quicken, for though small by nature and hidden away under a swath of muslin beneath my voluminous shirt, I worried my female bosom might somehow be visible to a man of the cloth.

"Mr. Frick?"

He licked at the trickle of seawater that made its way down his face to his lips.

"Mr. Frick, is something amiss?"

He shook his head, flinging droplets of water in both directions. "No, not at all. Pardon me, I must go search for some comforting passages." He bade me a good day, tearing his eyes away at last.

As soon as he had turned his back, my eyes flew to the front of my shirt. It was properly buttoned, and dry, thank God, revealing no pink nipples.

Did he suspect, I wondered. And if so, why?

* * * * *

Brian Dalton was the one man aboard who knew my secret and whom I trusted with it, yet I actually knew very little about the gunner's secrets, if he had any. I was ignorant of even the most basic facts of his life, which I imagined most courting couples shared with one another over long walks in the garden or over their teacups in the parlor. Our courtship, if you could call it that, had been subversive by necessity, our conversations brief and restrained, leaving me longing for more. This I knew; Brian was the man I wanted, the man I thought about in my hammock at night.

We had met aboard *Canopus,* the ship on which I hid myself in order to get to Barbados, where I had hoped to claim my late father's estate. I was someone else entirely in those days; too rash for my own good and all caught up in my imagined entitlement. Yet, Brian was the same man, or so it seemed. He befriended me then, keeping my secret and he kept the secret of my identity, here on *Richmond*. He had rescued me in Havana, when I was sick with the fever and could scarcely walk, and the bombs were bursting all around us, the Morro Castle crumbling at last. I trusted my life to Brian Dalton and knew his heart to be true.

Yet, I didn't know the particulars of his life. The gunner was a man of few words, didn't talk much about his past, and our time together was short. A few words here, a few words there, all I knew was that he had grown up in the north of England, as was evident by his manner of speaking. That he was of Irish stock, his family having migrated to Northumberland before he was born, in search of work, I supposed. All he had in life he had worked for. In contrast, my childhood was a very privileged one in every way—except for the lack of a mother and a profligate father who lived an ocean away. All we had in common was our situation, and a mutual desire for one another, a physical attraction that grew every time we were together.

* * * * *

The sun climbed high, the temperature rose, we were not yet out of the tropical climes. Squalls were already forming on the horizon. Freeman and I were nearly finished with sick call, my stomach rumbled with hunger. Any minute now the gentlemen would come on deck with their octants to take the noon sight, followed soon after by the bosun with his shrill pipe to call us to dinner.

The last man in line was a seaman old enough to be my grandfather, reluctantly reporting a severe case of constipation. I was measuring out the calomel and jalep when Neptune came scurrying through our line-up chased by Henry, who was in turn chased by Frank (or perhaps it was Henry chasing Frank, I never could tell them apart with any reliability), nearly knocking the bottle out of my hand.

Hoping for sanctuary, the dog tried to hide between Dudley Freeman's legs but Freeman grabbed the terrier by the scruff of the neck and held it high.

"Ha! Now I've got you now, you good for nothing little turd-maker!" He strode to the larboard rail, dog in hand.

The boys were aghast. "Don't throw him overboard, please Mr. Freeman! He didn't mean it, it wasn't his fault."

Freeman relished their anguish and worked to prolong it, holding the terrier high over his head. "Say bye-bye to little woof-woof."

"Don't do it, Mr. Freeman," said Goodwillie, coming on deck just that instant. "Put 'em down, he won't bother you no more."

"Come on, Dudley," I said. "We've got work to do." But Freeman just grinned and made a motion as if to toss the pup over.

The men paused in their work, all eyes on Freeman. He wasn't serious, at least I don't think he intended to drop the dog into the sea, but he was enjoying his little charade, to the discomfort of everyone.

Suddenly, there was Dalton, knocking him to the deck with one blow. Freeman howled his outrage and the dog scrambled to safety as the two men grappled, spit and blood flying. The sailors dropped from the rigging and crawled up from below, forming a circle around the spectacle, hooting, cheering them on, and calling bets. For them, it was all a lark. I stood as though paralyzed, bottle of physic still in hand, unable to tear my eyes away from the flurry of fists. I hate it when men brawl; especially when they're both men I care for. The fracas was soon broken up by the sergeant at arms and Lieutenant Mason, who came storming down from the quarterdeck.

"Mr. Dalton! Mr. Freeman!" barked the lieutenant. "On your feet this instant."

Dudley and Brian stood, huffing and blowing, glaring at

one another like two bullocks, separated by the sergeant who held each man by the back of the neck with his big red hands.

"What do you have to say for yourselves?"

"He started it," Freeman sputtered, wiping a string of bloody spittle from his chin. "He attacked me without cause."

"I can nae stand a bully," Dalton said."

Mason looked from one to the other. Sunlight poured onto the foredeck, illuminating their faces, hard with masculine wrath and shiny with sweat. Two young men, both about the same age, ruffled as gamecocks. But the commissioned officer had the command.

"I don't even care to know the particulars. You men disappoint me. Did we capture Havana so that we could fight like schoolboys amongst ourselves? We can't have gunners and surgeon's mates acting like drunken idiots. I don't give a damn who is at fault. You will, in the future, settle your differences in a manner becoming to your station. Now apologize at once or I'll have you both before the Captain."

"Sorry for the disruption, sir," Brian muttered, touching his forehead.

"Likewise," Freeman sniffed, studiously ignoring Dalton.

The lieutenant looked from one to the other, biting his lip. "Sergeant, release them. And all of you, what are you looking at?" Lieutenant Mason snapped, removing his tricorn and wiping his forehead with his sleeve. "Go on about your business. Get back to work at once, or loose your ration of spirits."

The men were fairly bursting, trying to hide their gleeful sniggers behind their hands. Nothing like a little fisticuffs to raise a sailor's spirits. But Dudley Freeman took his fat lip and black eye and stomped below without a word.

A look of triumph flashed across the gunner's face as he picked up his bucket of tools and returned to his work without even so much as a glance in my direction. The spark between us had been smothered by something darker.

The people reluctantly returned to their duties and the mischievous little dog was secreted away somewhere, likely given to the women below to keep out of harm's way. And I was left with a bad taste in my mouth, feeling somehow responsible for what had happened, yet not knowing how to remedy the situation.

Chapter Six

The bosun sounded the call and we all hurried below to eat our main meal of the day. My accustomed place was next to Freeman at a worn smooth slab of knotty oak suspended from ropes, on the aft part of the gun deck, three tables forward of the wardroom. Below us in the gunroom, Dalton and the other warrants messed. With nearly everyone below decks at once, it was elbow to elbow, the odor of sweating humanity mingled with salt beef, old cheese, and a whiff of steaming fresh manure from the manger, where the officers' remaining cow ate the last wisps of hay.

No matter the smells or the crowding, eating is one of the pleasantest things you can do aboard a ship. However, that day my stomach was in knots. The chunk of dried beef floating in a pool of salty grey water made me think of Everett Lee's leg and I was quite unable to put fork to mouth.

The sail maker glanced at me as he stabbed a lump of meat with his knife. "What's the matter, MacPherson? Not feeling well?"

"A bit bilious," I admitted.

Goodwillie eyed my plate hungrily. "If you're not going to

eat your dinner, can I have it?" He was effectively on half rations, as he was sharing all he had with Neptune. Yet I didn't want to mention the dog, as it had been the cause of the trouble between Dalton and Freeman, so I simply pushed my wooden plate toward the gunner's mate.

Freeman was well aware that Goodwillie wanted the extra meat for his dog, but he too, pretended not to notice since Dalton had trounced him and they both nearly ended up in irons over it. He chose not to see the gunner's mate surreptitiously putting hand to plate, then under the table. The others kept on eating.

Across the table, the carpenter's mate's woman smiled at me kindly and I smiled back. Every time I looked at Iris Wickham, I felt like I was looking into a bewitched mirror, one that showed a glimpse of how my life might have been under different circumstances.

Though not yet thirty she looked much older, already missing a few teeth and hair going to gray. However, Iris had a smile that lit up her careworn face, as if she expected at any moment her fortune to change.

"Well, it's been nice knowing you sods," Freeman announced, smacking his lips. "MacPherson and I'll be leaving this mess. We're moving to the aft cockpit mess with the senior midshipmen. I've been given permission."

"But why?" I said, taken aback.

"Because it has been made possible." We all knew he was referring to the recent deaths of the master's mate and two midshipmen, but death was seldom spoken of aboard a ship. "Mr. Sloane has invited me," Dudley elaborated, licking his teeth, clearly pleased. "The both of us, actually. You and I, MacPherson."

"So you'd leave us, just like that?" Mr. Wickham said with a complicit sidelong glance at the others of the mess.

"It's our rightful place," Freeman maintained. "No slight intended."

"Don't you think it's a little close and smelly down there, with no port to open?" The carpenter's mate continued, dunking a cement-like biscuit into his bowl of watery broth.

"We can't just go barging in there," I said. "Why do you want to change messes?"

"We're not barging in, we've been invited."

"But I don't want to eat down in the orlop." I had grown comfortable with my messmates and I didn't want the scrutiny of new ones, sizing me up.

Freeman took a slug of warm grog and lowered his voice. "Trust me, MacPherson. You want to mess in the orlop. Think of it as a sort of private club."

"But I like these fellows."

"Hell, I like 'em too. But we have a chance to move up a half step in this brutal world and I intend to do it."

"Move down, you mean." The idea of taking my meals in that stuffy dark hole in the bowels of the frigate, at the very same table on which we operated, made me a little queasy just then.

The others continued to shovel in their food, ignoring Freeman's pretensions. Maybe they'd be all too glad if he left their mess and took me with him. The midday meal was not a leisurely, chitchat affair aboard *Richmond*, for there was a long afternoon's work yet to be done. Throughout the deck, the sound of spoons scraping in bowls and the clunk of tankards striking tables could be heard, as the people filled their bellies.

"I'm only looking out for you, dunderhead," Freeman said affectionately, sucking on a chunk of meat. "Since you don't seem to know how to look out for yourself. There are some lively good fellows in the aft cockpit mess. And the food is better, or will be once we get to New York and can obtain some extras for our table. Mr. Sloane is most generous with his personal supply of spirits and the card games down there are notorious."

"Dudley, you know I don't play cards."

He looked at me with tender pity touched with shame, as a gifted boy might regard a beloved but idiotic younger brother. "I'll help you, Patrick, you dear dunderhead. Haven't I taken you under my wing from the day you came aboard?"

Indeed, he had.

* * * * *

Dinner over, I escaped to the deck hoping the sunshine and breeze would settle my nerves, and hoping for a brief word with Dalton. Instead, it was the chaplain, Mr. Frick, who hailed me and fell in step beside me as I walked. I sensed he had something to say to me, yet I was in no mood to talk religion just then.

I spied Brian through dozens of men, and he saw me. For an instant, I was aware only of he and I, as if all the others were but background in a painting. I stopped in my tracks and a lurch of the ship caused me to loose my balance. The chaplain caught my arm to steady me, a natural enough response if I was a woman, but over solicitous, I felt, between two young men such as us. My face reddened and I forced a manly laugh.

"Ha! Pardon my clumsiness, Mr. Frick, but since my bout with the fever, I've lost my sea legs. My former agility has been slow to recover."

He said nothing but looked at me intently and let go of my arm too reluctantly, I thought.

Gathering my wits, I stood tall. "Excuse me, but I've just remembered a matter of importance I must attend to in sick berth. Might we speak this evening, after supper?"

"Certainly. My pleasure, sir."

I was impatient for the chaplain to go. My attention was

focused on the man waiting for me in the waist at the lee-ward rail, alone; it was there I made my way as soon as Mr. Frick had taken his leave.

"G'day MacPherson," Dalton said, a bit tersely.

"And to you, Mr. Dalton." Was he somehow salty with me because of the unpleasant incident over the dog this morning? Was that somehow my fault? Above us and below, the ship's company went about their afternoon work. All too soon we'd be joined by someone else, all too soon our time together would be spent.

He offered me his pouch of tobacco, which I declined, though I loved the sweet, smoky vanilla scent that I associated with his person. Dalton put a pinch of the stuff into his cheek and leaned against the rail.

"How goes your day?"

"Distressing," I admitted. "I am to amputate Private Lee's leg tomorrow morning."

"Ach, poor devil. Are you up to it?"

"No. But Mr. Brantigan has assigned me the task."

"A test of sorts?"

"Possibly. Yes, I think so."

"Then I wish ye courage. And speed, for the poor lad's sake."

I swallowed hard.

He pressed my upped arm with his fist, a symbolic punch, as if to infuse me with courage and strength. It was a masculine gesture and I leaned into it, glad for the contact between us.

"And how goes the gunner's day?" I asked.

"Oh, the same. Counted shot, aired stores, and cleaned guns. Saved a poor mutt from drowning and nearly got clapped in irons for it."

"Really, I don't think Mr. Freeman would have actually

dropped the dog overboard. He was just teasing. I don't know why it came to blows."

As soon as the words were out of my mouth, I knew it was the wrong thing to say. I felt Brian bristle.

"Why do ye defend him? He's nae but a bully."

For once, I was at a loss for words. Indeed, why did I defend him?

"He can be, yes. He's insufferable at times. But I don't approve of fighting, it's unbecoming."

"Then perhaps you shouldn't serve aboard a frigate, Mr. MacPherson. It's what we do."

"Not to each other," I snapped.

"Do you always have the last word?"

Seeing the captain's boy approaching with a message, I leaned against the rail and studied the horizon. This put me in a devil of a spot. Was it too much to ask for the man I loved and the man I worked with to get along?

"G'day sirs. Mr. Dalton, Captain Elphinstone wishes to see you in his quarters at four bells. He says to bring your account book."

"Thanks Mr. Grimsby. It must be nearly four bells now. If ye'll excuse me."

I nodded curtly. "Duty calls."

"Have a peaceful afternoon, Mr. MacPherson," Dalton said, looking over his shoulder.

* * * * *

That afternoon in sick berth, I dispensed Peruvian bark to 14 men and vinegar to six for symptoms of scurvy. I wrapped a broken toe, splinting it against its neighbor, and I examined 12 wounds, one of them Everett Lee's.

Capillary refill below the wound was slow. Probing about the malodorous wound, I saw no new pink granulation tissue forming, the signs of a healing wound. This fixed in my mind what I already knew; there were no miracles in store for this young soldier.

Everett was groggy from the laudanum I had given him and kept dozing off, even while I was probing his flesh. I took a good look at the sickly limb to decide where I would make the cut and guessing how much pressure it would take. I imagined the procedure, envisioning the anatomy of the thigh. Femur, the largest and longest bone in the body. Sartorius, the longest muscle, snaking its way across the thigh from the iliac crest down to the tibia. The femoral artery, becoming the popliteal artery, above the knee where I'd be cutting. The great saphenous vein, the long saphenous nerve.

I imagined how it would feel to carve through the layers of skin and the custard-like adipose tissue beneath. Down through the tough, glistening membrane of fascia to the underlying red muscle and past that to the femur itself; hard, yes, but alive and pliant as a young tree limb.

Havana came back to me in a brief, horrific flash. I pushed the vision away, not wanting to relive it or even remember it. Yet, that had been my training ground for amputations. Remember, I must.

Chapter Seven

Surgeon's log, October 22, 1762. New cases: Treated three men for boils, five for purulent rashes, one for inguinal hernia, and one for toothache (offending lower left molar removed). Assisted Mr. Brantigan in relieving able seaman Parker of a bladder stone. Of note, there have been no new cases of yellow fever since we left Havana. Twelve colonial soldiers remain in sick berth in various stages of recovery from tropical fever and war wounds.

— *Patrick MacPherson, Surgeon's Mate*

* * * * *

That evening I readied my instruments by the candlelight, making certain that every tooth of the bone saw was free of rust and that the catlin's edges were razor sharp, the tenaculum's hook gleaming. Then polished the bone handles and the screw of the tourniquet before returning them to their velvet lined case.

Pulling back the curtain to the sick berth I looked into the makeshift quarters where a dozen men lay in hammocks and hanging cots. These were the worst cases, the recalcitrant. Those who were showing signs of improvement had been moved out; the sailors back to their accustomed berths and the Colonial soldiers temporarily quartered with our marines.

From his suspended bed, Everett's eyes flew to mine expectantly, as if I might be bringing a small miracle in my pocket.

"My leg pains me less," he said quietly, so as not to disturb the others. The hope in his voice was pathetically touching.

I assessed the temperature of his skin, the pace and quality of his carotid pulse before unwrapping the dressing. There was no improvement, no sign of eleventh hour, miraculous intervention. "You must prepare yourself, Everett, " I said, steeling my own self for the task.

The shudder ran through him like a wave.

"It can't be saved?"

"No," I said as firmly as I could. "It cannot,"

Everett looked down at the ragged edge of his cut-off pant. He wiggled his toes. "Look, I can still move them."

"No," I said coldly, though the tears pushed against my eyes. "You'll die." Knowing he might die even so. I could smell it in the air, the whiff of sweet decay.

"How can I go on without my leg?"

I groped for something comforting or wise to say but had no wisdom and no comfort to offer. The hanging beds rocked in unison with the rhythm of the ship and from above came the rubbing sound of a rope under load. Amplified by the ship's hull, it sounded for all the world like a sob.

From outside the canvas divider, a polite cough. "Mr. MacPherson?"

I recognized Mr. Frick's voice. "Come in," I said, rather glad now for the chaplain's presence. He entered, Bible in hand.

"Oh Lord," said Everett. "Are things so bad you've sent for the parson?"

Mr. Frick smiled humbly. "Why is it the chaplain is never a welcome sight?"

"Because he so often has the undertaker lurking in his shadow."

"Not I, son. Not tonight. I stopped by so that you would know you are not going through this ordeal alone. And. I." The chaplain too, seemed to want for the right words. "I thought perhaps to share a few words of comfort and strength from the Good Book. That is, if you so desire."

"An eye for an eye? Vengeance is mine? The sins of the Father are visited upon the son?" Lee's voice was curt with sarcasm but Frick would not be baited.

"No, I was thinking more of a more hopeful passage. A psalm or perhaps something from Christ's life. *Fear not, for I am with you always*, something of that nature. But if you'd rather not, I'll just wish you well and say goodnight and apologize for the intrusion." He turned to leave.

"Wait—don't go." Everett said. "It's just that biblical quotes and talk of religion reminds me of death and judgment day and eternity, and I can't bear to think of that right now."

The ship moved abruptly, a new rhythm, and the chaplain shuffled his feet to regain his balance. "Mr. Lee, I may be chaplain but I'm not one to judge any man. I'm a sinner too, but one who believes in the power of God's love and redemption."

Everett chewed on his lip. "Sir, do you know the works of *Marcus Aurelius*? He was a pagan, but I draw strength from his words. I have a copy of *Meditations* in my kit, I have carried with me all these months."

"Marcus Aurelius?"

"What, you think a bumpkin of a foot soldier from Rhode

Island is ignorant of the classics? We might be backwoods Yanks but we value our books. My mother couldn't afford to send me to college but she taught me to read and she taught me to question what I've read. My father published a newspaper. He was a scholar, a thinker, though he never attended university."

I felt a twinge of shame. All I knew of Marcus Aurelius was that he was the last of the succession of "good" Roman emperors and that his physician was the revered Galen who contributed so much to the science of medicine. My late husband had been a great admirer of the Greek physician who had been so keen on careful observation and dissection to further our understanding of the workings of the body. Aeneas had urged me to study Galen's writings on epistemology, though sadly, I had not, for I found them tedious at the time and not at all relevant to my own life. I had been so full of myself, at seventeen.

Frick bowed his head and seemed to contemplate the leather cover of his Bible, worn thin by the worrying of his thumbs. I wondered if he were going to launch into prayer.

"Let me see if I can recall," he said at last. "'*Loss is... Loss is nothing else but change and change is nature's delight. Ever since the world began, things have been ordered by her decree in the selfsame fashion as they are at this day, and as other similar things will be ordered to the end of time.*' From book nine of the *Meditations*, I believe?"

Everett's face was filled appreciation. "Yes, Book Nine, I know it well. Thanks, Mr. Frick." Lee offered a slight smile that showed his chipped tooth. "I was afraid you were going to call down a thunderbolt or something." His voice had lost its bitter edge and I was struck by how a simple gift of well-chosen words is well spent.

"I'm not adverse to the Stoic philosophy, though I find it much more dour than Christ's promise of life everlasting. "

Frick's long white thumbs ran up and down along the Bible. He cleared his throat and recited again. "Prophets come in various guises. Wise is the man who considers all philosophies, seeks truth in all religions, and examines his own heart."

"Marcus Aurelius wrote that?"

The chaplain shook his head, smiling self-consciously. "Benjamin Frick, actually. Although I may have inadvertently plagiarized it. I read too, you know. And not just the Holy Bible. I have brought quite a library aboard which I am happy to share with you during your recovery."

Everett allowed his head to fall back on the pillow. He stared at the light flickering on the overhead. "Mr. Frick, I'm ready to hear what other words of comfort or courage you might have for the likes of me."

The ship's bell struck the half hour and the call sounded for lights out. Someone approached sick berth, I could hear the footfalls and I felt a tingle of recognition. I stepped outside the canvas partition, nearly into his arms.

"Tis a fine evening," Brian said softly. "Can ye join us on deck?"

And so, I left the patient and parson talking philosophy and religion to join the gunner and company of men enjoying the night air. While we could not touch hands, nor lips, nor talk of our feelings, we could make small talk and get drunk on each other's proximity.

Some half a dozen of the warrants and petty officers were standing by the lee rail talking. Someone mentioned the scuffle on the foredeck this morning, but Brian (who had been unanimously accorded the victor) laughed it off modestly.

"I heard a rumor we're to be sent to the Pacific Ocean," said the carpenter, biting a quid off his tobacco twist. "To Buenos Aires or Manila Bay."

There was a moment of silence as everyone considered this piece of news.

"More chance for prize," said Humphries, the armorer. "A train of Spanish galleons laden with gold are crisscrossing the South Seas and I'd like a piece o' that. Retire as comfortable as Anson's armorer, I would."

"More likely we'll be sent down to Martinique, on blockade duty."

"I don't care where we're sent," offered Goodwillie. "But I hope we go back to England first. So's I can get paid and see me poor old mother again. If she's still alive."

"I hope we go back to England first too," said Bannock, the master's mate, "So's I can get paid, and throw a leg over that poor girl I left in pining for me in Portsmouth."

The men laughed heartily and I could feel the charge of their pent up energy, like St. Elmo's crackle in the air.

"Hey lads, why think of England or Manila when we have the New York beauties so close at hand?" The carpenter spit a stream of tobacco juice expertly over the rail.

* * * * *

Below, I discovered the chaplain had gone and the sounds of men breathing in sleep. I moved quietly to Everett's bedside. He was awake, staring into the darkness.

"Well, goodbye old leg," he whispered, looking down at his thigh. "You've been a good limb, taking me everywhere I wanted to go and never complaining. I never gave you a second thought until now."

Tears pressed at my eyes, I was glad for the darkness.

"You will do the cutting?"

"I will."

"That's a relief. The surgeon is half blind, I hear. And his hands shake like he needs a drink."

"He's an excellent surgeon," I said. "And the shaking has nothing to do with want of spirits."

"All the same, I'm glad it's you and not Mr. Brantigan or Mr. Freeman who'll be doing the job. Mr. Freeman is too boastful and hard-hearted. I don't much like him."

A dry laugh escaped me. "You're not alone in your sentiments. But you don't have to like the man who saves your life. Mr. Freeman is quick and good with his tools and I've learned a lot from him."

"You're quick and good with your tools as well, aren't you Mr. MacPherson?"

"Like lightening." I touched his shoulder, pressed firmly, wishing to hell it were true. "It'll be over before you know it."

A long moment passed in which we listened to the mournful dirge of the wind in the rigging.

"A tot of rum to help you sleep, Mr. Lee?"

"Aye, that would be the thing," Everett said, settling himself into his pillow. In the feeble yellow candlelight, his face shone like the moon.

I went for his rum. Was tempted to pour one for myself, for confidence, but I knew it would only fuddle my head. The ship's rhythm was interrupted as she slammed into a cross swell and I reached to the beam just overhead to keep from falling. On the main deck the guns strained against their breeching. I hoped the sea would be smooth tomorrow and wished now I had asked the chaplain to say a prayer for me.

Back in sick berth a young lad in the cot next to Everett cried out in his sleep. Whatever nightmare he was experiencing, it could not be worse than the one we had lived through. Satisfied he was breathing, I pulled the flannel sheet up over his shoulders and tucked him in, feeling more like a sister than a surgeon's mate.

Less than ten days to New York, if the winds hold. May they all live, may we all make it to shore. Lord, give me strength and a steady hand. With that prayer in my mind and heart, I left sick berth and returned to my own hammock.

All around me hammocks swayed with the ships' movement, like cocoons on a tree branch. Freeman was not yet in bed, he was still enjoying his drink and his cards. The chaplain approached out of the shadows, as if he had been waiting for me.

"Earlier you asked to speak with me."

"I could use an infusion of strength before I turn in," I admitted. "But Marcus Aurelius won't do it for me. I'm more of an epicurean than a stoic."

Frick smiled. "You seem unduly troubled, by the upcoming procedure. Is there something you want to confess?"

Was I overly suspicious or did this man suspect?

"You are very perceptive, Mr. Frick. I do have a confession. I confess I'm uncertain about my ability to saw a man's leg off in a quick and competent manner. I confess I'm afraid."

"I worked with you in Havana, Patrick, and I well remember those hellish weeks when we were sent ashore to help the foot soldiers. It seemed a question of what would kill us quicker; enemy mortars, lack of fresh water, or tropical fevers. I was in awe of you then and I'm in awe of you now, Patrick MacPherson." His voice nearly broke and I was sure now, he knew for why would he be in awe of me unless he knew I was a woman? I had done no more and no less than any other man. Fatigue had softened my resolve and I fought an impulsive desire to blurt out the truth to him.

He put his hand on mine in a fatherly fashion. "I have no doubt you will be as quick and competent as ever you need to be, and I pray God give you strength, guide your hand, and ease your mind. And should you ever want to talk to me, day or night..."

"Thank you chaplain, for your confidence in me. Now I had better turn in so I'll be rested." I affected a yawn. "See you in the morning."

Yet I couldn't sleep, I was wide-awake, listening for the striking of the bell every thirty minutes. When the watch changed at midnight, I went up on deck again.

Chapter Eight

We stood in the main weather chains, just the two of us, leaning against the shrouds. Overhead clouds pushed and shoved, blotting out the stars. We both shivered in our worn-thin jackets, yet the sting and cold were exhilarating.

"Can't sleep?" Brian said, studiously regarding the sails.

I shrugged and shook my head.

"What's on yer mind?"

"I just hope I'm strong enough to get through the bone quickly. I fear my hands will be shaking more than Mr. Brantigan's."

"Nae. The soldier's lucky its you doing the cutting and not Brantigan or that sliving coward who sleeps next to you."

"Mr. Freeman is a good surgeon," I insisted. "Even if he is a bit full of himself."

"Mr. Freeman is full of something, that's certain."

"He can be obnoxious, yes. But I've learned a lot from him."

Brian stiffened. "I don't know about bone saws, but I know something of human nature and can spot a sogger when I see one."

Then we were no longer alone. A seaman on watch came by, checking the tautness of the lifts and braces. Nearby on the quarterdeck the officer of the watch was speaking to the man at the helm. We stood in silence, wanting to make amends. Our time together was too scarce to be spent arguing.

The squall was already passing, dragging scraps of clouds along with it. Above us now, a scattering of stars. The wind was shifting.

"They'll be setting t'gallants," Dalton predicted.

Moments later the second lieutenant barked a command. The topmen on watch scrambled aloft and those on deck hurried to their appointed stations for the coordinated work of setting sails. The *Richmond* crew could do it as fast and efficiently as any. It was a pleasure to behold. I loved the orderliness of it all, the synchronization and the team work, and I rather wished I were out on the foot-rope leaning into the yard untying gaskets.

When the sails were set and trimmed and the topmen down from the yards we caught a glimpse of the newly risen moon, an eerie glow behind a thin veil of cloud.

"Let's go aloft," I said, the words flying recklessly out of my head. I remembered our first embrace, on the fighting top of *Canopus* on a night such as this.

His eyes widened, I could feel them dilate, taking me in. On the fighting top, we might press our hands together, interlace our fingers, risk a quick kiss. I dared not imagine anything beyond that. A warm rush of eagerness flooded me, overriding my worries about tomorrow. Of course, there was always a man posted aloft, but seldom on the mizzenmast.

Brian made a pretense of examining the stern chaser while I climbed the ratlines, as any idler with insomnia might do on a fine night. Scrambling up onto the platform, my heart surged. We had it to ourselves. The mizzen tops'l hid us from the lookout aloft on the main mast. Still, we had to be cautious for the chaplain already suspected me.

Brian followed a few minutes later, climbing the futtock shrouds as agilely as a cat climbs a tree. I smiled at the sight.

Brian was gazing intently, but not at me. He was looking past me, at something on the horizon. My hopes fell and I mouthed a curse.

"Ahoy the deck!" Brian called down, his voice charged with something other than lust. "A vessel to leeward"

"Where away?"

"Just abaft the larboard beam."

Along with our kiss went any chance of sleep tonight.

Chapter Nine

"Back the tops'ls Mr. Mason. Let us keep the advantage." The captain had come up on deck, his hair undone and flying in the breeze. "'Tis a small vessel. A lugger it appears, but we'll take what we can get, eh?"

"Aye sir." The lieutenant gave the command and the men jumped to take in sail and loosen sheets. The only sound was the soft swish of hemp sliding through sheaves.

"These skies are clearing, we should soon have a good moon to see by."

"Shall we take her at night, then?"

"Why wait? She's headed for shore, by daylight she'll be inside the shoals and wagging her tongue at us."

The young lieutenant seemed bemused. "Such a small vessel. Fishermen? Do you think she's armed, sir? Do you really think she'll resist a frigate?"

"You never can tell. She looks like a fishing boat but she may be armed. A stern chaser or a musket can be as deadly to the man it hits as a 12-pounder, and we cannot afford to lose another man."

The clouds parted, revealing a bulging gibbous moon. Taking advantage of the light, Elphinstone put his glass to his eye. "Look at that, Mr. Mason. It appears she has spied us. She has eased out her sails and fallen off, she's trying to slip away; but she can't outrun us."

The captain turned and spied me by the ratlines. "Is that Mr. MacPherson there?"

"Aye, sir." I was surprised he recognized me in the moonlight.

"We may need your services if these fellows resist. Go to your station and await further orders."

"Aye, sir."

* * * * *

I had just gone below when the drum roll sounded, a sound that sent a surge of fear and excitement through everyone's heart. All around me, men leaped into action. This was the well-rehearsed routine of a fighting frigate; and though it was only a small boat we were taking, the drill was the same.

Every man to his battle station. Freeman and I hurried to the cockpit where Mr. Brantigan was making ready our table; his practiced though palsied hands moving expertly in the dark, taking over the work of his eyes. The loblolly boys brought buckets of sand ready to be scattered on the floor to keep us from slipping in blood, though tonight we would hopefully not need it. Soon we were joined by the chaplain wearing his bands, and a handful of haggard women who waited in the shadows, in case their help was needed.

"All of this for a fishing boat? I don't like even like fish."

"Hold your tongue, Mr. Hollister," barked Brantigan. "Keep still and await orders."

The whole idea of taking private vessels smacked of piracy, yet the rules of this grand game allowed for it. The Spanish, the Dutch, and French had taken many of our merchantmen and fishing boats so why shouldn't we retaliate? It was tit for tat, the world was up for grabs, and no one wanted to be caught empty handed.

Then came the boom of one of our larboard guns, a warning shot fired over their bows, and though I had been anticipating it, I flinched.

In the shadows, I could see Mr. Frick bow his head.

"Now, will they answer?" Freeman whispered to me. I prayed the people aboard the shallop wouldn't be so foolish as to resist.

In the closeness of the dark, hot cockpit we waited, our armpits dampening, the acrid smell of perspiration rising. There was not a sound, save Brantigan's raspy breathing.

The waiting is always the worst. The slow rise of dread, wondering if you can stand what is to come. The stories I had heard about prize taking was that it could be difficult and sometimes deadly; and it almost always involved work for the surgeons. Often they resisted being taken. A well-placed shot could disable the aggressor's rigging, but a single barrel of langrage shot across the deck could maim or kill half a dozen men.

We could hear Captain Elphinstone's voice through the speaking horn commanding the boat to heave to. Then came the clatter of the marines running across the deck.

"Boarders make ready," came Lieutenant Mason's voice. "Lower away the pinnace!"

We could hear the squeak of the davits the boat was lowered. Deep in the cockpit of the frigate we stood ready at our stations, listening to the rattle of the oars placed in the locks, then the coxswain's command to shove off.

"I agree with young Hollister," said Freeman. "This is too much work for a leaky little boat stinking of herring, or whatever variety of fish they catch in these waters.

"Silence, Mr. Freeman!" Brantigan snapped.

* * * * *

Four prisoners were taken aboard; we could hear their shoes against the hull as they scrambled up the ladder. They were placed under guard somewhere near the captain's quarters, by the sound of it.

"High ranking fishermen," quipped Freeman under his breath

Those of us at the ready in the cockpit were then ordered to stand down. There had been no injuries and the prisoners were healthy and declined our services. The night's excitement was over for most of us.

Or so it seemed.

Aboard His Majesty's ships, news travels as fast as flame. Word spread that the fishing vessel was the escape ruse for a Spanish nobleman fleeing Havana to the obscure haven of Florida. He would have made it too, had Dalton not spied the vessel, for the coast was but a few miles away.

The real excitement was in discovering what the fishing boat carried. Not fish at all but a fine catch of silver plate, gold bars, and Spanish doubloons the nobleman was attempting to take with him! A fortune, rumor had it, to be transferred in cargo nets as soon as the sun came up. Once aboard, the prize would be catalogued and stored behind lock and key—and marine guard. The boat itself was of some value. Too big to be brought aboard the frigate, it would be sailed to Charleston, the nearest friendly port. Mr. Mason and the coxswain were given that privilege; after delivering the prize, they were to find passage to New York to rejoin us. I envied them their holiday.

The ship's company became riotous with the victor's bravado. Without anyone dying, without so much as a scuffed toe, we had taken a Spanish vessel containing a fortune and every man who served the *Richmond* would be rewarded with his little share of the prize. The ship was humming with speculation about how much it was worth, the figures growing by the minute, and money was spent in many a man's imagination before it was even in hand.

Too elated to sleep, most of the officers and men stayed up until the sun rose. The seamen were given a tot of spirit and in the wardroom, the officers were felicitous over their bottle. Freeman tried to get me to go down to the orlop with the older midshipmen to celebrate, and if it hadn't been for the upcoming ordeal, I surely would have.

Though I had been born to a wealthy man, I had never had money of my own. Since becoming a man, I still had none, for I had not yet received my pay. However, back in England, once we were paid off, I meant to find out what it felt like to carry a pocketful of coin.

Yet, it all seemed like a dream and I thought I might better appreciate it tomorrow, after the amputation. Once again, I took off my shoes and topcoat and climbed into the canvas sling. Outside, the sky was lightening. There was no sleep for me now, how could I sleep? I intended to just rest my eyes for a few minutes...

Chapter Ten

Freeman was shaking me, laughing, his breath stinking of stale liquor, rousing me from the land of forgotten dreams.

"Seven bells! Get up, MacPherson, a rotten leg awaits you!"

I shot out of the hammock, fully clothed, and rifled through my sea trunk for the cleaner of my two aprons.

"My, my! Such a white apron!" Freeman chaffed. "You know you shouldn't wash it so often. The dirt and stains are your badge of experience, my good fellow. Have you ever seen a butcher with a snow white apron?" He clapped me on the back, good-naturedly.

"I'm not a butcher, Dudley." I fumbled to tie the strings.

My mate just laughed. "Today you are, my friend. Today you are."

"Do I have time to shave my face?"

"Ha! All three of your chin hairs? Go on and shave, if you must." He bent his head forward to fasten his stock around his neck, and I wondered how he could be so blithe about it all.

"What I need is some coffee. When I am surgeon proper, I shall mess in the wardroom and have real coffee served to me by my very own boy. Where are those good-for-nothing loblolly boys, anyway? Hollisters! Frank and Henry!"

"Leave them to their duties, Freeman. Go get your own coffee—and fetch me a cup while you're at it."

"My, my! Getting into your role so soon, ordering me about as if I were your coachman."

"Could you just go away Dudley, and give a fellow a few minutes of peace to collect his thoughts?"

Freeman's laugh was unconcerned. "A little irritable, are we? A fat head from last night's celebration? Well, calm yourself, MacPherson. Pretend it's a mutton bone you're about to carve."

"I'll pretend it's your neck," I snapped.

He laughed blithely as he made his way toward the galley for some burned and bitter brew.

* * * * *

No wonder it's called an operating *theatre,* for indeed I felt as if I were making my entrance onto a macabre sort of stage. Everett Lee was already on the table, thanks to Freeman and the boys. The table was equipped with holes into which leather restraints would be tied. The patient, wearing only his shirt, was covered with a navy issue blanket that I would soon remove.

Six lanterns with mirror reflectors swung overhead. I had hoped for following seas, but that was not in the script, for the ship bumped along with a most irregular and unpleasant rhythm. Mr. Brantigan, Thomas, and Frank were standing by, as was Mr. Frick, hands clasped behind his back. His eyes caught mine; *take courage*, they seemed to say.

Brantigan pulled me aside. "You'll want to collect some

more men to help hold him down. A couple of stout waisters with strong stomachs, I'd advise. Even with the restraints he may buck enough to impede your work."

This task I delegated to Freeman so that I could concentrate on making ready.

"At your service, sir. Two thugs, coming up." He bowed deeply to mock me, but disappeared and soon returned with two big fellows who already looked green at the gills anticipating their assignment.

I opened my instrument kit on the tray just to the side of the operating table. At my feet, a bucket of water and the waste kid, waiting to receive the amputated leg. My stomach was in my throat and the scenes of gore and agony that had been Havana began flashing in my head. Somehow, this was worse because of the orderly environment, the careful preparation.

My voice warbled shrilly. "Mr. Freeman, you shall retract the skin and otherwise manage the affected leg, if you please. Thomas, you are to assist Mr. Freeman. Mr. Brantigan is observing. You men, what are your names?"

The waisters whom Freeman recruited were staring dumbstruck, their mouths agape.

"Your names," I snapped.

"Bonner, sir."

"Goff."

"Bonner, you are to hold the patient's shoulders. Firmly, I say. Goff, you are to hold the left leg down. Do you understand?"

They grunted and moved to their respective positions and immediately pinned Private Lee against the wooden planks until he cried out.

"Not yet, for God's sake, give the man some air to breathe. And not so roughly. He's a patient, not a criminal." I braced myself as the ship hit the side of a steep wall of water, jarring us all.

If only there was a way to make him totally insensible! To force him into a deep sleep, a complete oblivion, until the work was done. But there was no known bark, herb, or powder that would induce a safely reversible coma. Strong spirits were generally not given, for they made some men wildly uncooperative and prone to swinging their fists. The best we could give was laudanum, to blunt his pain and smooth the surface of his horror.

Dipping a sponge in the bucket of water meant to wash the blood away later, I began to wipe down his thigh, above the injury.

"Are you a surgeon or a washerwoman?" Freeman jeered.

"Hold your tongue, Mr. Freeman," Brantigan said. "But that will do, Mr. MacPherson. The patient's appendage appears quite clean and I'm certain this young man will appreciate all due speed."

"Aye, sir. Pressure on the femoral artery, please."

"Fingers trembling, I tied a strip of muslin around his thigh, indicating where I was to cut, two fingers width above the line of demarcation. Then placed the tourniquet high around his right thigh, the big quadriceps quivering like a lamb awaiting slaughter, and tightened the screws. I briefly glanced at Lee's face and saw he was biting down on a knot of a rag someone had the foresight to give him.

I looked round at my assistants, and gave them a nod. A quick glance at Mr. Frick, who looked quite pale and solemn but gave me a thumbs up.

I forgot the man whose leg it was, and I forgot my superior officer watching my every move. The moment I made the initial incision, I forgot everything but the task at hand. Concentration cleared my mind and I was able to focus on the technicalities apart from the whole man. As Freeman pulled up the skin of the right thigh, I neatly carved through the flesh to form the flap of skin that would cover the stump. Intent on the mechanics of cutting, I quickly and cleanly severed the layers of tissue and muscle, now thick and warm in my hand, and was through the periosteum, with two flicks of my wrist.

"Do be brave, lad," I heard Brantigan say. Though he was talking to the patient, I took his words to heart for myself.

Everett quieted except for his breathing. I could hear him panting like a sick cat. Picking up the bone saw I went in for the femur, pressing hard, fully intent on getting through with all due speed. Everett screamed through the rag, struggled against the restraints, then fainted.

"Thank God," Freeman said. "Sure is easier once they pass out, eh MacPherson?"

The lower leg fell onto the table, oozing blood. "Remove it, please," I said, picking up a file to smooth the rough edges of bone, feeling more like a carpenter's mate than a surgeon's mate. Now to tie off the ends of the severed blood vessels with catgut and cauterize any persistent bleeders with scalding pitch.

As I dressed the stump, his eyes fluttered open. Brantigan and Freeman had gone for their coffee, and the others, too, had been dismissed.

"Is it over?" Everett mumbled.

"It's over."

"But it feels like its still there." He struggled to sit up, to have a look for himself, but the effort caused him to faint again and his face went gray with shock.

"Frank! Thomas!"

One of the twins appeared.

"More blankets, at once! And hot broth. When he comes around you are to give him as much as possible."

"He don't look like he's going to come to his senses any time soon, Mr. MacPherson. Do you think he'll live?"

I grabbed the boy by his shoulders with my bloody fingers and shook him. "You just pray to God he does, Mr. Hollister.

You just pray to God he does." And then I hugged him fiercely and kissed the top of his head.

Chapter Eleven

Dinner in the orlop mess was a felicitous affair, the men still joyous over last night's prize. Bottles of Madeira and French brandy were shared round and the cook served up a plum duff that was especially tasty I tucked up to the table where I had earlier amputated a leg with a newfound ease and sense of belonging. *I was a surgeon's mate in His Majesty's Royal Navy. These men were my family, this ship, my home. We were victorious in Havana, and we would be rewarded with prize.*

Time slowed, paused, and hung suspended for a supernatural moment. The relief, the gratification, the happiness, was indescribable and I felt as if I were looking down at myself from afar. I *was* living and I was *watching* myself live, both at the same time. I was content.

All around me the warm hum of talk, scraping of knives, the clink of tankards, and the rich *a cappella* of men's voices all talking at once. Someone shared a joke and the entire company roared in masculine laughter, like a great wave breaking against the rocks. Someone poured me another glass of wine.

* * * * *

The afternoon passed, Everett Lee slept. Later I looked in on my patient to make certain he was not hemorrhaging, and not in undue pain. I marveled at his breathing, the very fact that he was alive. Though the source of infection had been removed, I wondered now if it should have been amputated sooner. Had the poison already spread? I could not bring myself to leave his side, and I held a vigil until late into the middle watch when the chaplain came in and relieved me.

We exchanged no words; only a look that told me Mr. Frick was sympathetic to both Everett and me. Then I left the sick berth, hung my hammock, and collapsed, leaving the patient in good hands. For the first time in many a night, I slept.

* * * * *

The next morning we examined the fresh stump.

Brantigan put on his spectacles and peered at it like a falcon over his prey. "Well done, Mr. MacPherson. Mr. Lee, can you hear me? Everett? Are you awake?"

Everett's eyes fluttered open and he tried to focus on us, his pupils were constricted from laudanum. He muttered something nonsensical then lapsed back into his opium dream. I was glad he was so heavily under the influence because at least for now he didn't have to face the fact that his leg was gone.

"He has survived the shock. Now, if the blood poison doesn't kill him, he's a fortunate man. Mr. MacPherson, note it in the log, sir."

The day passed slowly, marked by the ship's bell announcing the passing of each half hour. Everett Lee lived and I decided I would apply myself more studiously in learning what surgical skills I could. I vowed I would study Branti-gan's books; I would listen more closely to Mr. Freeman's gory tales of glory for any advice I could glean. The surgical kit that had belonged to my late husband was no longer just the means of eking out a livelihood. They represented the tools of my profession. When we returned to England I would take my exams. I would pass them. I would be a bona fide surgeon, as my namesake Patrick MacPherson had been. I would no longer be a sham.

Having resolved that, I approached my duties with a renewed sense of purpose.

Chapter Twelve

The euphoria of taking our Spanish prize soon faded. We were only a day or two at the most, from landfall when the wind backed and strengthened, driving black clouds before it and whipping the seas into spume. The next day we treated two for chilblains, seven for catarrhs, thirteen for rheumatic complaints—all due to the worsening weather. Having grown accustomed to the heat of the tropics, the drop in temperature was a shock to us all. My teeth rattled, my bones ached; I was wet to the core and couldn't be warmed. Our spirits were as damp and ragged as our clothes.

The ship's cats had disappeared, seeking the few remaining rats deep in the hold. The last cow had been butchered for the officers and the prisoners (who were treated well and would be exchanged once we made New York.) The rest of us existed on salt beef and biscuit, our stinking moldy cheese no longer eatable, our salt pork and dried peas all consumed. Landfall could not come soon enough.

For those soldiers we were transporting, New York was home, or close to it. For the rest of us New York meant the novelty of land and a day or two of pleasure, before the work of replenishing much needed supplies. Brian and I looked forward to a consummation of our desire. There had been few opportunities lately for us to exchange a look, much less a word, but soon, in the dark privacy of some rented room near the waterfront, there would be no need for words nor looks.

The gale beat us miserably and at last made us change our direction. We braced yards and wore ship, heading out to sea, away from our destination, away from New York, for the winds were in our teeth and we could not hold our course. The ship took on water as the sea swept across the deck, the pumps were manned continually, and the creaking of the chains could heard throughout the ship, like large metallic crickets.

* * * * *

I woke from a deep sleep to Iris Wickham hissing in my ear. "Mr. MacPherson, please sir, you must come at once!"

"Who? What's going on?" I fought to clear my foggy head.

"It's one of the women, sir. She's bleeding. It can't be stopped. Please, can you come to the fo'c'sle with me?"

I tumbled to the floor, clumsily knocking into Freeman, sending his hammock swinging. He slept on, his snores undisturbed.

"I should wake Mr. Brantigan," I said, fumbling for my coat. "He'll want to know."

"No, you must not, sir! He'll tell the captain and she's not authorized to be on board, she'll be put off in New York."

If we officially treated the women on board, we'd have to officially recognize they existed, and report them in our logs. If they weren't one of the warrant's wives who were authorized to be here, they'd almost certainly be sent packing at the very next port.

"What's the matter? Why is she bleeding?" Fumbling with my jacket, I stuffed my bare feet into my shoes.

"A seven month baby. The placenta came first, and in pieces."

I stumbled after her, grasping for handholds as the ship lurched and plummeted into the deepening troughs. High above us the wind screaming in the rigging, sounding for all the world like a woman wailing. Ducking, I making my way through a swaying forest of hammocks, like some great arbor, heavy with fruit. Before I even laid eyes on the woman, I smelled an extravagance of warm blood overriding the other strong smells of the fo'c'sle.

I called for a lantern and someone brought me a candle in a sconce. The cone of flickering light illuminated the woman's face. The girl's face, I saw now. I knelt down beside her, my heart knocking. I had only ever attended one delivery, an uncomplicated one, and had done nothing whatsoever useful at that.

"Patrick MacPherson, miss. Surgeon's mate, I am sympathetic to your circumstances." I supposed I should have addressed her as madam or missus, but she was ridiculously young.

"Thank you," she said. "Iris told me you would come."

"What's your name?"

"But I don't hear it crying. Why doesn't it cry?"

Iris dropped to her knees beside me, and stroking the girl's damp hair away from her face, whispered, "I'm so very sorry Maggie, but the wee one never took a breath."

I noticed it then, a small bundle of rags tucked next to the bulkhead. I crawled over to have a look and found a baby, a girl, eyes swollen, skin cool and grey. Someone, likely Iris, had wiped it clean of membrane and blood before hastily wrapping it in a scrap of canvas. A wooden pail next to it held the placenta and the twisted, ropey umbilical cord.

Maggie's sob was lost in the shriek of the wind in the rigging. "Lad or lassie?"

"It was a girl," Iris said, grasping Maggie's slim white hand and pressing it between her own. "She's with God now. The angels are rocking her."

"Let me see her, Missus Wickham. Please might I hold her?"

Iris looked to me and I nodded. Iris brought the bundle and placed it in the girl's slim arms.

Maggie struggled to sit up and unwrapped the dead infant, touching it all over as if to inspect it, then hugging it to her breast. "She's better off with the angels than in this cruel world, " she said, rewrapping the body and handing it back to Iris.

"Maggie, might I examine your pulse?" I took hold of her thin, cool wrist. Finding no beat there, I placed two fingers over her carotid artery alongside her neck. Rapid and weak.

"She's in shock," I said to Iris. "We must consult Mr. Brantigan."

"No!" Maggie grabbed my sleeve in alarm. "You can't sir, please! I'll be thrown off the ship in New York."

If you live to see New York, I thought. She should be bled, of course.

Bleeding was the answer to nearly every ailment, yet it was counter-intuitive in a situation like this, to cut a vein and remove even more blood. No matter what Hippocrates, Galen, and those other long-dead Greek sages said, it just didn't make sense. Yet, the women looked at me hopefully. They clearly expected me to do something, to take charge, to manage the unmanageable.

There in the dark on the deck I performed a pelvic exam, discovering naught but a boggy post-partum uterus. The blood continued to flow. "Where's her man?"

The women looked at me, their faces grievously haggard in the flickering light.

"Aloft, " came a voice from the shadows. "Reefing sail."

"The watch is nearly over, the bell will be striking soon," said another.

It was impossible for anyone to alert him while he was engaged in such a task. He would come below when his watch was over, to find his baby stillborn and his wife near death

"She needs warm fluids to restore her," I said to Iris. "Tea, if its to be had. A quart of warm, weak tea. And find another blanket." I looked at one of the bystanders, a pale, slack-jawed girl. "You, Miss, go fetch a blanket. Your own, if necessary."

"But it ain't mine, sir. It's my husband's. He'll want it when he comes off watch."

"This woman needs it now," I snapped.

The group of women began to busy themselves, scavenging the fo'c'sle to find blankets and sneaking to the galley to make a furtive pot of lukewarm tea on the still-warm stove. On my knees beside the girl, I massaged her tender abdomen, as if I were a baker kneading dough. I'd learned the old technique from Aeneas after Mrs. Blake had given birth. If Aeneas MacPherson were here now, he'd know what to do.

Some of the hammocks stirred with life as people woke and were peering out over the edges of their canvas beds to see what was going on. They would know, of course, that one of the women that lived among them was with child. They would have guessed that she was in labor, and that things had not gone well.

"Shall I send for the chaplain?" I said.

"Sir, she's a papist," another said.

"At a time like this..." I began, but Maggie grasped my sleeve. "No officers, no chaplain, I beg you!" She held on tightly and whispered, "Our secret, please sir!"

"She's afraid she'll be given the boot, sir," another girl explained. "And we'll all be thrown off the ship." All were afraid of bringing attention to themselves, of being deprived of their floating home. To them New York was not a welcome shore leave, but a potential pitfall.

Iris returned with a pot of lukewarm tea, from whose stores they came, I cared not. From out of the shadows, girls brought blankets.

"Good. Now see that she drinks all this, and more."

"We have no more. Those leaves was obtained from the steward's rubbish, they was."

"Hell's teeth!" I cursed under my breath. "Do you have any grog? Any rum? Any broth?"

They looked from one to another.

"I have a bit of grog saved," came a man's voice from the darkness.

"She must have it," I said. "And I must go get my kit." I hurried across the lurching ship, stumbling into swaying hammocks heavy with sleeping seamen, oblivious to the situation. What I would do with the instruments, I wasn't sure, but I was in a panic to do something.

* * * * *

"Dudley!" I hissed.

He slept on, oblivious. I grabbed his shoulders, shaking him until at last he opened his eyes.

"For God's sake, is the ship a'fire?"

"I need your help. There's a woman, a sea wife. She's just been delivered, the infant was stillborn. They came for me, they don't want the captain to know; but maybe I should go wake him anyway, what do you think?"

His yawn was extravagant. "I think you should let me sleep Do I look like a midwife?"

"But she's bleeding, she's..."

"Birthing's a messy business, more blood than an amputation," he mumbled as he turned in his hammock, snuggling in. "Let the women handle their own kind. Smart as cats, those sea wives."

"She's in shock, she's hemorrhaging. We can't just stand by and watch her expire."

"Alright, I'll come then," he groused. Yet, he was slow to get up.

I left him, making my way through the forest of swaying hammocks to the fo'c'sle where a young seaman in a ragged Monmouth cap was now on his knees beside her. He looked to me for help, his eyes wide, his jaw slack. I had no idea what to do.

"Where is Mrs. Wickham?" I said. "Somebody fetch her! I need dressings, tows, muslin gauze, old petticoats, rags, anything to staunch the flow!"

The seaman squeezed his girl's hand and pressed it to his lips. "Hold on, Maggie dove," he whispered. "Mr. MacPherson is here, he knows what to do. Everything will be alright."

Where was Freeman?

"Send for Mr. Brantigan at once, and rouse Mr. Frick," I shouted out to anyone who might obey, but they all simply stared at me, as if I were mad. "Mrs. Wickham!"

She appeared from the darkness and handed me a freshly torn roll of lawn, the hem of a petticoat, probably her own. "Iris, you must rouse Mr. Brantigan and Mr. Frick and tell them I've sent for them, they must come at once. Do as I say now, be off with you! The rest of you, bring me your blankets."

What had gone wrong? What could cause this much blood? If we can cut off an offending leg, pull a bad tooth, why couldn't we fix a bleeding uterus? Yet to cut her open was unheard of and might hasten her death.

Not knowing what else to do I slipped a fistful of cloth

into the birth canal, up against her open cervix, hoping through the pressure of my hand I could stop the bleeding. Still the blood ran down my arm, pooling and congealing on the deck at my knees. The girl began to convulse, her bare feet twitching a macabre dance. Her man cried out and wrapped his arms around her thin shoulders, lifting her up as if he could keep her alive through his embrace. "Oh, my Maggie girl!"

Kneeling between her legs my fist buried inside her, I felt the river lose its force, slowing to a trickle as her heart stopped beating.

Chapter Thirteen

Surgeon's log, October 31, 1762: Called to the fo'c'sle to see one of the women who had just been delivered of a still-born female. The young mother suffered postpartum hemorrhage, but although she was bled of half a pint and given warm tea and compresses, she expired just before two bells (5 o'clock A.M., ship time). Captain and chaplain notified. At sunrise, both mother and infant were buried at sea.

— Patrick MacPherson, Surgeon's Mate

* * * * *

Maggie (I never did learn her last name) was not the first person who had died under my care; many men had, including my own husband, nearly two years ago. Instead of hardening me, making me more insensible to the vagaries of fate it seemed instead to have made me more vulnerable to my emotions. I had succeeded in amputating Everett Lee's leg, yet I had been able to do nothing to save Maggie. Might something more have been done for the woman? The next afternoon I decided to unburden myself on Mr. Brantigan.

The gales had abated and I found him walking the quarterdeck conversing with the captain. I stood by the leeward rail, gazing out on the grey North Atlantic, still unsettled and choppy. The sky was already dark but for a gaping hole of red, a fresh wound to the west where the sun had set. I waited until the captain took his leave before approaching my superior.

"Well then," Brantigan said after we exchanged our good evenings, "I suppose you'll be wanting liberty when we reach New York?" He was surprisingly warm and magnanimous, not his usual irascible self. On his clean white cravat, a telling burgundy stain

"Aye sir," I said truthfully. In fact, I was counting on it.

"Once we get the Yankee soldiers delivered, you and Mr. Freeman shall have your holiday ashore, you have earned it."

"Thank you, sir. But I have something else to ask of you."

The ship's bell rang four times, followed by the bosun's call, signaling the second dogwatch. Those men who had not yet supped were relieved by those who had just done so.

"Speak up, Mr. MacPherson. What's on your mind?"

"Might you tell me the most efficacious treatment for, ah, post-partum hemorrhage? Profuse uterine bleeding?" I blurted out.

He blinked and rubbed his rheumy eyes. Had he heard me? I dared not repeat myself.

"It seems a theoretical question, and rather irrelevant, I should think. We so seldom see such occurrences aboard His Majesty's warships. You would further advance your naval career by focusing on procedures such as amputation, trepanning and cystotomy."

I shuffled uncomfortably at his chiding, but not wanting to drop the matter, I pressed on.

"Well, there are occasionally wives of officers and warrants aboard that go to childbed, perhaps prematurely. And then there are the others."

Linda Collison

He looked at me, narrowing his rheumy eyes. "The others?"

"The fo'c'sle wives. " My ears burned with embarrassment for even mentioning them.

"You are too generous with the term wives," he said, wagging a gnarled finger at me. "And if you're referring to that unfortunate creature who so recently passed away, I don't know of anything else you might have done for her. We're naval surgeons, Mr. MacPherson, not *accoucheurs*. The perils of childbirth are the unfortunate lot of their sex, I'm afraid. We don't hold the power of life and death in our hands as some of our profession would like to think."

He had my ear and seemed eager for an audience. "You're young, not yet twenty, am I right? You still want for experience. Even after that ghastly siege we endured, you need more seasoning. You still have much to learn, but your skills are improving immeasurably, you are temperate with your bottle, you show a genuine desire to help your fellow man." He paused, his face relaxing into an expression of indulgence and favor and I realized he was already into his cups.

"Patrick, my boy," he said, squeezing my shoulder with his trembling paw, partly for balance, as the vessel rose and plunged on the chop, "You will make an excellent ship surgeon and I intend to write a letter of recommendation. My career has been long enough that my word is well respected. I have some influence and a man does not get his own ship without it, that's certain. However, you must learn to draw the line, MacPherson, and not take every death so personally. Nor every triumph. Oh, if only I could have trained you from a young age..."

I was speechless, trying to grasp what he had just said.

"Tomorrow we should raise New York, and none too soon, I say. So glad to be out of those ungodly climes and away from the Spanish mortars and the tropical miasmas, eh? Tomorrow, after sick call, come to my quarters. After we have caught up with the log we must inventory our supplies, we have nearly depleted our stores of Peruvian bark and guiacum, that much is certain."

"Aye, sir."

"Now then, my supper awaits and another bottle of claret with the good captain. If you'll kindly direct me toward the companionway, my eyesight is no good once twilight descends."

I helped him to the ladder and bid him a pleasant evening, feeling only slightly comforted. Brantigan had absolved me of any official wrongdoing in Maggie's death, yet he had never answered my questions: *What else might I have done? What would he have done? Had I been negligent in my duty to another human being?*.

I supped with my new messmates where the talk veered from end-of-war rumors to a comparison of the inherent sexual prowess of various races and nationalities of women. I was silent on the issue but didn't blush, for my ears had become accustomed to such ribald, boyish boasting. All I could think about was the young woman who bled to death shortly after giving birth, and of whom nobody spoke. To hear them talk, sexual congress was a sporting game, a conquest, and the only danger it held for these men was a wife and brat or a dose of the clap.

I missed my old messmates, especially Iris, and when my glass was empty, I left the aft orlop for the berthing deck to have a word with her. But I found that Mrs. Wickham had turned in early and was asleep behind a canvas partition that served as the only provider of privacy for her and her husband.

"How fares your wife?" I asked Wickham solicitously.

"Fairly worn out, she is. All that business with the topman's woman and all. She has taken it to heart."

As had I, yet apparently it must not be spoken of. Though we lived and worked in close proximity, depending on one another for our very lives, never did we discuss death aboard a ship. God forbid we should share our fear and sorrow in this uncertain world! Feeling conflicted and confused, I went up to the spar deck with a mind to climb the rigging. Aloft, the sharp wet wind would blow my mind empty and sweep my heart clean.

The chaplain stood at the rail, alone as usual, and I thought I might ask him if I had done right by the girl. What good was a surgeon or surgeon's mate, really? If neither life nor death were in our hands, what role did we play? However, Mr. Frick had no answers for me either, just an allegory to share, the biblical account of Jacob wrestling the angel. Though I found no comfort in his tale, and no parallel to my own questions of conscience and duty, I thanked him for his council and wished him a good night.

"I am sympathetic to your situation," he said as I turned to go. "And I promise to keep whatever secret you might tell me in confidence."

My breath caught in my throat, but I kept my equanimity. "Thank you, Mr. Frick. I'll keep that in mind, should I ever have a secret that burdens me; but just now I'm going aloft to the main fighting deck to be closer to God. Care to join me?"

Even in the dark I could see, or feel, his self-effacing smile. "The very thought of climbing aloft makes me bilious. Do take care, Patrick. And put in a good word for me while you're up there."

* * * * *

One of the loblolly boys had strung my hammock for me, a small act of kindness, or amends for some minor offense I had yet to discover. Had I not been so exhausted I would have found them in the darkness and kissed their sleeping faces, both. Instead, I climbed into my hammock and collapsed. Now the tears came and I indulged them, my pathetic little sobs sounding like a kitten drowning. I was feeling every bit as sorry for myself as I was for the young woman who died and the topman who loved her, until I realized that Freeman, hanging in his hammock just fourteen inches away, was not asleep as I had thought.

"I'll let you in on a little confidence, MacPherson," he whispered in the darkness. "I was once like you, overly solicitous of my patients, overly tender-hearted. Every death I took personally, as if I had somehow failed in my duties." His laugh was a dry crack, a branch snapping. "Many was the night I wept myself to sleep. Oh, I know you're probably thinking, *Dudley Freeman weep?* Yes, Dudley Freeman wept."

This was indeed a night of revelations. I sniffed my tears and dried my eyes with the hem of my shirt.

"My advice to you, Patrick, is to drop it like a bundle of faggots, this load of worry you're carrying. Those fo'c'sle girls have a wretched existence. It's probably best she's gone to be with her little mooncalf. There's no profit in what-ifs, my friend. If you want to be a good surgeon, you must carry nothing from patient to patient. And you must build a strong box around your heart to keep it from breaking."

"Oh, but I..."

"And if you ever tell anyone I ever cried myself to sleep, I shall vehemently deny it. In fact," he added, his normal persona regaining control, "I will personally thrash your sorry freckled hide. Now then, good night sir, and may you enjoy sweet, wet dreams of those New York girls awaiting us."

"Thanks, Dudley. Good night." I was imagining the stout sea trunk that he had built around his poor neglected heart; a box already overgrown with barnacles, the key lost, the lock rusted.

From above, the sounds of the men on deck, the voice of the captain o' the tops relaying directions, the creaking of yards braced round. The ship's motion eased and now rolled along on a following swell. I took comfort in knowing the morning sun would rise and shine upon the green shores of North America.

My mind was still a confused sea though, as I grappled with the meaning of professional duty and moral obligation, and of my feelings for the gunner, which was a physical desire, a growing need that would drive me into his arms as soon as we found the opportunity. My biggest fear was that I should be found out. The chaplain obviously suspected, how should I deal with that? This much was certain: I must maintain the ruse, for I absolutely wanted to become a legitimate ship's surgeon. I realized this clearly, with a joy of discovery, as if a ray of light had illuminated the hidden desire in some dark recess of my being. It was like finding a crown in the gutter.

Chapter Fourteen

Well into the middle watch, I got up to use the head as I often did at that hour, when most of the ship's people were sleeping. The wind had dropped, a cold fog had materialized, and it was starting to drizzle. The ship's great sails hung limp as bed sheets on laundry day.

Brian was waiting for me in the waist by the boats that were lashed to the gallows amidships.

"I'm sorry to hear about Maggie," he said. "Her man is on the crew of one of my guns, he was much affected by it."

I nodded.

"He expressed his gratitude for what ye did."

"I did nothing," I said, almost angrily.

"Nae, ye came and ye tried to help."

"It wasn't enough."

"Ye aren't God."

A short laugh escaped me. "Thank you for reminding me. And that seems to be the consensus."

"How's the soldier, the lad whose leg ye had to take?"

"I believe he's going to make it."

"Well mark that down on yer score card, Mr. MacPherson. One win, one loss. And have ye thought how will ye spend yer wages and yer share of the prize money?"

I hadn't. But now I allowed myself to consider it.

"I'll buy a horse and a saddle, that much is certain. A fast horse and a fine saddle."

His laugh was soft. "Aye, if ye're going to dream, might as well dream in color. And where will ye keep this horse?"

"In a stable, of course."

"A stable on land?"

"Where else? Of course on land."

"But I thought ye were a man of the sea. A ship surgeon's mate." He gave me one of his enigmatic smiles.

And that did give me pause. "For the moment," I said, contrarily.

"Inconstant, fickle female."

"Explain yourself."

He shrugged. "I was jesting. Nothing more."

Suddenly I was tired of the jesting, the teasing, the everlasting mating dance. I wanted something more definite. Something sure.

"What will become of us, Mr. Dalton? Do you have any idea?"

He shrugged. "With any luck, we'll live to see our payoff. And with even more luck we'll know a bit of happiness before the reaper taps our shoulder."

"Once we get to back to England, I mean. What, specifically, will we do?"

Brian laughed softly. "Myself, I plan on getting hard over at the Highwater Mark Tavern. And ye?"

"I am perfectly serious."

"As am I. When navy men reach port that's the first thing they do."

"Must you be so literal? I'm talking in more general terms. As in what will be the nature of our association?"

Just then, the cook and his boy came clambering up the companionway lugging a cauldron of greasy water between them. Soon it would be daylight. The cooks grunted as they heaved the contents of the enormous pot over the leeward rail, not far from where we stood.

"Damn this fog, it'll keep us out of port if it gets any thicker," said the boy to the older man.

"Thick as soup already."

We stood in silence as they dipped up pails of seawater to scrub the cauldron clean, and then dumped the dirty water into the scuppers. They cursed cheerfully as they worked, then disappeared below again without a glance at us.

"What of us?" I persisted, not wanting to let the matter drop. "What of me? When we get to England, what will I do?"

"What of ye? Ye'll do as ye please, I expect. Just like ye always have. But if ye're going to dress like a man and act like a man, then..."

"But I don't do as I please, not at all," I interrupted, my impatience growing. "How can you say that? Do you think I enjoy living this charade?" I was surprised to realize we were at odds. Why was I forcing an argument on the eve of our arrival into New York?

"It appears so." He glanced at me then looked away.

"I do what I must to get by," I protested. "You know that."

"But there are so many ways of getting by, Princess. There's always a choice to make. Ye make it every day."

I felt the blood rise to my face. He did not understand after all, and I thought he had. "I'm not talking like a philosopher now, or even a surgeon's mate. I'm speaking as a woman, from my heart. And I want to know when we get to England, will we live together or do I take my own lodgings? Shall I give up my trade?" There, I had said it.

His eyebrows shot up. His voice changed. "This frigate is my home, ye know that well. This warrant is a plum, it's what I've wanted my whole life, I'd be a fool to give it up. And I'm entitled to keep a wife, ye know. In my cabin."

"If that's a marriage proposal, Mr. Dalton, it was not well put," I snipped.

"I was just stating a fact, *Mister* MacPherson. I'm sure the life of a gunner's wife is far beneath ye to ever consider. Once a princess always a princess."

That took the wind right out of me.

"Just as I thought," he muttered, when for once I said nothing in response. Within a storm of conflicting feelings, I was still trying to imagine myself as his wife.

The silence broadened and I didn't know how to close the growing space between us. A kettle of contrasting feelings roiled in my mind. I loved the man, yes! However, I didn't want to live as the women below did. Though Dalton indeed had a cabin of his own, it was a tiny, airless box. The two of us, we'd be all shoulders, limbs and feet; we'd be bumping into one another constantly.

However, it was more than the tiny living space. I didn't want to give up the respect I had gained or leave behind the freedom I had enjoyed as Patrick MacPherson. It dawned on me that I actually liked my new persona; and I wanted to become a good surgeon, the best of surgeons. Yet, I also wanted Brian Dalton's love and I realized at some point I might have to choose between them.

"Ye're shivering," he said.

"It's wet and cold, I'm going to bed for a wink of sleep."

As I started to take my leave, he reached for my sleeve, pulling me into his arms, my hat falling to the deck. I didn't resist but returned his kiss with an eager mouth, nearly bit-ing him at first. Then giving in, my arms around him, lips open and soft, all my anger and frustration drowning in the rogue wave of our embrace.

Chapter Fifteen

Long Island was raised at first light; on the larboard, New Jersey's green shoreline. Soon we entered the narrows where a slight shift in the wind brought seductive smell of land. Oh, New York!

Those soldiers who had the strength for it, crawled up the ladders from the underworld to witness their triumphant return. Their wizened eyes were sunken into pinched faces—faces etched with both joy and unspeakable sadness, the irony of homecoming. Buttons having been lost back in the muck of Havana trenches, they held their homespun jackets against the cold autumn air with trembling hands.

A pilot boat came alongside and a man clambered aboard to conn us into port. Rising up from behind the busy clutter of masts the smoke from hundreds of chimneys beckoned us like waving arms. Glimpses of warehouses, taverns, stables, churches, houses—the rich diversity of sights was a delight to our eyes after the monotony of the sea. I gazed upon the scene as if it were a great landscape painting come to life and growing larger by the minute.

Allow and aloft, the men worked the sails and readied the

anchor with a diligence and vigor that bespoke their pride in the ship and in themselves. I felt it too, I was full-to bursting with pride, certain that everyone on shore was looking at us and thinking *now there is the finest of frigates that ever came into our port.*

As the ship drifted closer an onslaught of smells reached our heads and we sniffed the air like hunting dogs, mad for more. The ripe odor of the fisherman's catch, the autumn tang of fallen leaves, the stink of sewage in the gutters. It was all novel. It was all delightful.

The women too, were in high spirits. They slipped to the rail or put their faces to the ports for a glimpse and a whiff of land. Everett struggled up the companionway with the help of the Hollister boys, to look upon the shore. Very soon now, I'd be saying farewell to him, yet the pain of leaving my young amputee was overshadowed by the glee of landfall and the prospect of my tryst with Brian. Our little quarrel, if one could call it that, had been purged by last night's kiss with the promise of more to come. I had already pushed it to the back of my mind and Brian wasn't one to hold a grudge. Nothing could keep us apart, I was certain.

The wind was a knife's edge, penetrating my worn-thin coat. My teeth chattered happily and I could not remember ever being this cold or this happy. Let it be cold, the colder the better, for Brian's arms would feel that much warmer when our opportunity came. And who cared about what would happen, I no longer gave a thought to how we would live once we got back to England. At this very moment, we were arriving in New York!

The thump of hawser being flaked on the deck, the shriek of the bosun's call. The great boom of the cannons firing a customary salute thrilled me, the grand orderliness of it all! Yet, so much work to be done before we could enjoy our liberty ashore. We surgeons had to transport the colonial soldiers to the hospital, then clean and fumigate the sick berth.

Freeman and I were to take inventory of our nearly depleted supplies and procure what was needed.

For the sailors the work was even more laborious; the vessel was to be stripped of everything in preparation for breaming. Every barrel, every trunk, every cannon and keg of powder would have to be removed from the ship and stored in a warehouse on the waterfront. The frigate would then be sailed up to the careening yard at Turtle Bay where sails would be unbent, the topmasts removed. The ship would then be winched over on her side exposing half her hull at a time, to be cleaned of the barnacles and seaweeds that attached themselves below the water line. These beard-like growths hung on tenaciously and slowed us down considerably. Above all, a frigate must be sleek and fast.

Once the underside was scraped and burned clean, the ship would be set to right. Then she must be reloaded again and new supplies taken on. The barrels and casks must be carefully arranged to balance the ship's weight and to prevent the stores from shifting while underway. Finally, the rigging must be made right, the topmasts and sails replaced, the water and stores brought aboard.

All this work was said to require at least four or five days (the longer it took, the better, by my way of thinking), during which time the ship's company would be billeted in nearby inns and houses where we would take our meals and sleep—at the navy's expense, of course. The officers would have private quarters, the midshipmen and we petty officers would share rooms, and the sailors and marines would be quartered in lofts, warehouses, and livery stables.

Not that any man planned on spending much time in his own bed. New York beckoned us, a seductress with a clamorous siren call. We were all in love with the city and ready to do her bidding.

* * * * *

"Easy now, mind your step," Freeman said as we helped the first of the ambulatory soldiers onto the gangway, bobbing and swaying with the harbor swell. "Mind you don't fall and break your leg."

"You're in a jolly mood, my friend." I had never heard him be so solicitous as now, when we were discharging the patients.

"Hell, yes! The quicker we rid ourselves of these lubbers, the sooner we'll be free to enjoy ourselves. I know a fine little tavern, MacPherson. Good drink, good company, good gaming." He enjoyed being the knowledgeable one, the old hand in New York, and the one to show me around.

Truthfully, I didn't mind, I needed a guide, having never set foot on this continent before. And a tankard of ale was going to taste awfully good by the time we finished delivering our patients and helping the transport ship unload theirs. But our job was relatively easy; the gunner and his mates would be busy until dark. I might as well have a drink with Dudley for there would be no chance of seeing Brian until after supper.

Overhead, the seagulls wheeled and cried. The wharf was a lively place with sailors loading and unloading their cargo, hucksters advertising corn, apples, and pumpkins. Clusters of people waited anxiously, scrutinizing each soldier we offloaded, looking for a familiar face. Underfoot pigeons chortled, profiting from scatterings of spilled grain

We pushed a cart between us, Freeman and I, carrying a soldier from Connecticut who was recovering from the fever, but still too weak to walk more than a few steps. For once Freeman didn't complain about having to do menial work but lent his shoulder to the task without a grumble or an excuse. The chaplain shepherded a company of men in rags, stumbling along on blistered feet. The Hollister boys looked like little burros, laden as they were with tin cups, haversacks, and powder horns.

The surgeons from the transport *Aeolus* were shuttling patients too and we called to them in high spirits, inviting them to join us for drinks later. The air was charged with the excitement of landfall and the new variety of sounds invigorated me. The smart clip clop of horseshoes, the jingle and rattle of harness and carriage, I had missed these noises and they contrasted delightfully with the weary moans and groans of the frigate.

Agents and procurers approached us, offering every service imaginable. I could have had a hot meal while my shirts were washed and pressed. I could have known an hour's joy with the renown Brewster sisters while my shoes were being repaired. What a city, I marveled.

Half a dozen church bells pealed the hour, in different pitches and not quite in unison, like some enthusiastic but ill trained country choir. New York welcomed us, she seemed big bosomed and generous, more vital than I had anticipated—and more prosperous. It was evident that war was good for commerce. The stores and counting houses had an air of business about them, and the warehouses were filled to bursting. Army officers aplenty walking the streets in their smart red coats, their side arms gleaming in the sun. Merchants, sutlers, privateers and smugglers, all looking like perfect gentlemen, all getting rich off the war.

Of paupers and street urchins, there appeared to be none. Even the more rudely dressed folk, the servants and stable boys out on their errands, had a look of hope about them as if their luck was about to change for the better, and the very pigs and dogs rooting in the rubbish heaps were fat and glossy. Here in New York even the roosters seemed to crow more boisterously.

My first disappointment came on Front Street where we found not a proper hospital, but a converted warehouse. Row after row of rude cots, were still not enough to hold all the men from the *Aoleus*. Many would be forced to lie on the floor. Those that weren't so ill or injured stood in groups, talking, waiting to be released. They were waiting to return to their wives, their mothers, their workshops, and farms.

I wanted to save Everett's transfer for last, to prolong our farewell as long as possible. However, he was in a great hurry to meet his family and insisted on going under his own power, with the help of the crutches Wickham had made from scraps of timber scavenged from the carpenter's locker.

"My brother is an impatient man, Mr. MacPherson. He'll want to be picking me up and getting on."

"Your own brother? Surely he'd be only too happy to wait a few more hours to welcome you home," I said.

"Half-brother, actually." Everett said. "And he's not inclined to wait for anything or anyone. He'll be wanting to get on."

With a knot in my chest, I helped Everett gather his few belongings into the haversack. His shaving kit (which he barely needed, but for the sparse beginnings of a moustache), a tin cup, a spare shirt, stained and worn at the elbows and cuffs, and his precious book of Meditations.

It took us the better part of an hour to cover the quarter mile to the hospital, for he insisted on going under his own power and the crutches slipped on the cobblestones. When at last we reached the brick warehouse, he was pale and trembling, barely able to stand. A gathering of people stood outside waiting, but I could tell by Everett's face his brother wasn't among them.

Inside the hospital doors, a harried clerk dressed in homespun took his name and company, entering the information into a ledger book.

"Row 16, cot number 23," he directed, motioning vaguely over his shoulder with his thumb. "If someone's in that space, take the nearest one to it."

"Has Private Lee's family inquired about him?"

The man shrugged.

"His family are merchantmen," I explained. "Aboard the schooner *Andromeda*. Have they come for him?"

"It's a regular circus here sir, as you can see for yourself. The Royal Family themselves could be here and I wouldn't know it." He turned from us to log in the next wave of patients waiting for admittance.

Everett was already hobbling on his crutches to find his cot, down the long row of occupied beds, and collapsed into an empty one. I hurried to his side, saw that fresh blood had saturated his dressing and was seeping through his coarse woven breeches.

"Where's the receiving surgeon?" I demanded of a man carrying a bucket of water and a dipper, but he just shook his head. I preempted a female nurse carrying a bundle of dressings, taking what I needed to redress the wound.

Though tender and bleeding, the stump's suture line was still intact and showed no signs of infection. Satisfied, I redressed it and gave Everett the dram of laudanum I had saved just for him. Still, I was reluctant to leave him.

"I only did it for the money, you know," he confided. "To get out from under my brother. And now I'm more dependent on him than ever. I never should have joined up."

I couldn't bear to hear him talk this way; but I didn't know how to shore him up. I could not recite Marcus Aurelius, had no words of comfort or strength, nothing at all to offer.

"Everett, my friend." There was a thickness in my throat. "Write me. Send me good news of your recovery."

He nodded.

I swallowed hard. "Get well. Promise me."

"Thank you sir."

"Your family..."

"They'll be along."

"I'll stop by later."

"You don't have to."

"I will."

I knelt by his cot and we hugged like brothers, clutching one another with warm ferocity. Forcing a smile, I bade him farewell.

Chapter Sixteen

The tavern was close-packed and steaming with body heat, infused with the smell of burning tallow and tobacco, humming with the timbre of men's voices. I lost myself in the sensory onslaught and the easy togetherness of men talking of their day over their pints of ale.

Soon Everett Lee's face, his freckles and chipped tooth, the grief in his eyes when we bid farewell, these details were starting to blur. The pain of farewell not so exquisite as it was a few hours ago, but dulled to a blunt, hard fact—a fact now trying to lose itself in the muddle of my brain.

Directly across from me, Freeman's face was starting to look rather flat and squished. I rubbed my eyes but his features remained distorted. There was a ringing in my ears, a dull swish actually, the sound water makes against the ship's hull. The room pitched and rolled pleasantly, the after-effects of being at sea.

The surgeons mates from *Aeolus* arrived to join Freeman and I, all of us glad to have delivered our patients, glad to have a few hours of liberty, glad to be on land in this prosperous little city of New York. Drinks all around, and again, each of us standing our round.

The closeness of their bodies made me long for Brian Dalton and I wondered with a pang, where in this bustling town he was just now. Still at work, unshipping the cannons from the frigate, or enjoying his draft at some alehouse? I wished we were together, he and I, instead of these fellows, yet even my wishes were dulled. I felt pleasantly lethargic, protected from pain. As if I were wrapped in layers and layers of invisible padding.

The innkeeper's boy went from table to table lighting the candles, and from the kitchen came the hearty smells of roasting beef. A fiddler and a fifer truck up a tune and the locals burst into song, one I hadn't heard before. The ditty ended, the crowd cheered and clamored for more drinks. Up from the cellar the tavern keeper carried another cask.

Someone among us ordered our supper and before I knew it the boy carried out trenchers of steamed oysters and plates of roast beef, and fresh bread and butter that we tore into like wolves. To us it was ambrosia and we devoured it with the privilege of demi-gods; mythical heroes we imagined ourselves to be, having won Havana for the British and delivered the broken soldiers at last to their homeland. We chased our food with more flagons of yeasty, bitter ale.

My thoughts returned to Brian, as they always did at the end of a long day's work. Soon. Soon. Like a soothing balm, a trick of the mind, a young girl's daydream. Sometimes it was enough just to imagine him, to know that we loved one another, to believe in the magic hours we would spend in each other's arms. In my imagination, our love knew no bounds.

Freeman's voice broke into my thoughts, a rude interruption. It was loud enough now to be heard above the din of conversation, the clink of tankards, the riotous laugher enveloping us. He was telling a story, recounting a gory battle aboard the *Richmond,* a battle that took place before I signed on. At the end of it, he waved to the tavern keeper, signaling another round.

Mr. Isaacs and Mr. Gordon, the surgeon's mates from *Aeolus,* countered with stories of their own; but because their deeds had taken place on a transport ship rather than a frigate they didn't have quite the clout that Freeman's tales did.

Freeman had a way with taking over a conversation. He could tell a good story, one in which he was always the main character, always the hero. Yet, when it came to surgery, he really was as quick and as sure as he claimed to be, for I had seen him in action. However, the best storytellers know how to laugh at themselves; and they know when to end. Freeman knew neither.

The looks of ennui on the faces of our companions were unmistakable—blinking, squirming, and yawning—yet Dudley's response was to become more animated in his dramatization, as if to whip them into paying attention. I was embarrassed for him, yet I knew not what to say or do to rescue him. Besides, I had drunk too much to trust my tongue.

Isaacs and Gordon excused themselves, bid us a good morrow, and made their escape. But Freeman wasted no time collaring two young officers, recently arrived, their noses and cheeks still red from the raw outdoor air. I watched, as he struck up a conversation, eager for their attention, hoping for their favor. It shamed and saddened me, yet I had no idea how to correct the matter.

I had drunk too much, my head had grown thick, and the room whirled around me. It was no longer a happy feeling and I wished the evening were over instead of just beginning. Life was perfect after two ales, but now it was a whirling headache to be endured. I had lost track of how much I had consumed or how long we had been there.

And then I noticed it was he and I at the table. Together. Alone. I sat like a stump, afraid to move, knowing I had drunk far too much. Yet I didn't want to go back to our room, the room we shared, for it had only one bed for the two of us. That too, was meant to be shared, as men of the middling sort are accustomed to when traveling. Though I had been sleeping next to Freeman these many months, we had separate hammocks. There was only one man with whom I wanted to share a bed.

Freeman was talking, still. It was hard to focus on his blurred, flat face, but his voice somehow penetrated the fog.

"I hear there's better gaming at the Beef and Bird. What say we go in search of superior entertainment?"

I shook my head. "I... you know... hell, I'm no good at cards Dudley. You know that. I'm no bloody good at cards."

He frowned, annoyed. "You always say that, though I'm willing to teach you."

"How many times do I have to tell you, I'm not a gaming man." I could scarcely hear myself over the din in the room, the roar of drunken voices, the clink of tankards.

"You're better at games than you let on."

"What do you mean?" (Was that *my* voice? Was I shouting?) "Explain yourself."

"The little game you're playing with me and Brantigan." His voice took on an accusatory tone. "Brantigan's *my* cousin. You're no relation to him. None at all."

"Of course I'm no relation! What the devil are you talking about?" My voice was garbled, as if mired in quicksand. I tried to separate and enunciate my words, to pull them out of the sludge in my brain and pass them through my numb mouth with my incompetent tongue.

"I'm quite content in my station, I've no designs on anything. I'm happy just to do my duty and make my wage."

"Oh, that's rich. Old Brantigan has taken a shine to you; he's giving you all the glory tasks. You're the golden one now. I dare you to deny it."

Anger flared up, setting my oakum-stuffed brain on fire. "Glory tasks!" I sputtered sloppily. "You call amputating a... a... 16-year-old's leg a glory task?" I took a long pull of ale to drown my anger, or fuel it, I'm not sure which.

"Brantigan thought I needed the experience," I said as calmly as I could. "You're much more the man for the job than I am, and I told him so."

"I'm just warning you, don't push me off the teat, Patrick. That post is mine, I've been groomed for it for years. Long before you ever came along."

A hoot of laughter escaped my mouth. "What are you saying? I don't want to be bloody chief surgeon, I promise you that." However, even as I said those words I knew they were no longer true. I wanted to be *Patrick MacPherson, Naval Surgeon,* with a ship of my own. And why not the *Richmond* some day? My heart leapt at the possibility.

"It's been a long day, I'm off to bed. Goodnight Dudley." I stood and immediately realized I had no control of my legs. I felt myself swaying, toppling. Like a spruce tree cut through by the ax, I crashed to the forest floor. This happened to be an adjoining table, scattering cards, spilling tankards, and nearly catching my hair on fire from the candle I knocked over. There was a great buzz of angry hornets around my head and I fought them off—fought to remain conscious.

Amazingly, Brian Dalton's face appeared out of the melee, peering into mine.

"He's a mate of mine, I'll take him. Sorry for the trouble. Sorry lads, I'll stand ye another round of drinks for the ones on the floor."

Brian, making my apologies. Brian, lifting me off the table and carrying me over his shoulder outside, into the street where I puked like a cat into the gutter.

"How did you know where to find me?" I gagged, wiping the spittle from my chin.

"I searched every damned public house on the waterfront,

that's how. Might've known I'd find ye lifting your tankard with that worthless sogger what calls himself surgeon's mate."

"I wanted to leave, I wanted to find you, but I... drank... too... much." My words poured out sticky, like treacle. "I'm sorry," I sobbed pathetically. "Please don't be angry with me."

"Nae, I'm not angry with ye, Princess," he said, his voice still hard. "But I don't know how this is going to work itself out. I can handle ye dressing like a man and doing a man's work. But the thought of ye carousing around the waterfront drinking with the men, especially that cowardly bastard, well I just don't know if I can put up with it." He kneeled beside me and wiped my face with his neck scarf.

"Come on, let's get you to bed. Where are you quartered?"

I pondered this, grasping for the name of the establishment I'd been assigned to. "I don't know. Some sort of bird. A stork with a fish in its bill."

His laugh was a snort. "The Hungry Pelican?"

"Yes. Pelican. That's it."

What a mess I'd made of things. Freeman was angry, Brian was jealous, and I had made a complete fool of myself in front of both of them. To my horror, I started to cry.

"Hush now Mr. MacPherson, ye'll give yourself away."

I felt his arm around my waist, buoying me up, guiding me down the dark, cobbled streets toward the inn.

"Let's get ye to bed."

But when he found out I shared not only a room with Dudley Freeman, but that the room only had one bed in it, he led me back down the stairs and out the door. Out into the raw air of the night, down to the waterfront and onto our ship, now deserted but for a single marine, asleep, leaning against the mainmast.

* * * * *

Brian put me to bed in his own cabin, with a bucket close by, and strung a hammock outside the door for himself.

Sleeping in the gunner's bed at last, but alone, how sadly ironic was that? And no one to blame but myself for I had squandered my evening on drink and Dudley Freeman, whose company I didn't even enjoy.

Tears of remorse slid down my face dampening his pillow. Though we were secured to the dock, the ship spun like a child's top. I fought a rising tide of nausea and soon gave in to the kind hammer of oblivion. The forgiveness of sleep, a sot's blessing.

Chapter Seventeen

Freeman was still in bed when I returned to our billet the next morning.

"Where in God's name did *you* pass the night?" He muttered from beneath the blanket, his voice hoarse from spirits and tobacco. "Or do I even want to know?"

"I very nearly spent it in the gutter," I said, neatly avoiding his question. "Never again will I drink that much. Never, ever."

"Ha! Better men than you have made that vow and to no avail." He buried himself deeper in the bedding and soon was snoring softly.

I poured a basin of water, lathering up my handkerchief with the sliver of soap from my kit. Then turning my back to the bed where Freeman lay, I unbuttoned my shirt and made a few swipes at my hidden parts as quickly and discreetly as I could. What I needed was a good hot bath, but it was too cold here for such a luxury, I'd surly catch my death. Besides, there was no privacy—no place I could walk in as a man and risk having someone find out the truth beneath the clothing.

Freeman slept on. I closed the door behind me, venturing

out into the bright morning to find a coffee house, the small advance I had gotten from the purser ringing cheerfully in my pocket.

With a pot of steaming coffee in front of me, and a New York newspaper in hand, the pounding in my head eased. The coffee house was packed with other men discussing the news as they stirred sugar into their cups and packed their pipes with Virginia tobacco.

I skimmed the paper and half listened to the conversations around me. Now that peace talks were in progress, now that Great Britain ruled the sea-lanes, the talk was of economics. Our victory over the French had come at a great cost, apparently. England was deeply in debt, the cost of maintaining navies and armies was enormous, and the New Yorkers worried they would be stuck with a large bill.

From fraternizing with them and pretending to be one of them, I had learned this much about men: You don't take away what a man has coming to him. You don't take away a man's earnings or tax him without his consent, for he won't put up with it. Not a freeborn British subject. Yet, I had no vested interest with the Yanks. I just hoped Parliament wouldn't decide to make up the deficit out of my wages or my share of the prize.

The door opened with a blast of chill air as a group of the *Richmond* warrants entered, among them Wickham, Hicks, and Humphries, the armorer. I waved to them.

"MacPherson! Just the man I wanted to see." Wickham's cheeks were red from the cold and he blew into his hands to warm them.

"Come join me. They brew a fine pot here."

"MacPherson, I've a great favor to ask of you, seeing as you're one of the very few of us who has his freedom today."

The others ordered their coffee and drank it standing at the bar, for they were off to work soon and had no time to sip it leisurely. The ship had to be made ready for breaming.

"Would you be a good man and escort my wife and her friends about town this morning? They'd like to have a look, you know, and do a bit of spending." He smiled indulgently, thinking of his Iris. "There's a market today and the purser has given me an advance."

"A market?" I gulped my coffee, not wanting to commit to the task. I knew nothing about New York, nothing about markets. Yet we surgeon's mates were among the few who enjoyed a day off today.

"Our women can't go running about on their own. It's only for a few hours this morning. They'd be so happy, sir; and I'd be much obliged."

"I'd be delighted to go a-spending with the women," I said as earnestly as I could.

"You're a true gentleman, my friend." Wickham clapped me jovially on the back. "I shall buy you a pint at the grog-shop this evening."

* * * * *

Out on the street the sea wives waited, dressed in their shabby, soiled, oft-mended gowns, eyes bright beneath their bonnets. Bright with anticipation of a day on the town. Looking to me to squire them about. I felt like a goat-herder.

They were five, one with a babe in arms, and one chasing a tow-headed toddler across the dirty cobblestone street. Among them, Iris Wickham, was the most fortunate of the lot.

"Now then, ladies, where is this market we're to explore?"

Embarrassed smiles and giggles all around.

"Why sir, there are five of them, we're told," a bold brunette spoke up. "Along the waterfront, at the end of each major street."

"And I suppose you'll be wanting to peruse all five?"

"Why, yes, of course. That is, if you can afford the time, sir. We don't want to keep you from your duties." She gave me a smile that was at once flirtatious, yet coyly yielding. A smile that could not be refused.

"At the moment my only duty is to you lovely creatures," I said gallantly, taken in by her charm, yet recognizing it as a way to manipulate me, an effective use of feminine force disguised as charm.

Our cajoling smiles and pretended deference, our beguiling flattery were little devices which when used at exactly the right moment could sometimes bend a man's will to do ours. Sometimes. An indirect, attenuated, unreliable sort of power were feminine wiles, and I never learned to successfully employ them (which is why I made a better man, at least in that respect) but I could recognize them.

The women giggled with excited pleasure, glad to have persuaded me, yet I felt uncomfortable in the situation. They knew it was only patronizing banter I flattered them with, for they were but fo'c'sle wives, most of them not even proper wives, and all of them in patched, salty, sea-worn clothing with handmade shoes and bonnets pieced together from scraps of canvas purloined from the sailmaker's locker, their capes fashioned from woolen blankets looking suspiciously like those issued by the purser. To be squired about New York by the surgeon's mate was likely quite a treat for these depreciated women.

If they had known me as I had been born, the natural daughter of a baron's son and raised to be a lady, they would have been even more cowed. In my former life I would have considered the company of a surgeon's mate to be beneath me, indeed any man who had to work for a living would have been a step below. Yet, I soon found out my status was precarious. There are so many rungs on this imaginary social ladder we climb, and always one higher and one lower than the one you find yourself clinging to.

Linda Collison

* * * * *

The lively marketplace invigorated me, chasing away the last of my fat, groggy head, and my morning-after ennui. I marveled at stall upon stall of produce: burlap sacks of potatoes, turnips, apples, onions—and cider aplenty, in every conceivable container. Fish—silvery slabs of perch, buckets of squirming live eels, rack upon rack of dried kippers, bushels of oysters still wet with mud and smelling of the bay. Blocks of yellow soap, tallows, buttons of all sorts—bone, wood, pewter and brass—dented copper pots and chipped porcelain plates, wooden trenchers, needles, and used but serviceable clothing, some of it home-spun but much of it fashioned from finer, imported fabrics.

Coin was scarce in the colonies and I'd have been wise to hold onto the advance I'd received from the purser. But I sorely needed new clothes and had nothing (no war booty, no tobacco, no liquor) to barter with. On impulse, I bought a lightly used ruffled shirt, French made, I'm certain, and a pair of serge breeches, scarcely worn and fitting me like it was made to order.

At the next market some of the women bought a few trifles and I purchased a greatcoat, rather worn at the elbows and missing a button, but cut of good quality English wool and well tailored. A gentleman's coat. Having tried it on over my threadbare frock coat I couldn't bear to take it off again, it felt so good against the New York chill. But I got it for a good price (at least I thought so at the time).

On the way to the third market, we entered a dry goods store, the women drawn by the fabrics displayed in the window. Rolls of imported silks, brocades, and colorful cottons were brought out for us to look at. Such a delight for the senses, the colors, the hand, the smell of the cloth. I secretly admired a bolt of silk, the color of a peacock's feather, the same shimmering sheen. I imagined how it would look as a gown of the latest fashion, and how it would feel against my skin, the voluminous folds of cool fabric, and the rustle and swish it would make as I walked. The way I would feel wearing it—almost pretty. I was nostalgic for that aspect of femininity. I missed the fineries that defined a woman's realm; the pretties, the fancies, the glittering baubles that catch a woman's eye and keep her entertained in her captivity.

The indulgent shopkeeper brought forth the sketches of the latest fashions from Paris for the women to see. They studied them closely, remarking on the details of the bodice, the ruffles, and furbelows. I caught a glimpse of myself in the mirror on the wall and turned away in disgust. My face, a mass of freckles, my jaw set firm, my hair plaited into a mannish queue.

What on earth did Brian Dalton see in me? How could he have feelings for one as rough as I had become? I dared to raise my eyes again back to the looking glass. Looked myself in the face, the pale-lashed green eyes staring back and a shiver of recognition went through me. Patrick or Patricia, the eyes were the same.

Of course, the women couldn't afford the fabric or anything else in that store. They mumbled their apologies and shushing the babies shrank back next to the door to wait for me while I perused the men's stockings.

All over town, the church bells of New York were announcing noon in a racket of dongs, clangs and chimes. Shopkeepers closed their doors as they retired to the back room or a nearby tavern to have their dinner. I led my little covey away from the waterfront taverns in search of a humble yet respectable boarding house. An affordable place, yet proper, not some seedy pothouse. It was hard to know myself, for I had little experience dining at public houses.

We chanced upon a likely establishment across town, next to the Quaker Meeting House, a sturdy but welcoming cottage where the widow MacNichols served a hearty pork and apple pottage, with bread and apple butter on the side, and apple cider to drink. "Apples have come into season," she laughed. "We'll be serving them morning, noon and night."

A fire crackled in the dining room fireplace and it felt very homey at our table, where I was the only man. I missed female conversation, the sympathetic nods, the "do tells", the gossip, the endearments, even the vacuous chatter, the nit-picking over details. The young mother nursed her baby and the toddler ate from his mother's plate, sneaking scraps to the dog waiting hopefully under the table. *This* was a woman's domain. I knew its comfort and felt its pull, yet I wanted both worlds. A home of my own, the love of my heart, *and* the freedom to explore the wider world.

Walking back to our quarters, our bellies full and our arms filled with our purchases, I began to anticipate night-fall, wondering if this would be the night. I flushed warm with eagerness at the thought and vowed I would have no more than one glass of ale with my supper. Tonight I'd not make a fool of myself.

The small child could no longer walk and the mother weary of carrying him so I stooped down and he climbed on my back, glad for the ride. The dank smell of the harbor hit our noses with the chill air from the bay; the frigate was in sight, her rigging down, her topmasts removed. She looked disabled and vulnerable. I winced, embarrassed for her as if I had seen her naked. My ship, my pride, my home. Soon she would be put to rights and filled once again with her people. Soon we'd be setting sail and New York would disappear behind us.

The ring of hooves on cobblestones sent us scurrying to the side of the street as an elegant coach-and-four came upon us at a fast pace. A dark-skinned driver held the reins in white-gloved hands; a footman in livery stood on the step ready to leap down and open the carriage door when needed. As they passed, I caught a glimpse inside of a young girl's profile. A young woman about my own age. She had porce-lain skin, hair well coiffed, and a hat of the latest fashion, yet the look on her face was one of sheer boredom contained as she was inside her fancy carriage.

She might have been me, before my skin was ruined with freckles, before my life was undone. That was the life I had been born to, a life of wealth, leisure, and finery, with a carriage, well-bred matching horses, and servants to attend. I had been born as lucky as that stranger in that carriage, lucky as a porcelain doll. But I'd lost it all when my father died, for my privileges had all hinged on him; his bloodline, his wealth, his influence in the world. I stood and watched as my other self passed me by.

One of the horses lifted his cream colored tail and shat in the street, without ever breaking its stride.

"What I wouldn't give to trade places with the likes of her," one of the fo'c'sle women commented, lifting her skirt and dodging the golden brown nuggets, still steaming.

The others laughed at the absurdity.

Chapter Eighteen

The sun had already dropped out of sight, signaling the end of the workday, short in these latitudes this late in the year. I arrived at the docks in time to watch the men finishing their work in the waning daylight, gathering their tools and making fast the dock lines. I sat on the edge of the wharf, hanging my long, weary legs over the edge, waiting for an opportunity to talk to Brian.

Our frigate was still in a state of dishabille, stripped as she was of her anchors, boats, cannons, and sails. Her truncated spars gave her a shockingly broken look. However, the stripping and dismantling was necessary in order to heave her over and clean her sides and bottom of the tenacious seaweed and barnacles that grew to her undersides like a crusty brown beard. Once burned and scraped clean, the ship would move faster through the water, and if nothing else, a frigate must be fast.

What a great lot of work a ship requires! It was miraculous that something made by man, of wood, hemp, and iron, could transport whole societies of people and their effects around the globe. Really, what kept it afloat with all those people, and all that weight aboard? It's a wonder more ships didn't sink to the bottom of the ocean, or drift helpless as a cork on the currents.

With a prick of guilt, I remembered Everett Lee and wondered if he was still waiting at the hospital, or if his family had come for him. I had said I would stop back, but in truth, I had forgotten. I scanned the harbor, purple in shadows, wondering if one of the myriad vessels was his brother's schooner. Perhaps they had already sailed.

In the deepening twilight, men called out to one another at the end of the workday. Among them I heard the gunner's voice, recognized its timbre. The sound of his voice infused me with a private joy. Along with the joy, I recognized a tension I couldn't understand. A conflicting need to be one of them, one of his friends. Not a lover, a wife, a possession, but a part of the grand purpose of what they were doing. Then all of this fizzled and dissolved, like sea foam and I was left with longing, stripped of any description. Just longing, down to its essence.

In groups of twos and threes the sailors left, heading toward the taverns and public houses. A gust of wind snapped the pennants and rattled the halyards of the row of merchant ships along the wharf. I hugged my new coat close; enjoying the protection it offered me, proud that I had purchased it with an advance on my own wages. Money I had earned.

It was then that I noticed her, a young thing, poorly clad, at that awkward age—all arms and elbows. Out of the corner of my eye, I saw her looking my way, sizing me up.

She edged closer, her cloak whipping back, the hood dropping off. I kept looking ahead, out at the water, at the ships; but I could see her at the edge of my field of vision. She was quite close now. Close enough for me to catch a waft of her, a mixture of warm body, perspiration, and the reek of gaudy perfume.

"G'd evening, sir."

She spoke to me, that could only mean one thing. Why else would a woman speak to a strange man on the waterfront? I dared to turn and look at her, to look as a man would look. Straight and without deference. As if I were entitled.

She was not pretty, but she might have been. Her limp hair, dull brown, uncoiffed, fell forward over her heart shaped face, like some wild thing. She had a slender nose, slightly upturned. Red, as if she had a cold. She sniffed, as if to confirm it. Her shoes were tied with twine to hold them together.

"Are you quite alone, sir? Would you like some company?" She glanced at me very briefly with guarded eyes, and then looked down again, inching closer all the while.

"No, thank-you. Actually, I'm waiting for someone," I said, crossing my arms across my chest. Feeling my heart pounding, reminding myself that I had the advantage. I was in no danger compared to the risk she was putting herself in; yet I couldn't help but identify with her.

"Well then, I won't trouble you sir, though I could perhaps make your wait a bit more pleasant?"

I had an impulse to give her something. To make her leave, to ease the uncomfortable feeling she evoked, the feeling that I should somehow help her. I felt in my pocket for a coin, but found them empty. On a whim, I gave her the bundle containing my new stockings.

"Here, take these. Now go."

Like a puppy, she lingered, wanting to please.

"I don't want you," I said savagely. "Just go." And turned my back on her, looking out over the masts. Above me a few swallows still wheeled and darted, or maybe they were bats.

After a long minute I glanced over my shoulder, then turned around.. She seemed to float away on the wind, her cloak fluttering like some dark wing, disappearing into the shadows.

Then from the other direction came Brian Dalton, bigger than life and striding toward me, looking at once tired and full of life. I forgot about the streetwalker. I forgot about Everett Lee. I forgot everything else as I walked toward him, intent on him, as if no one else existed. We said nothing, did not wave in greeting, yet I was electrified. His face was streaked with tar, his hair pulled loose from its braid and blowing. When he was within arm's reach, he spoke.

"I've been given permission to stay aboard ship again tonight. Will ye join me?"

"When?"

"Another hour or so. By then they'll all be in the taverns. They'll be a marine posted on board, but he'll have his bottle, he'll nae be a problem."

"Yes," I said, my ears ringing with the din of my own heart, the rush of my own blood. Tonight! Tonight, at last.

Chapter Nineteen

"Where have *you* been all day?" Dudley said the moment I entered our room. He stood in front of the mirror, a tin of hair powder in hand.

We were both still raw from our drunken argument last night; both of us nursing bruised feelings.

"Who are you, my nursemaid?" I closed the door with my foot and tossed my new purchases onto the bed. "I had a day of liberty, just as you did."

"Liberty! Brantigan found me and put me to work. The old goat is as blind as a salamander, you know. Instead of a day of liberty, I was forced to inventory our supplies. Meanwhile you've gone on a whoring holiday, I suppose."

"If you must know, I was pressed into service myself. Wickham asked me to escort his wife and some of her friends to the market."

Freeman rolled his eyes; I could see them in the mirror's reflection. "You didn't have to oblige him, I certainly would have refused. That's not an officer's work and those molls don't belong on board anyhow. You should've been helping me instead."

"They aren't prostitutes, Dudley."

"Alley cats, fo'c'sle wives, whatever." He shrugged and sprinkled some powder onto his head, dusting it with a brush. "I must purchase a wig here in New York; and you as well. We look like a couple of backwoods chuckleheads wearing naught but our own hair."

"Suit yourself. I've spent my advance. See my new greatcoat?"

He gave me a quick appraisal in the mirror. "A dead man's, I presume?"

"Perhaps. But it's good quality wool, and well-stitched."

"I could have used your help today, my friend."

"I'm sorry, Dudley. I'll help you tomorrow. I'll do whatever needs to be done." I was eager to repair the rift between us, for I didn't want anything to spoil my evening.

"Tomorrow? Ha! I don't give a damn what you do tomorrow. Tomorrow I am taking my liberty and I'll not be found, I promise you. Mr. Sloane and I are going off for the day to see some of his relations. Well-to-do relations, by the sounds of it."

"Bully for you," I said, taking off my great coat and hanging it on the peg. "Would you like to see the fine linen shirt I bought?"

"How fortunate you are to have had to leisure to replenish your wardrobe while I was slaving away."

"It becomes you, the hard work and slaving. You should do it more often." I kicked off my shoes and sat on the edge of the bed to examine my aching, blistered feet. What I wouldn't have given for a pair of comfortable shoes!

Dudley brushed the hair powder from the front of his shirt. "What are your plans for this evening?"

I hesitated, not wanting to tip him off, and above all not wanting to get swept up in his plans.

"Actually, I have none. I'm done in. Bloody exhausted and still hung over. And my feet are killing me."

Linda Collison

"Say, Patrick, can you lend a hand here?"

He handed me the powder and brush and I obliged him, getting powder all over the both of us. "Wait, let me brush your back. There's more on your shirt than in your hair."

"A manservant would be the thing, wouldn't it?"

Unbraiding my own queue, I rubbed my scalp with my fingertips.

"Powder?"

"No need for that. I'm staying in tonight." Anything to get him out the door. It was dark enough now to need candles.

"Won't you at least come sup with us first? Have a pint?"

I shook my head. "No carousing for me tonight, thank you just the same." I remembered all too well how supping with Freeman had gotten me into trouble last evening and I wasn't about to loose this opportunity to be alone with Brian. Happiness fizzed in my veins like champagne and I didn't want Freeman to spoil it.

He frowned as he fastened his stock and slipped on his waistcoat. "If you're that tired we could take our supper downstairs, though everyone else has gone out."

"I've absolutely no appetite tonight, Dudley. In fact, I'm going straight to bed. I'd like to sleep for a solid 24 hours, I would. Sleep like a dead man, I will." I collapsed onto the bed face down, to illustrate my point.

"Patrick?"

I affected a rumbling stage snore.

"Well then, Mr. Killjoy, go to bed with the sun if you will, just like an old woman you are. Tonight will be my night for gallivanting."

"Enjoy yourself," I said. "And should you happen to meet up with a gay young blonde named Nancy who waits tables at her brother's establishment at the far end of Broad Street, tell her I send my very best regards." I turned my head to give him a sly grin.

Snorting his disbelief, Freeman snatched his coat and hat off the rack and left, banging the door behind him. Thank God!

The minute I heard his footsteps going down the stairs I leaped to my feet and started readying myself, pouring a bowl of cold water from the pitcher to wash in, then combing my long, tangled hair. It was far worse than I realized, I had done little besides running a brush over it since leaving Havana. At least there were no signs of lice. A few more tugs and finally I gave up, for getting all the knots out would have taken all night. Out of habit, I braided it up again, my fingers all clumsy tonight.

Looking in the glass I smiled, pouted, stuck out my tongue and examined my teeth—at least they were all intact and my gums, healthy and pink. And how my eyes shone!

Quickly I dressed, stockings all twisted, fumbling with the buttons on my breeches, missing a button on my waistcoat, and having to start over. At last, I was ready, and giddy as a filly. Wanting to skip, to leap, to dance my way to the ship, I forced myself instead to saunter casually down the stairs and out the door, tipping my hat to the innkeeper's wife. Out into the crisp cold night. I looked around me and over my shoulder, seeing no one I knew. The bells of New York pealed the hour, six o'clock. I quickened my pace, no longer sauntering, but going faster and faster now, my blistered feet fairly flying down to the docks where Brian waited.

Chapter Twenty

Brian had relieved the guard, sending him off to supper with his companions. There was no one else aboard and, except for the cats, the ship was deserted. Even the squawking chickens were gone. I had never seen the *Richmond* so still, so quiet. No creaking and groaning of bulkheads against the great press of ocean. No shrill boson's call, no voices, no footsteps. Even the ship's bell hung silent.

He appeared from below decks, clean and freshly shaven, his hair out of its tail and loose on his shoulders. He looked carefree, joyful, his perfect self. As he approached, I could see his eyes alight with desire and my very bones hummed in anticipation. It was as if we were surrounded by an invisible globe, a magical bubble that isolated us from the rest of the world; a protection fashioned for us by some benevolent god who had made us wait long for this night, but now was to allow us what we most desired.

I followed him below to his cabin, as fine to my eyes that night as any lord's bedchamber. Outside, the bustle of the city had faded and we were alone at last.

He had lit a candle and by its light, I saw his bed. (Again, and this time sober.) A proper bed it was, built into the bulkhead with a straw mattress, a flannel sheet, and a navy issue woolen blanket folded neatly at the foot. Next to the bed, a barrel covered with his striped neckerchief, as fine as any linen tablecloth. On top was a bottle of wine and two empty glasses, waiting to be filled. Next to that was a chunk of fresh cheese, and a loaf of bread—fresh bread from a New York baker. A whiff of the yeast and my mouth watered.

I was touched beyond words. He was wooing me (as if I were reluctant!) Well, let him woo, let him lead. With a pop, he pulled the cork with the screw end of a gunner's worm.

"Are ye as hungry as I, Princess?"

My breath caught in my throat. "Aye, Mr. Dalton. I am surely famished."

And I was. Both hungry for him—*and* for the bread, cheese and wine. Hungry for all that life had to offer.

"I gave the servants a night of liberty," Brian joked, affecting a gentleman's accent, and not succeeding very well. "So I shall attend ye myself. Do, have a seat, Princess." He made a sweeping motion with his hand to one of two smaller staves that he had found for chairs. I sidled past to take my seat, breathing in the clean, soap and sunshine smell of his shirt, the whiff of tobacco that was always a part of him.

He poured the wine and raised his glass. I lifted mine and we touched them with a little ring, the contact charging us both. I had been longing for this night since I had met him. Though it took me some time to realize it, I had wanted him even then.

We sipped the wine and ate chunks of bread and cheese, saying little, but savoring every mouthful. We were making ourselves wait; satisfying one hunger while the other grew.

I tore my eyes away from his face to glance around his small Spartan room, more crowded than usual tonight with the temporary dining set. Painfully neat, yet most definitely a man's space, a shaving bowl and razor on a fiddled shelf, a cracked mirror the size of my face hanging above it. There was a small desk where he kept his records for the Ordinance Board, which had the appearance of having been hastily arranged for my visit. Propped in the corner, a gunner's sponge and worm.

"This is perfectly elegant, Mr. Dalton. Why, I fully expect for you to serenade me now, like a Renaissance courtier."

He shook his head, and then laughed aloud. "Well I could sing ye the ballad of the gypsy davey, but it might not have the desired affect. Nae, I won't sing, love. But that's the only thing I'll refuse to do for ye tonight."

The low hum of his voice joined forces with the wine, warming me, priming me.

* * * * *

Small spaces and confinement have always made me feel a sense of panic, but not tonight. Tonight this gunner's cabin was all the space I needed. Tonight I wanted nothing more than to lie down with Brian here in this room, to feel his full weight on top of me. That was not confinement, that was ecstasy.

Outside on the wharf, we heard drunken laughter as a group of sailors passed. Further away, the tolling of a church bell, answered by another. The candle flickered; the heat of our bodies filled the room.

"Would ye mind unloosening your hair? I would love to see it tumbling down."

I fumbled to untie the ribbon at the nape of my neck, unbraided the plaits, and shook my head, feeling the hair fall across my shoulders.

"Ye're lovely," he whispered.

"It's the wine," I quipped, for I knew I wasn't lovely at all. But I wanted to be, and it was warming to know he thought me so. Indeed, in this flattering candlelight, I might even believe myself to be what he said I was. I felt both shy and bold at the same time.

"I have something for ye," he said, reaching under his bunk and bringing forth a bundle, something wrapped in a scrap of old sailcloth.

"What on earth? For me?"

"Go on. Open it."

It was a dress of aquamarine silk, with a low neckline, two rows of ruffles on the sleeves. Quite beautiful, though probably a little too small.

I smiled for him. "It's lovely, Brian. Thank you."

"Will ye wear it for me? I want to see ye in it. And then I want to help ye take it off again."

My blood rushed, roaring in my head. I stood up and he did too, the two of us nearly upsetting our table. The cabin was so small there was scarcely room for the both of us to turn around in. He moved the makeshift table and chairs aside and slid into his bunk to give me room. I turned away from him, facing the cabin door, for I felt suddenly shy about undressing in front of him.

"I won't look if ye don't want me to. I'll turn and face the bulkhead. But do hurry, Princess."

Fumbling with the buttons, I removed my breeches and shirt and stepped into the gown, pulling it up over my hips, up to my waist. Then unloosened the long strip of bandage that bound my breasts against my body, I unwound it and dropped it on the floor. Groping for the sleeves I tried to pull the bodice up over my naked breasts and heard a rip as a seam pulled apart against my struggles. It had been so long since I had put on a dress, I had forgotten how.

"Easy now," Brian laughed. "Save the bodice ripping for me."

My giggle sounded like a silly schoolgirl's, but I didn't care. "Don't peek!"

"I'm not," Brian insisted. "But I'm lighting another candle to better see you when you're ready."

"Actually, I might need some help with the laces," I admitted.

"Ah, that would be my pleasure!"

But instead of lacing me up he slid the sleeves down over my arms and deftly pulled the bodice to my waist. He stared at me; his eyes riveted on my breasts, and then cupped them, one in each hand, as if they were rare treasures. I felt transformed into something beautiful and desirable under his gaze. His fingers, his lips, and the stubble of his chin against my skin set me a-fire and my head dropped back in pleasure as I allowed him to do what we both wanted.

But at that very second there was a loud crack as the cabin door was forced opened and three men came tumbling in. I gasped and stepped back, tripping on the hem of the gown, knocking over the table, the wine, the candle. My worst fear had just come true.

Dudley Freeman held the lantern high, the yellow cone of light falling on my breasts. Once let loose from their bondage, the pink, pert nipples refused to be ignored. Now, instead of feeling beautiful I felt hideous. Dudley's eyes bulged as if he were seeing the most gruesome of creatures. Indeed, he looked as if he were going to be sick or faint. "You're a... a... oh my God, Patrick, how *could* you?"

Mortified, I folded arms across my chest and dropped my head.

Chapter Twenty-One

Brian sprang, leaping at the men like a wild thing. "Ye bastard, I'll kill ye!" He went for Dudley, shoving him back outside the cabin. The lantern swung, casting wild shadows as Dudley stumbled and fell into the gunroom.

Feeling like a freak and wanting to hide, I grabbed for something to cover myself, found my shirt in a tangle on the floor.

"Halt!" The master-at-arms shouted, grabbing Brian from behind. "Don't make me have to put you in irons, Mr. Dalton."

"Put *me* in irons! Ye're the ones that broke down the door of my cabin! What the bloody hell is the meaning of this?" He jerked free of the man's grip. Sloane helped Freeman up off the deck just outside the cabin.

"Begging your pardon, Mr. Dalton," the master-at-arms apologized, obviously embarrassed. "There's been a mistake. I can't believe I was drug away from my pint for this. A thousand apologies, sir. Buggery, indeed!" He glared at Freeman.

"All this fuss for a romp with a moll," Midshipman Sloane said, brushing the sleeve of his coat. "It's what I'd be doing myself now, Freeman, if you hadn't talked such a good story." He was clearly disappointed not to have found what he had expected to find in the gunner's cabin.

Dudley spat blood from his mouth. "You idiots! This isn't just any little waterfront whore, don't you know who this is?"

Again, Brian lunged toward Freeman but Sloane and the master-at-arms jumped between them, fending off the gunner's blows as they rushed Freeman out of the cabin, up the companionway and off the ship. Dalton cursed them, shouting threats, but didn't follow. In the end, he didn't want to risk losing his own warrant. And I sat feeling aloof, yet somehow ashamed, like some sort of circus hermaphrodite.

The night had shattered around us and we stared at the scattered remains. One of the glasses had broken and my waistcoat lay in a heap soaking up the spilled wine.

"He'll get a thrashing he won't soon forget, the interfering bastard," Brian swore, kicking the empty wine bottle, sending it crashing against the bulkhead. "A north-country ass-booting, I promise ye."

His eyes were no longer soft and wide with desire but black and impenetrable. He had thrown up his shield and I felt like some low, vile creature to be despised.

Numbly, I finished buttoning my shirt, found my breeches, and shook the broken glass out of my waistcoat.

"Where are ye off to so suddenly?"

I paused at the door of the cabin. "I have to speak to him."

"What, to Freeman?" He choked. "You want to speak to Freeman?"

"I must. He'll ruin everything."

"Ye'll go running after that bastard so you can beg him to keep his mouth shut?"

"My whole future is at stake, surely you can understand that? I must find him before he betrays me."

"Don't you see, love?" Brian's voice cracked. "He already has."

Chapter Twenty-Two

Dudley Freeman was not to be found that night. It was as if New York had swallowed him up. I searched the streets and back alleys, asking for him in every tavern and grogshop along the waterfront, but having no luck. At last, I went back to my assigned lodgings, my feet burning with blisters, my heart heavy. He would surely return sometime that night. I lay in wait and every step I heard on the stairs I thought might be his.

I woke to the cry of the water boy below in the streets. It was dawn and I was still alone in the bed.

He was not downstairs at breakfast with the other petty officers. Goodwillie, Hicks, the Hollister boys, they all looked at me strangely, or was it my imagination? They invited me to join them, but I had no time, I was out the door, I had to find Freeman.

Out into the brisk, busy morning, raucous with clanging church bells and rattling wagons, the cry of hucksters advertising their goods. I strode down to the wharf, intent on only one object, one man. Catching sight of Captain Elphinstone, I abruptly turned the other way, not wanting him to see me, waiting for him to pass. I was afraid to be seen until I could clear this business up, come to some sort of an agreement with Dudley. If only I could talk to him, explain myself, offer him my share of the prize money, a month's wages. What would it take to buy his silence?

Meanwhile I was a man on the run, searching the coffee houses of New York, looking for my messmate, my mentor; the man I hoped might still be my friend.

I moved single-mindedly, driven by desperation. Up and down the streets, dodging carts and porters, calling to figures I mistakenly took for him, pushing past them rudely when I realized my mistake.

The sun climbed, generous with its heat. I panted for breath, sweating in my great coat, and wishing I had left it behind, for it slowed me down. I took it off and slung it over my shoulder, continuing my search.

Down to the waterfront again.

The ship was hove down on her starboard side and a crew of seamen was afloat in the boats, burning and scraping the bottom. A horrid smell of burned barnacles filled the air and there was no breeze this morning to disperse it. Dudley surely would not be here, not with such work going on. Maybe he had gone off with Mr. Sloane.

Already exhausted, I returned to our billet to wait for him, the noonday sun bright and too warm. He had to show up sooner or later. The smells of roasting meat tempted me and I took my midday meal with Goodwillie, Wickham, Hicks, and some of the marines. Though I was famished, the food seemed to stick in my gorge. *Did they know? Or had Freeman for once kept his mouth shut? Freeman and Sloane and the master-at-arms—that all three would keep tight about it was too much to hope for.* But if my old messmates had heard of the goings on last night, no man said a thing. As soon as I was finished, I hurried upstairs to wait for him

The afternoon wore on slowly, hour by hour, and I paced

the floor anxiously, looking out the window again and again, to see if I could see him. Still Freeman did not return. Although some of his effects remained, his sea chest sat in the corner and his great coat hung on the peg behind the door, his razor and strop were not on the press where he had left them. His comb and hair powder were not to be seen, nor his haversack which yesterday had been hanging beneath his coat. It seemed he had found lodging elsewhere, but eventually intended to return. I wondered what he was up to.

Chapter Twenty-Three

The next morning the captain's cabin boy knocked at my door to summon me to his master's quarters. My heart was thick in my throat as I grabbed my coat and hat. I wanted to vomit, so great was my dread.

On shaking legs, I went to the Commodore's Inn on Water Street, where Elphinstone and his lieutenants were lodged. I knocked and waited an interminable few seconds for the captain's voice to answer.

"Come in!"

I did so, nodding and touching my forehead in respect. Standing awkwardly, heart hammering, waiting to be addressed.

The captain was in the midst of other matters, judging by the looks of his secretary, piled high with sheaves of paper and stacks of books. He sat with an open log-book in front of him, quill in one hand, scratching furiously, a cup of coffee in the other, poised half-way to his mouth. He wore no wig. His natural hair was un-powdered, untied, uncombed.

He looked up, regarding me through his spectacles as if I were a mosquito that was humming in his ear, and then returned his attention to his work.

The cabin boy was dismissed with one curt word, the door clicked shut behind him, and I found myself alone with the captain. My knees nearly buckled beneath me.

The captain spoke without looking up from his writing. "Be seated, Mr. MacPherson." His voice had a Scotsman's burr, reminding me of my late husband. If only Elphinstone would be so compassionate.

I sat in the only other chair in the room, the one facing him on the other side of the secretary, taking hope at the way he had addressed me. *Mister* MacPherson. Perhaps I had been summoned due to some other matter entirely. Hadn't Brantigan said he would write me a letter of recommendation? Maybe Dudley had kept his mouth shut about me.

The morning sun streamed in through the windows, warming an orange cat that dozed on the floor in a square of light. The room was so quiet I could hear it's throaty purr, a rumble of contentment quite in contrast to the nervous rumblings in my gut.

The captain looked much older on land somehow, than he had appeared on the quarterdeck of the frigate. Puffy bags under his eyes, like fluid-filled blisters, age spots on his forehead and hands, a sheen of white stubble on his chin. Gone was the flush of glory I had seen on his face after the siege of Havana. Only his nose remained red; perhaps from drink or from the damp New York chill.

"Now then. I'm a busy man and this is a busy ship," he said at last, putting his pen down and removing his spectacles. He held my face in his gaze, sizing me up.

"Mr. MacPherson, ye are accused of being an imposter. I have three men who say ye are neither surgeon's mate nor man, but a female."

His words rang in my ears, deafening me.

Linda Collison

"Well MacPherson? What have ye to say for yerself?"

So they were all three so quick to expose me, even after I had performed my duty as well as any man! I took a deep breath, found my voice, and spoke the truth.

"I *am* a surgeon's mate, sir. And a good one, as Mr. Brantigan will attest."

The captain's face was unreadable. "Are ye male or female?"

The simple question hung in the air like a blade, ready to destroy me. A few feet away the cat purred. I was once told that a cat will purr to the terrified mouse it holds in its teeth, to sooth it.

Elphinstone spoke. "Ye have answered my question without saying a word. For if ye was a man ye'd have been insulted by it. Ye would have defended yer honor and yer name."

Still I said nothing, not wanting to seal my fate. Yet anger began to smolder, burning the fear in my gut to ashes. Heat rose up to my face.

"I have three reliable witnesses who claim they have seen your person in intimate circumstances. Three reliable crew-members who say they have seen beneath your clothing and that you are, in fact, female."

Our eyes locked and I did not look down, I did not blink. An eternity passed in the space of a deep breath.

"Well? Do you deny it?" He thundered. "Shall I have you stripped of your clothing here before me?"

Gone was my fear. Now I nearly choked on my rage. "No, sir. I do not deny having the body of a woman; but a surgeon's mate, I am, and a good one. Ask Mr. Brantigan, ask anyone on board."

"Tell me your name."

"MacPherson. Patrick MacPherson."

The captain struck the table with his hand. "Damnation! I

will not be toyed with! What is your real Christian name? What name were you given at birth?"

"Patricia." I blushed at the intimacy of it, at hearing it spoken aloud, for the first time in so long.

He nodded. Satisfied. His face softened.

"Now tell me Patricia, what brought you to this state of affairs?"

"Necessity, sir."

"Well I wouldn't think you would do it as a lark. Would you be so kind as to elaborate?"

The floodgates opened and the words poured out, for I had nothing to lose now. I told him the circumstances of my birth to a wellborn man who owned a sugar estate in Barbados. I told him how my mother died when I was young and that I was sent to England to be educated. (I did not tell him that I was a natural child, that my father didn't marry my mother, in fact was married to another woman back in London.)

"I grew up believing myself to be well-provided for, I believed I would someday inherit his plantation, in dowry. However, when my father died I discovered I was destitute, all his promises were empty. He had squandered his wealth leaving me penniless and without influence. There was no kindly uncle or brother to take responsibility for me. I was on my own."

Captain Elphinstone hit the side of his head with his open hand. "Ye Gods, of course! So naturally, you did what any young girl who finds herself alone in the world and wanting does. You put on a man's costume and went off to become a ship surgeon's mate. It's completely understandable." His sarcasm burned.

"Sir, I might have ended up in the workhouse, or the brothel, or under the thumb of some unscrupulous sponsor as has happened to many a girl in a similar situation. Had I beauty or charm, I might have attracted a suitor, yet I had none. My impetuousness saved me, luck intervened, and I married a good, kind man, a Scotsman like you who had been trained as a physician. Aeneas MacPherson was his name and he taught me a ship surgeon's skills, for which I am grateful. He made me his mate, though of course it was unofficial; but like many wives I shared his workload."

"And what happened to change your good fortune?" Elphinstone asked.

"He died, and I continued to perform my duties and his, for a time. But through a chain of unfortunate circumstances, which I can see by the look on your face you don't wish to hear recounted, all that remained to me was his instruments, the tools of his trade—our trade; and he left me the skills he taught me and all of my hard earned experience. So, I decided to make the most of this inheritance; and that's how I've gotten along in the world. As a man. For at least a man has his natural born rights and can earn his living and have say over his possessions."

I stopped, out of breath and out of words. Only a thread of hope remained.

The clock ticked heavily. A minute passed.

When he spoke, his voice was level and absolute. "I have listened to your story and I am heartily sorry; but the navy doesn't employ women, not as surgeon's mates, nor can we tolerate imposters. You have deceived me, you have deceived your fellow mates, and you have deceived the Royal Navy. For all I know you could be an agent of the French, for a person such as you cannot be trusted. You must quit this ship MacPherson, or I'll have you jailed."

"Quit the ship? But sir, where would I go?"

"I would advise you return home aboard a packet or a merchantman, by whatever means possible. I will not have you aboard my vessel, not as a man, not as a woman. T'would set a poor example, undermine my authority, dampen the men's spirits and jeopardize my command."

"But the *Richmond* is my home, I have no other."

Now his face hardened again. His eyes became glittering marbles and I knew I had absolutely lost the game.

"Ye're a cunning lass, I've no doubt ye'll find another. Return to your home parish or stay here in New York. There seems to be plenty of opportunity here."

Still, I sat.

He looked up from his shuffle of papers.

"Dismissed." A word as sharp as flint and ringing with finality. "And if I catch ye near my ship, miss," he paused, furrowing his brows for emphasis. "Ye'll have hell to pay, I can promise ye that."

Chapter Twenty-Four

I knocked on Mr. Brantigan's door, apparently waking him from a nap. He was whiskered, his hair askew, his breath foul.

"Sir, I must see you."

He bade me to enter, rang for a pot of tea to be delivered, and asked me to open the shutters. Sunlight flooded his dark den.

"Now then, MacPherson. What's on your mind?"

"I've just come from Captain Elphinstone's quarters. I assume you know the reason I was called before him?"

"No, I do not."

"I've been given the boot."

"Why? My God, lad, what sort have trouble have you gotten yourself into?"

"I was born female," I blurted out.

His face transformed before my eyes. His rheumy eyes widened, then narrowed suspiciously, his mouth twisting and pursing as he registered shock, denial, and disappointment. Just then, the girl came with the tea, placing the tray on the dresser and leaving in a soft rustle of skirts.

"Cup of tea?" He offered, ridiculously.

I shook my head, unable to sit, much less swallow tea! I paced the floor, hoping he would come around, once the shock wore off, and accept me as I was.

"Well, you had me fooled, I'll give you that, MacPherson," he said ruefully, spilling tea into the saucer as he brought cup and saucer, shaking, to his lips. "If my eyesight hadn't deteriorated so, I'm certain I would have spotted you for what you are."

"Mr. Brantigan, you talk as though this were a game and I bested you. I assure you, this is no game; my livelihood and future are at stake. Did I not perform adequately at Havana? Did I not properly amputate Private Lee's leg? Did I not keep the logs diligently and attend the sick?"

He smiled, abashed. "Somehow, you did all that. You're a clever girl, no doubt; but you had to know your days were numbered. 'Tis unnatural."

He stirred his tea thoughtfully. "One can't get away with a ruse forever. You've had your lark and now its over. If I had the eyesight God gave me in my youth I would have spotted you straight away."

"What would you advise me to do now, sir?"

"Why, I wouldn't presume to know." He slurped his tea noisily. "Whatever females of your kind do when their number's been called. Turn a new trick, I suppose. Or find a man to make an honest woman out of you."

"Sir, I was born and raised a gentlewoman. My father was the third son of a baron."

"Then what on earth are you doing on a frigate, for God's sake? You have fallen far, that's certain."

"I'm simply trying to earn my living."

"There are other ways for women—women of good backgrounds. Surely you have a brother, an uncle..."

"It's not fair!" I interrupted.

"Not fair?" He laughed a dry and humorless cough. "No, the world is not fair, my dear. Whoever said it was? It's not fair that I should loose my eyesight and become palsied at five-and-forty. It's not fair that I be forced into retirement before my time. This is my last campaign, did you know?"

"You hinted as much. You also hinted you were grooming me to be your replacement," I added brashly, having nothing at all to lose.

He flushed scarlet. "Oh, come now, don't delude yourself! What an embarrassment to the navy of the greatest country on earth. Though I will admit, you've a quick mind and a strong arm with the bone saw. A pity you were born of the weaker sex. Perhaps you would've made a better lad than a lass."

Saying this, he dug into his pocket and handed me a crown. As if he were giving a child a bauble. "There now. Go buy yourself a proper dress and bonnet."

And I took it, yes. I clenched it in my fist. For I had earned it and more.

"I wish you no harm," he said, rising to see me to the door. "And you were a help to me, I must say. Perhaps you could find work ashore as a nurse or an apothecary's assistant. Yes, that is what you should do, Mac..." He nearly choked on my name. Couldn't bring himself to call me by it.

"Yes, that is what you should do, Missy," he finished lamely. So I had even been stripped of the name for which I had worked so hard.

* * * * *

I left in a rage, determined to find Dudley Freeman; and this time I did. He was leaving the apothecary's shop on Wall Street, a package of supplies under his arm.

As soon as he saw me he blanched, then gave me a hard, contemptuous stare.

"Dudley..."

"Don't speak to me you vile bitch. You betrayed me. Made me a laughing stock. To think I loved you like a brother." He brushed past me, hurrying on his way.

"But it was you who betrayed me!" I ran to catch up and tugged on his sleeve, causing him to whirl about.

I was surprised to see the pain in his eyes. "I beg to differ. I trusted you to be who you said you were. I believed you, Patrick MacPherson. And you were lying all along."

"And you were jealous because Brantigan favored me. You wanted me out of the way. You would have seen me hung for sodomy, wouldn't you? You thought Brian and I were both men and you would have cheerfully seen us both hung or shot dead."

"You're right. But I hate you even more for being female," he said, curling his lip. "Get out of my sight." And he walked off.

"You are lower than a crab on the sea floor, Dudley Freeman," I called after him, my voice breaking; but I don't think he heard me. The wind had picked up and the signs swung on their rusty hinges, creaking a racket. I let him go, I was loosing the force of my anger. I realized I was tired, exhausted; but where to go? I took a circuitous route back to my lodgings, wandering. Looking for something, but I knew not what.

* * * * *

Back at the Hungry Pelican Iris Wickham was waiting for me, just outside the door. She wore only a shawl against the wind and her face was red and chapped from the cold.

"From Mr. Dalton," she said, handing me a package. The bundle was wrapped in brown paper, tied securely with hemp cordage. The same cordage used to make reef points, and knotted as only a seaman would.

Did Iris know my secret? Was it common knowledge amongst the ship's company?

"And this too," she added, reaching in her apron pocket and handing me a letter addressed to *Patrick MacPherson*. "I'll return shortly for your reply."

* * * * *

Upstairs, behind the closed door, I tore open the bundle, cutting the cord with my surgeon's scalpel.

It was the dress he'd given me the other night. My heart fell. I don't know what I was expecting, but not a dress. Laying it aside, I broke the seal on the letter and read Brian's handwriting.

Dearest Patricia,

Ship talk is that Freeman betrayed us and ye've been given the boot. I know that is what ye feared and I'm sorry things didn't work out the way ye hoped. He'll get his due, I promise ye that. I'll wait until we're off the ship, on some waterfront alley. I won't jeopardize my warrant.

I cannot bear to leave ye here in New York. Once before ye came aboard with the molly girls, why not tonight? I'll keep ye hidden below, I'll feed ye and care for ye as I once did aboard the merchantman Canopus. I know a gunner's cabin is a rude home, but I love ye and I'll do right by ye, so help me God.

P'raps someday I'll have saved enough to keep an apartment in Wapping for ye to live in, if ye don't fancy living below decks and sharing my cramped bunk. The gown is not befitting of ye, Princess, but twill serve ye well enough until ye can have something more suitable made.

Besides, I think ye look bonny in the dress.

Yours, aye,

Brian Dalton

I collapsed on the bed, reading the letter again and again until the words blurred together and the tears ran down my face. I cried for my imagined freedom, the last of my independence. I cried for the shame of discovery and I cried for the love Brian Dalton so freely gave.

There was a tap at the door, a woman's polite knock.

"Mr. MacPherson? Might I have a word with you?"

"Come in, Iris." I wiped my face roughly on my sleeve. "It's not locked."

There was a click of the latch, the squeak of hinges.

"What do you know, what have you heard?" I looked at her with my swollen eyes.

"My mother taught me to believe only half that I see—and nothing that I hear." Her face was sympathetic. Her eyes smiled with complicity.

I threw myself onto the bed. "What am I to do?"

"The only thing you can. Wear it. Wear the dress. I've altered it to fit you better, and added four inches of sailcloth to the length so that your ankles won't show."

I had taken no notice of the alterations and it touched me that she had troubled herself to do it. That she had been observant enough to see that it was too small for my big-boned frame.

"Why? Why have you done this for me?"

"To help you remain on the ship."

I buried my face in my hands, but there were no more tears to shed.

"It won't be so bad as a woman. You'll see." She put her two hands on my shoulders, those strong little hands like the tough, wiry feet of a sparrow perched on a limb. And she pressed her sharp fingers into my flesh, giving me both comfort and strength.

I looked at the woman who had befriended me, the woman whose ranks I was about to join. "Thank you."

"What shall I tell Mr. Dalton?"

I took a deep breath. "Tell him I will come."

"You sound like it's your funeral you're announcing. Do you not love the man?"

The simple question shook me. "Yes. With body, heart and soul, I do."

"Mr. Dalton's a good man. I believe he loves you as much as a man can."

Iris laid her shawl on the bed, the mended holes looked like black starfish caught in a net. "Now then, take this and wear it tonight when you come aboard."

"I can't take your shawl. You'll catch your death."

"It's just for tonight. To get you aboard. Then Mr. Dalton can hide you away in his cabin until we set sail, which will be very shortly, from what I hear. As soon as the wind is favorable."

"So soon?"

"That's the rumor. The ship has been breamed and put to rights. Tomorrow she'll take on water and supplies. Maybe as early as tomorrow evening. Though of course I'm not privy to the weather, nor the captain's wishes," she added with a laugh.

"Where are we bound? Portsmouth? London?"

She shrugged. "I'm not privy to that information either. But wagging tongues say we're headed back to Havana before we go home to England."

Iris untied her bonnet and lifted it off her head, smoothing into place the tired strands of hair come loose from the coif, a touching womanly effort. "Here, take this too. You don't want to be bareheaded." She examined my hair a worried frown, fondling the thick auburn queue with concern. "Would you like some help dressing your hair?"

I forced a laugh. "Making me presentable would take hours and I don't have hours—not now. What I really want is to go out to a part of town where no one knows me. Have a pint, clear my head. Enjoy my last supper as a man, in a tavern, as men can do. My last night of freedom."

She smiled, a puzzled look on her face. "Well then, I'll see you later, Mr.—uh—MacPherson?" She reddened. "Oh, but what shall I call you? By what name do you wish to be known?"

"I don't know," I said. And that was the truth.

I had come to like Patrick MacPherson, he was a confident young man with a promising career ahead of him. I had the respect of *Mr.* in front of it, as was due a man of my station. I had grown into the identity, or it had conformed to fit me. Now who was I to be? What was my name?

Chapter Twenty-Five

I intended to find a quiet tavern where I wouldn't see any one I knew, and after walking some distance found just the place on Nassau Street, up near the Common. The warm den was nearly empty, but for a handful of tradesmen talking shop matters over their pints. I took a seat at a small table in the corner with my back to the crackling fire. The innkeeper came over and lit my candle, asked me what my pleasure would me.

"Ale, sir." My mind was in a turmoil, my feet hurt, and my heart was breaking. A pint of ale was just the remedy I needed. Waiting for the innkeeper to serve me I watched the candle wax melt, pooling around the blue base of the flame. Ran my finger through it as I had done as a child, marveling that it did not burn.

The door opened and in burst the chaplain, clutching his hat, his cheeks ruddy from the chill wind and scattering of dry leaves that blew in with him. Frick! My heart stuck in my throat.

He spied me immediately; there was no escape.

"May I join you?" His face looked so very grave, as if he

were a schoolmaster set on giving me a scolding, and I noticed he was wearing his bands, which at sea he had only worn on the Sabbath.

I sighed and nodded my head, for indeed, how can one refuse any man, much less a parson, such a simple request? Like a wild hare, I had been deftly snared.

"Good evening, Mr. Frick. How did you find me?"

"I followed you," he admitted. "And you set quite a pace." The chaplain smiled kindly as he settled into the chair, as if to soften the heavenly reprimand I feared was coming.

Resigned to his company, I held up two fingers, signaling the host to bring not one pint, but two.

"Tell me, Mr. Frick, what has inspired you to dog me so far on this bitter All Hallows Eve? Is my soul in that grave a danger?"

"May I be blunt?"

I managed a weary smile. "By all means, sir."

"Mr. Dalton has come to me, he has asked me to intervene."

The chaplain lowered his voice. "He wishes to marry you. He has asked me to speak with Captain Elphinstone on this matter. So that you may stay aboard ship."

"And you would do that?" I asked. "For Mr. Dalton?"

He looked dismayed. "Of course, I would. For Mr. Dalton, for you, and for myself."

"Yourself? What interest do you have in the matter?"

Just then, the man brought our pints and I was glad to take a long pull. The chaplain stared into his brew, as if he was a diviner and there were answers to be found in the golden brown liquid. The candlelight illuminated his face, his sandy eyebrows, furrowed in concentration, his fringe of pale eyelashes. He is a fine looking gentleman, I thought, and well intentioned. Not at all your holier-than-thou sort of parson, nor a hypocritical wastrel, like some aboard His Majesty's warships.

"I have known for sometime, Patrick." His eyes held mine and I felt my strong will crumbling.

"Was it you then? Was it you who told the captain?"

His fair face flushed. "Of course not. I have always been sympathetic to you and your situation; I thought I made that clear on more than one occasion. It's just that I've long suspected."

"Why? What gave me away?"

He shrugged. "Perhaps because I alone aboard a warship have the leisure to observe and study those around me. In fact, that's part of my job, the way I see it. And perhaps because I once loved a woman who was very like you, in some ways."

"Was she a surgeon's mate too?"

"No," he smiled, ruefully. "She was not. She was another man's wife, and not free to marry me. Our love was furtive and secret, when it should have been something beautiful and fine."

I blushed at this admission. "Why do you tell me this?"

He laughed and wiped his eyes. "Indeed, I don't know! Maybe it's to draw some sort of parallel, to urge you to follow a particular course of action. Maybe I'm unburdening my own heart on one I hope will be understanding. In truth, I've never related my story to anyone, although an ugly version of it is common knowledge, I'm sure. One thing certain, I'm not here to judge you for my sin was the greater. I too, am not what I appear to be, my friend. I am ordained. I do a chaplain's duty, and I am paid for it. Yet, I'm a sham, Patrick. What's more, I am performing a service any other cleric could do; hundreds of failed parsons without parishes of their own could fill my shoes. Yet, who could ever love my Evalina better than I? Certainly not the rascal that calls her his wife!"

He paused to collect himself and the air between us, surrounding us was charged with grief and regret.

"But sir," I said. "Not knowing all the circumstances, what choice had you? You had to make your living, I presume. You could not have just run off with her to some fairy tale land. I too, had to make a living, for I had no man to support me. I was raised for a life vastly different than the one I'm leading, but I'm getting by."

"Life can be much more than getting by, my friend; and where there is love, there is always a way. I might have found a way with Evalina but I'll never know. Instead, I left her with her cold and unloving husband. I left her because I was remorseful for what I had done. I was self-important in my sin. But leaving her has brought me no redemption and no peace of mind."

He smiled though his eyes were shining with unshed tears.

"And now for my sermon, its short but sweet. Surgeon's mates there are aplenty, but there is only one woman who can love Mr. Dalton as you can. Follow your heart, my dear. Put on the dress, I will speak with the captain, he will allow you back on board as Mrs. Dalton, the gunner's wife, I assure you. And I shall be overjoyed to properly marry the two of you."

After we supped, Mr. Frick walked me back to my billet at the Hungry Pelican. I marveled that I had spent more uninterrupted time with him this evening than I have ever spent with Mr. Dalton. I knew I could count him as a true friend, along with Mrs. Wickham, and Brian himself. Three true friends, I should count myself lucky and I knew I must cross over, give up my wages, my imagined freedom, and my silly pride. From somewhere in the street a watchman called the hour. Eleven o'clock and all was well.

* * * * *

Alone in my room, I prepared to don the dress, laid out across the bed.

A clumsy clatter on the stairway, then a loud knock at the door. "Mr. MacPherson!" It was Everett Lee.

I opened the door and we embraced, cuffing one another on the back like two young bears.

"Everett, why are you here, and at this hour? Did you brother not come for you?"

"Yes, and I've come to beg you your services," he panted. "Can you please come see her?"

"See who?"

"My sister-in-law, she's very ill. Please sir, won't you come and have a look at her. There must be something you can do. She's a good woman, truly a sister to me, and if she dies the wee one will be without a mother."

"Are there no doctors to be found?"

His face fell. "I'm a stranger here, I don't know of any doctors, but I know you, Mr. MacPherson. I was sure you would help."

"I don't know what I can do," I stammered. Brian would be expecting me shortly. "Is it a fever of some sort? Did it come on suddenly?"

"I couldn't say, but my brother is beside himself, and I told him I'd find help. If you could just come and have a look. Maybe bleed her or tell us what remedy we should apply." His voice faltered, he paused to catch his breath. I could see he was still weak from the amputation.

"But how did you find me?"

"Sir, you told me yourself you were billeted at the Hungry Pelican. Only it seems your ship is put back together again, and I took a chance you would still be here and not aboard. I beg you sir, will you please come and have a look? I'm afraid it is serious, I've never known her to take to her bed in illness, and we are off on a long passage soon."

My heart was rent in two, but I couldn't say no, for I couldn't have lived with myself had I refused.

"Of course I'll come, let me fetch my kit, but I must warn you; I'm no physician. I have no medicaments, only a surgeon's tools."

"Thank you, sir," he said, greatly relieved. "Thank you."

"Mind you, Everett, I cannot stay long, my ship will be sailing soon. As soon as the wind is favorable, she is off."

"I understand, of course. We'll be off with the next tide ourselves. If you will only look at her and tell us what must be done, I'd be ever grateful."

"Wait for me downstairs, I must gather my effects." I bundled up the dress, bonnet, and shawl, stuffing them into my haversack with my toilet kit, folded the letter, and put it in my breast pocket. Then snatching up my surgeon's kit, I was off.

* * * * *

The *Richmond* looked her old self again; the topmasts mounted, the sails bent on, the boats back aboard. Lights flickered in the captain's quarters and on deck a sentry paced, his musket on his shoulder. From below decks came the sound of laughter. I thought of Brian, waiting for me, maybe on the spar deck now, watching for me to approach the ship, wearing my dress and Iris Wickham's bonnet and shawl.

Up the docks we went, as fast as Everett could swing those crutches, past the warehouses, to a landing quay.

"Here's our skiff. And there she is, *Andromeda*." He pointed out to the darkness of the East River, though I couldn't distinguish his brother's schooner from all the other vessels anchored out there. "The wind's against us, I'll have to row." Then tossing his crutches into the little tender, he managed the ladder, half falling into the bottom of the boat, and putting the oars into their locks.

I handed him my surgeon's kit and the sack with my belongings, untied the painter from the piling, climbed into the bow, and pushed us off.

Chapter Twenty-Six

I scrambled aboard to find four men, their faces indistinguishable in the darkness. Woolen caps pulled down over their ears, dragon-like puffs of vapor from their nostrils, they stared at me suspiciously. It was not the greeting I imagined.

"This here is Mr. MacPherson," Everett said, panting from the exertion of climbing aboard with his one leg. " He's a surgeon's mate aboard *Richmond,* the frigate that carried me home. This man saved my life, he did."

The others continued to stare mutely.

"I only did what any surgeon would have done," I mumbled.

The largest of the figures stepped forward and thrust out his paw, nearly crushing my hand in his grip.

"I'm Dominic Hale, captain of this vessel. My wife is very ill and, if you can save her, I'll pay any price you ask."

"It's not a question of money, Captain." I said indignantly

"What, then?"

"I come out of compassion, and as a favor to Mr. Lee. But

I make no promises." I found myself shivering, as much from nervousness as from the cold sea air. "What's the nature of her illness?"

He lifted his broad shoulders. "She's feverish. Delirious."

"How long has she been ill?"

"I don't know, she's not one to complain. A few days, maybe. But this morning she hadn't the strength to get out of bed. And the rash has worsened."

I didn't like the sounds of that. "Is there coughing? Vomiting?"

He frowned. "I don't know. I'm short-handed, there's no one to attend her. The ship makes her own demands, as does the cargo."

"Well then, if I may take a look. I haven't much time. My ship will sail soon, wind and tide permitting."

"John, will you show this man below."

"The name is MacPherson," I said, resenting the captain's rudeness, the way he took me for granted when I was going out of my way for him. "Patrick MacPherson, surgeon's mate, His Majesty's Ship *Richmond*."

The captain was unimpressed. "Take him below. Show him where she lies." Hale left abruptly, going forward to take care of some business on the bow.

"I'm John Eli," said the first mate. "Pleased to meet you, Mr. MacPherson. We're glad you've come out of your way to have a look at Mrs. Hale. You'll have to pardon the captain's brusqueness. He's got a lot on his mind."

Eli motioned me to follow him down the narrow aft ladder that led to the cabins. The air below decks was a rich stew of odors; wet wool and fresh manure, and a strong stench of humanity, worse than aboard the frigate where at least hammocks were washed regularly, decks scoured, and vinegar liberally applied.

"Wait here, Mr. MacPherson," Eli said, "while I go to the

galley for a light." And he left me standing in the stinking
darkness holding my surgical kit, listening to the muffled
nickering and blowing of horses, and the bleating of sheep in
some compartment nearby. I was regretting that I had bothered to come.

Eli returned with a lantern that cast its warm glow and
showed me that his face, at least, was kindly. He knocked on
the door of the aft cabin on the starboard side.

"Mrs. Hale, we've a doctor here to see you, ma'am."

No answer.

"Mrs. Hale?" he called loudly. But there was still no answer.

The first mate then lifted the latch and pushed the door
open. The room had been unlit until he hung the lantern on
the hook just inside the door. "There you are, sir. Call if you
need anything." I heard his footsteps on the ladder.

A new odor now reached my nose, blending with the fetid
stew. It was the distinctive sweet-sour smell of the sickbed.

The woman was dressed in a cotton shift, her hair spread
upon the pillow like a dark fan. She was slight in build, star-
tlingly young, with delicate features almost obliterated by the
pustules that clustered like some exotic growth on her face.
Her breathing was raspy and laborious, almost song-like in
its rhythm. A work song, a chantey.

"Mrs. Hale?"

The form on the bed gave no indication she had heard
me.

"Mrs. Hale!"

No answer but for a gurgling sigh.

She appeared to be in death's embrace, there was little I
could do for her, yet I had to do something. Make some effort, bleed her, go through the motions. People put great
store by the physician, the surgeon, and the apothecary. As
Aeneas MacPherson used to say, sometimes what a person

believes is the most powerful nostrum of all. For Everett Lee's sake, I must do something.

"I'll need more light," I called out to no one in particular. The ship was small enough I could hear the murmur of the men talking on deck, just above my head.

It was Dominic Hale's voice, curt as a whip, which answered me. "You shall have it." He brought me two tin sconces, with mirrors to reflect the light.

"Don't waste 'em. Good Rhode Island candles, these."

Stood in the darkness outside the door, I could feel his criticizing, mistrustful eyes watching my every move.

The sick woman moaned and mumbled something; I think it was in French. I held the lantern closer to her face and saw angry red pustules, so many they merged, coloring her face scarlet. Like the freckles on my skin, they no longer had borders, but had spread like a viscous continent of ooze across her face. A black scab had formed on her upper lip, beneath her slender nose. It might've been a beautiful face, but now it was hideous. I completed my examination, a cold knot in the pit of my stomach. I had never seen it before, not firsthand, but I had read about it, studied it, and I knew how to identify the dreaded symptoms.

"Can you open your mouth Madam? Might I have a look at your tongue?"

Her dark eyes, shining with fever, opened now and flew to mine. They seemed the eyes of a mad woman, bright with knowing what the rest of us could not.

"Does she speak English, Captain?" I said over my shoulder. The captain stood in the doorway, arms crossed, watching my every move.

"Of course. She's a Creole but she speaks English as well as George himself."

"It appears she speaks not any language. How long has she been in this state?"

"Not long. Not that I've been aware of. When we left Narragansett, she was up and about, minding the girl, darning stockings. Then last night she took to her bed, said she was ill."

I turned around to face him. Could a husband be so unaware of his own wife's health?

"It's not like I've been playing cards," he growled. "I'm a busy man. I've been occupied with the cargo, the vessel, and fetching my brother from the hospital. Actually, it was Everett who discovered her like this."

I busied myself with my instruments, preparing to bleed her. It was all I knew to do. It gave my hands something purposeful to do while my head adjusted to the situation.

There was a rustling in the doorway, a little whine. I turned to see her peering around the captain's legs. She was a wild thing, unkempt and uncommunicative, her dark curls a nest of tangles. She looked at me with eyes immense and round, two dark moons.

"Don't be afraid, Miss. I'm the surgeon, I'm here to attend to Mrs. Hale."

"Get back to bed, Chance," the captain said curtly. He gave her a little push, sending her whimpering into the shadows.

I dreaded to touch the woman. Her skin, hot and dry; those fluid-filled vesicles ready to burst. Yet, touch her I must. Carefully I took her hand and pushed up the sleeve of her nightdress, and found more eruptions on her forearm. She groaned at the slight pressure.

"Do you have any morphine aboard, Captain? Any laudanum?"

"Naught but spirits. Rhode Island rum or Martinique rum, take your pick."

"Whatever. Bring me some."

He brought me a flask and a spoon before leaving me

alone with my patient, his wife. I could hear his voice nearby, crooning to the horses. I could hear their snorts and knickers in answer from somewhere amidships. From the sounds of it, he cared more for the horses than any other living thing aboard.

The patient could not swallow in her comatose state, she seemed not aware of the spoon against her lips. So far gone, and what was I to do? I soaked a pledget with rum and dabbed it onto her lips, her parched tongue, then wrapped the tourniquet around her firm young arm and bled her, taking a full pint of her hot cherry-colored blood. *Was the blood tainted too? Surely, the air I was breathing was vile.*

I took the bowl of blood up on deck and dumped it over the side, into the black water. All the while, my heart was hammering like a wild thing in my chest because of what I suspected. My mouth was dry; my hands tingled. Death seemed close at hand, like a damp, cool breath on the back of my neck. Although I had no firsthand experience with smallpox, I knew its telltale signs and symptoms, and how to differentiate it from yellow and other putrid fevers. And like everyone, I had an innate fear of it—a revulsion.

I lingered on deck, breathing in the East River air as if to cleanse my lungs. The moon was obscured and there were no stars to be seen, and over on the shore, the lights of New York began to wink off as the inns and taverns shut down for the night. The bitter wind had come up rippling the water and the vessel tugged at her anchor, wanting to be off. I peered into the black night trying to make out the frigate, but could not.

Captain Hale appeared out of the darkness, a hulk of a shape. "Well? What is it? What's wrong with my wife?"

Fear tightened my throat, and the word was little more than a croak. "Smallpox."

Hale started at the word, I could feel his shock. The word itself was a curse, as bad as the plague. The yellow fever that had killed so many of our men in Havana had been horrible, but the prospect of a smallpox epidemic was somehow worse. The very word had etched itself in the memory of Europeans since antiquity; it was synonymous with suffering and death. Like the plague itself, smallpox could cross borders, climates, entire hemispheres and no place on earth was safe from it. Apparently, not even a New England schooner.

An icy mist seemed to fall out of the darkness, enveloping us; but Hale said nothing else. He simply left me standing there, the sound of his brogans heavy as Goliath's on the deck.

"Prepare to make sail," he thundered for all aboard to hear. "Down the river and out to sea, by the wind."

"Aye, Captain," came Eli's response. Below, the horses neighed nervous shrieks.

Assuming he would soon send me ashore in the skiff, I went below to gather my things, wondering where I should change my costume in order to get past *Richmond's* sentry. I was worried that Everett had survived his amputation only to be threatened by the deadly smallpox, yet there was nothing more I could do now, but to save myself.

"Stand by on the peak halyard!" I heard him shout.

I stumbled up the narrow ladder and to the foredeck where Captain Hale himself was working the windlass.

"Captain Hale, who shall row me to shore?"

"No one, Mr. MacPherson," he grunted, his powerful arms moving the handle. "You are to go below at once. Do everything within your power to save my wife."

"What?" I stared at him in disbelief. "I cannot! I must return to my own ship."

"Damn you and your ship!" he bellowed, still working the windlass to raise the anchor cable. "Go below. That's an order."

"You're not my superior officer," I said, incredulously.

"You cannot order me about. You must take me to the frigate *Richmond,* I demand it!"

Now he stopped, straightened his back, and touched my breastbone with his finger.

"I am captain of *this* vessel, the one you're now aboard. You'll do as I say, Mr. MacPherson, do you understand?"

"Are you are taking me hostage?" My voice became shrill now. I lost control and practically screamed. "Are you holding me prisoner?"

"We're all prisoners, no one is leaving the ship. This vessel is under quarantine. You said yourself it was the smallpox. Maritime law forbids you're leaving the ship, as does common sense. And you call yourself a surgeon?"

I gathered my wits, dropped my voice. "If we're under quarantine Captain, why are we setting sail?"

"Because time is money," he sputtered with exasperation. "And I'll make none sitting here at anchor waiting to see which of us lives or dies. I'm cleared to leave port and I've got a pair of Narragansett Pacers aboard that will surely wither away if they must stay at sea any length of time. We're bound for Martinique as quickly as we can. God willing, my wife will make it to her homeland."

"Martinique? Are you mad?"

He looked like he was about to strike me, but instead he dropped his voice and put his face close to mine. "No, you're the crazy one, Doctor. Would you really risk carrying smallpox aboard a crowded frigate? Would you even dream of endangering your comrades in that manner?" I was abashed. He was right, and there was nothing I could say.

"Should you survive, Mr. MacPherson, you'll get back to your frigate eventually. In fact, I'll see to it personally. But for now, I order you to go below and do the best you can to save my wife."

I stood rooted, unable to move. Thinking, *let the woman*

die, there's nothing I can do. Meanwhile the captain was in action, working the windlass, huffing and blowing from the effort.

"Bring the skiff aboard, and stand by to make sail! Hinkley! Wilson! Where the hell are those worthless boys?" After a few more turns the anchor was aweigh, and soon the ship was moving through the water. "We're underway! Hinkley! Wilson! Damn it you lay-abouts, I need you on deck at once! On deck with your lazy asses!"

"By God, Dominic, they've made off with our skiff!" The first mate's voice rung out from the darkness. "Those scamps have made a run for it!"

"What? A run for where?"

"I don't know but they're gone, and so is our boat.'

"Sons-a-lazy-bitches!"

A quick search of the schooner showed that they had indeed fled in the small boat, taking their belongings with them.

"I hope the damned pox kills 'em," the captain's curse thundered through the damp night air. "How in hell can we sail this tub with naught but a cripple and a dandy doctor for crew?"

I felt an acute stab of envy for Hinkley and Wilson, gone to shore, to freedom. Had I known they were jumping ship, I'd surely have gone with them. Had I been able to swim I would have braved the freezing waters. Looking back at the dark thicket of swaying masts that was New York Harbor, I hoped for a glimpse of the *Richmond*, yet I could not distinguish her. Had she already gone? Sick at heart, I returned to the patient's bedside.

Chapter Twenty-Seven

The hours crawled by, though no one rung the ship's bell to mark their passing. There was just the ebb and flow of the woman's breath, raspy as waves on a gravel shore, and the strange whimpering of the child in the adjoining cabin. It was an animal-like sound, the noise a puppy makes when left alone in the darkness. She would want to be here, with her mother, she must be frightened out of her mind, yet for her to be here, for her to breathe the foul miasma of the sickroom was not advised.

Above, the men worked the schooner, the first mate steering the boat while the captain conned down the river, through the narrows and out into the open sea. Everett was needed on deck to keep a lookout, for these waters were filled with obstacles. I was in no mood to talk to him, I felt as if I had been tricked on board by my former patient, though of course he had no idea it was smallpox. Yet here I was imprisoned aboard this squalid Yankee hell ship, quarantined by my own diagnosis! I wished I had never agreed to come aboard with Everett Lee! My sense of duty, my feelings of friendship had turned against me, my loyalty had been misplaced, and I was filled remorse and regret.

The night was long, unimaginably long, and there was no comfort in thinking of tomorrow. Exhausted, disillusioned, I stayed at the woman's side because someone had to tend her, and because I had nowhere else to go. Two perfect strangers thrust into intimacy.

The cabin was cramped and cluttered with a spare sail stuffed into one corner, coils of hempen rope, and boxes of tools. It seemed to be a storage space, a bosun's locker, not a proper cabin, with only a scuttle for air. My own flickering shadow was huge on the bulkhead. Nothing to do but press on. Go through the motions and let nature take her course. Pray no one else gets sick.

Having done all I knew how to do as a surgeon, I assumed the role of a nurse. Doctors, surgeons, and apothecaries all turned away when the end was near, shaking their heads as if the patient had somehow failed *them*. But someone had to stay to the bitter end. Someone had to manage the whole unpleasant business of dying. Someone had to sit in attendance, hold the hand, wipe the brow or the arse, standing by until the last breath was exhaled. Tonight it seemed I would be the nurse, the kindly angel of death. Indeed, no one else showed up for the task, for they were all busy on deck.

And so passed the night, breath by breath. I tried not to think about Brian aboard the *Richmond*, waiting for me. He would think I had chosen not to come, how that pained me! I brought my attention back to the woman. Found another blanket under the bed and covered her with it. At some point, I lay down on the spare sail and closed my eyes. I must have slept.

I awoke with a start, knowing exactly what was to be done. I leapt to my feet filled with a driving certainty that made my skin tingle. There was no time to be lost.

Chapter Twenty-Eight

"Captain Hale!

I heard his heavy footfall on the ladder, followed by the crack and groan of the cabin door as he flung it open. He looked at me with his fierce glower.

"We must save the rest of us," I said.

"How?"

"Inoculations."

I watched his face closely, for the very word was charged. Many believed wholeheartedly in the practice, yet many more feared it. Dominic Hale's stony face told me nothing. My own began to weaken, a tiny muscle under my right eye twitched spasmodically.

"I believe it's the best course, but there are no guarantees. In fact, it may be too late."

His eyes bored into mine. "Then there is no time to waste," he said evenly. "Proceed with it."

"You must understand, it might not work. It could be a failure, and..."

"Fatal," he interrupted, finishing my sentence for me.

"Yes, I know that and I'm willing to wager my life on it. Do it immediately."

"And the others?"

"I'm the captain, they'll do as I say," he growled. "It's for their own damn good." He turned to go, to return to some ship business, or to attend to his horses. The ship and the cargo, those were his obsessions.

"Wait! Don't go yet. Hear me out, sir."

He paused at the bottom of the companionway, not even giving me the courtesy of his face. "Go on."

"You must know this. I've never done it before. I've only read about it."

Hale muttered a curse and stamped up the ladder.

I tried to recall what I had read or heard about the various methods of inoculation, also known as variolation. In the Far East, scabs from infected persons were dried and crushed into powder, but then was the powder injected, inhaled, or taken internally, I couldn't remember. In Russia people were beaten with switches used on those who had the disease (which seemed unusually cruel.) The most common method, and the one I best recalled, was to inject a small amount of fluid from the vesicles of the diseased person beneath the surface of the skin of the one to be protected. If successful, the newly inoculated person developed mild symptoms of the illness in two or three days' time, recovered quickly, and was immune for life. Yet, no one really knew how it worked.

It had been the wife of a British ambassador, Lady Mary Wortley Montagu, who introduced the practice to Britain some decades ago. She had seen it done with effect at the court of the Ottomans. I had read of her experience with this method, which the Ottomans call engrafting. She described the process in some detail in her travel writings.

The procedure was not without risk. Though the ambassador's wife trusted it enough to have her own children engrafted, many others condemned the practice. Sometimes instead of a mild case of the pox, a severe form erupted and a number of deaths had been attributed to it. But was it the inoculation that killed— or was it the technique? Or did the person already have the virulent form of the disease within them at the time of inoculation? And what factor did hygiene play? The cleanliness of this vessel left much to be desired, that was certain.

My mind reeled with questions yet there was nothing to do but get on with it. I opened the latch of my kit and lifted the scalpel from its worn velvet bed. With tremulous hands, I wiped it on my shirtsleeve, rubbing it until it gleamed.

I would inoculate myself first, to try out the technique. Frightened as I was to cut my own arm with a blade tainted with the powerful fluid of this dying woman's pox, I was more terrified of *not* doing it. I thought of praying but cringed under the weight of my own hypocrisy. When was the last time I prayed? Why should God—if there was a God—help me?

A long ago conversation with Aeneas about Pascal's wager came to mind. *If you erroneously believe in God you lose nothing, should there actually be no God. But if you correctly believe in God, you have much to gain, being the salvation of your soul.* Yet according to Aeneas, the French mathematician's deeper message went beyond the wager. To Pascal's way of thinking, belief is a matter of will. *Act as if you believe and faith will follow.*

I wondered what Mr. Frick would say about Pascal and his philosophies and I fervently wished I had the chaplain by my side at this moment. What a good friend and counselor he had turned out to be, though it had taken me so long to realize it. I swore that when I got back to my ship I would be happy to be Mr. Dalton's lawful wife and keep his cabin. I'd enjoy the good company and counsel of Mr. Frick, and Iris Wickham, the cheerful Hollister twins, oh, my eyes stung with tears thinking of my *Richmond* family. Even Dudley

Freeman, who it now seemed, had just acted as a jealous, spiteful brother. Surely all our petty wrongs could be forgiven.

"Please, if there is a God in heaven." I spoke aloud, my voice sounding as thin and fragile as a teacup. "Help me." The words seemed to hang in the air. There was no answer from God, or anyone else. No sound at all but the rub of the anchor chain. Still, I felt it right to go on, and did so more calmly.

* * * * *

I picked the ugliest pustule I could find on her arm. Holding the lancet with steady fingers, I pricked it, releasing a drop of viscous yellow matter, which I gathered on the edge of the blade. Carefully I transferred it to my own left forearm, on the fleshy part halfway between the wrist and the elbow. With a fascination mixed with terror I pushed the handle, felt the sharp sting, and slid the contaminated blade completely under the skin. There I held it there several eternal seconds, my own blood started to ooze, trickling down my arm and onto the bed linen.

Had I just delivered my death's wound? Was this the final mistake in a string of mistakes I had made? Or would this action save me? Would it save us all?

Withdrawing the blade, I wiped it against the edges of the wound I had made. I wanted to make certain I had captured the substance, whatever it was—the heart, the black-magic essence, of smallpox.

Well now, I have either hastened my death or greatly postponed it. The blood rushed in my head, my ears rang.

The child's voice at the door brought everything to scale again. It sounded like she was talking, asking something by the inflection in her voice, yet it was unintelligible. Not French, not patois, but something inhuman.

"What is it? What do you want?"

She fled at the sound of my voice, and I heard the slam of a cabin door.

I looked down at my arm and dabbed at the trickle of blood. Suddenly it seemed like a foolhardy act, but it was too late. I had done it. The others were waiting. Everything depended on me.

* * * * *

"Your arm, sir."

I lanced another of the ugly pustules. Grasping Hale's thick wrist in one hand, I turned his arm over to its underside and with a jab, introduced the quivering yellow drop beneath his tar-stained skin. He never flinched, never made a sound. I withdrew the blade, reaching for a pledget to cover the wound; but in one motion, he shook down his rolled up sleeve and left, bandage be damned.

My own arm burned where I had made the cut. Was that good or bad, I wondered? I decided it was good. It had to be.

I did the same to the others, one by one, John Eli, Everett, and Chauncey. Chauncey trembled in fear when I reached for her arm.

"Just a little prick," I said as kindly as I could. "It'll be done in a flash."

She simply stared at me.

"*Tu parles francais*?"

Still no answer, no sign of comprehension.

I turned to Hale

"Chance," Hale interrupted. "Tell the doctor your name."

She hung her head.

"Say it!" His voice was hard as a marlinspike. He tilted her chin up in his powerful hand and forced her to face me.

"Tell him your name."

She blurted out an incomprehensible sound.

Hale shrugged. "Only her mother understands her."

"Yet she can hear," I mused.

He glared at me as if I were the cause of all his misfortunes. "Of course she can hear," he thundered. "She just did what I asked her to do. She can hear and she can think as well as any five year old. And she can write her alphabet, she can. My daughter is not an idiot, she's a mute."

Chauncey shot me a look of indignation followed by a piercing scream—which her father immediately stopped by clapping his hand over her mouth.

"Silence!"

She turned to bury her head in his chest and beat him furiously with her dirty little fists.

"I believe the child is tongue-tied," I said, having had a glimpse into her mouth and detecting a short frenulum, the fold of mucosal tissue that holds the tongue to the floor of the mouth. It was so short that it restricted the movement of her tongue. "I could fix that in two seconds with a nick of my scalpel, it would surely help her speech."

"Never mind the girl," he growled. "Tend to my wife."

His unfeeling arrogance deflated me; I was too exhausted to argue. I left him with his banshee daughter and returned to the sick woman's side, shutting the door behind me. Mrs. Hale's pulse was rapid and weak; her skin was hot to the touch. A good blistering agent might have some effect but Hale's medicine box contained little of value, and I carried no medicine at all in my own. I asked for a pint of vinegar and a pail of fresh water, having no idea if this would have any effect, but remembering that placebos sometimes work when all else fails. In these cases it was likely the patient's own mind that healed, yet the minds of most people seemed to need a potion, a nostrum, a laying on of hands. Not strictly in the Biblical sense, but the principle was the same. In any case, the bath of vinegar water would at least be cleansing.

What more could I do for the dying woman? I had dutifully bled her and cleansed her. Had I had at my disposal a full complement of blistering agents, but I knew of nothing that could help her now. She was beyond help. This was the hour when doctors and surgeons packed up their kits and went home. Yet, I had no home to go to.

I found a hairbrush amid the clutter and groomed the woman's wavy black hair, for want of something useful to do. Remembering with a flash of sweet pain when I had been aboard the merchantman *Canopus,* how Mary Blake had groomed my hair. How her strong hands wielded the brush and comb against my rebellious copper colored tangles, the tingle of scalp as she pulled against the roots, the way my eyes smarted and watered as she ferreted out a knot. To assist someone in grooming was such a simple, yet caring act, it brought tears to my eyes. Perhaps it was within all living creatures, this ability to care. Even cats, proud and aloof as they are, deign to groom one another.

* * * * *

Time seemed to crawl and there was no ringing of the ship's bell to mark its slow passage. Growing weary, growing bored, I looked around at the grim walls of my confinement. The rough-hewn bulkheads were devoid of decoration of any sort, and only practical items, nautical necessities, hung from the pegs on the wall. A tin sconce, a man's woolen overcoat, a tarred hat. There was not so much as an embroidered pillowcase or a homemade quilt on the straw mattress. Had the woman not wanted to hang a portrait, a primer of needlework, some sort of gewgaw to make the place home? Perhaps she had moved to this cabin when she first became ill, or maybe she lived invisibly in a man's world, making no adjustments; content to be a passenger on her husband's vessel.

Searching for clues I discovered a strange collection of

objects in the storage nook beneath the bed. A desiccated apple core. A milk tooth inside a sail maker's thimble. A collection of wooden spoons with faces inked onto them. The end portion of a cat's gray striped tail. I had chanced upon a raccoon's stash, a fairy's trove, or more likely the mute little girl's stash of toys. Puzzled, I shut the cupboard door and turned my attention back to the comatose woman, wondering now if it were too late for me?

Had I maintained a professional relationship with my patient, Everett Lee, I never would have gotten involved in this mess. But no, I had assumed responsibility for his very life. My own vanity had brought me here. Oh, how I wished I were the gunner's wife, keeping his bunk warm, sharing his portion of ship biscuit, darning his socks, bearing his brats. I imagined how it would be to drift off to oblivion with the weight of his leg over mine, the sound of his breath slow and satisfied in my ear, the rise and fall of our chests and the wild beating of our hearts slowing as they fell into step for the duration of the night.

Chapter Twenty-Nine

I went on deck to speak to the captain, who was taking his turn at the wheel.

"Mr. Hale your wife is not long for this world. I can do nothing more for her. If you want to see her while she still draws breath..."

Hale's face darkened. He looked as if he would let fly his clenched fist into my nose, and I flinched in spite of myself. But his rage quickly dampened and he sighed, the first sigh I had ever heard from him. The air came out of his lungs in a great whoosh and it seemed to deflate him. When he spoke, his voice was thin as a skim of ice on a puddle.

"How long?"

Who can say precisely? Some pass in the blink of an eye while others linger, reluctant to leave. More than a few wrestle with the dark angel, a fight that cannot but prolong the inevitable. I had seen enough people die to know the precise hour cannot be predicted, but there comes a point when death seems to shine from within, as if the angel already inhabits them and is preparing to take flight. At this point, the dying person seems resigned, they are quite ready to go, only the brave little heart has not given up its earthly job. It beats on and on, a blind but steadfast drummer, rallying the lungs to draw yet another breath, and another, all in vain.

"An hour or two," I said. "Or maybe twelve, I can't precisely predict. But your wife has passed the point of no return, Mr. Hale. There's nothing more I can do for her, and I daresay she'll not be alive this time tomorrow. If you wish to speak your farewells I'd advise you do so now."

Now it was he who flinched. The fortress of his chiseled face began to crack, and then fall in great slabs.

He stamped his foot three times on the deck and bellowed, "Eli, take the helm!"

Both Eli and Everett scrambled on deck to take over. I followed the captain below, but he turned me away at the cabin door.

"Leave us alone," he roared savagely.

I was happy to, and closed the door. But I could hear the wavering murmur of his voice, barely more than a whisper. It wasn't that I was purposefully listening; it just couldn't be avoided. I sat down on the bottom step of the companionway, exhausted.

The child appeared out of the shadows, tugging at my coat sleeve. Her dark eyes shone with questions she couldn't ask, her face was stricken with anguish. I felt the push of unshed tears, a dam of sorrows. This soon-to-be-motherless girl and I had something in common. You'll gradually forget her, I wanted to say, because you're so young, as was I. You'll forget too, the details of this dreadful night, but *Mother* will remain with you always. Her loving presence will become a part of your conscience that sits in understanding judgment of all you will ever do or become. Mother will be with you always, even if you can't remember her face.

"Chauncey?" But Chauncey squirmed past me and disappeared into her father's cabin, slamming the door. Behind it, I could hear her howl.

I didn't like this new attachment, this connection with the girl. I didn't welcome it at all. Much too complicated. I wished I had never come to this miserable floating prison, never succumbed to Everett's pleas for help. Maybe Dudley Freeman was right in one respect. I had grown too familiar with one of my patients. I had gone beyond the call of professional duty and now I was trapped on this little schooner with a crazed captain, his dying wife, an uncivilized, tongue-tied child, and the scourge of smallpox. I looked down at my forearm, beneath the rolled up sleeve. The inoculation site stung. It was red, swollen, evil looking.

And to think I could be hidden below decks in Brian Dalton's cabin, safe in his love, a woman protected, a wife. With each decision the road branches, and the road back home becomes so much more complicated.

The captain came out of the cabin and faced me squarely. He seemed huge. A bear with long black hair falling into his face.

"I've made my peace. She requires your attentions now, doctor. Call me when she has passed."

"And your daughter?"

"Chauncey!" As she came out of his cabin, he swept her up, hugging her to his chest, a chest as thick and hard as the mainmast. "Say goodbye to Mama, little one," he whispered. "*Dis-tu, au revoir.*"

He held her at the open door where she could see her mother, comatose on the bed. However, he did not take her to the bedside, would not let her breathe the contagion. Instead, he took her up on deck, into the cold, fresh air where she could cry out at the night. And he walked the deck with her for some time, then brought her below to his cabin and shut the door.

It was Everett who kept vigil with me, sitting inside the tiny cabin. We tried to stay awake, but kept nodding off. Through the bulkhead Chauncey's sobs and sniffles grew fainter then finally ceased as she gave in to sleep. Time crept, breath by ragged breath. Then shortly before sunrise Mrs. Hale drew her last.

* * * * *

"She hated the sea, I won't drop her over the side for the sharks to make a meal of," Hale said. "I'm taking her home to be properly buried."

"What shall we do?" Everett asked.

"Pack the body in salt and store it in the forward hold, with the barrel staves. Do it before Chauncey awakens." He put on his tarred jacket, pulled a cap down over his unkempt hair, and stomped up on deck to a wet gale, leaving Everett, Eli, and me with the gruesome task.

After we had stowed the body in a hastily made box filled with salt, I threw the dead woman's bedding overboard and fumigated the cabin with glowing hot loggerheads stuck into a bucket of pitch. This filled the tiny space with a bitter steam that would purify the vile air. As any good surgeon, I would have fumigated the entire vessel but the captain forbade it, because of the livestock. "I won't have them breathing that acrid smoke, it'll cause them to panic. One of the horses might break a leg and then I'd have to shoot it."

Chapter Thirty

I dreamed I was aboard *Richmond,* with Brian. I was pregnant and about to deliver. In my dream we were the only two people aboard, we had the whole ship to ourselves. We came across *Andromeda,* her sails all ripped and flapping. I got up from my childbed to hail her; but through the spyglass, I saw a horrible sight. I could see everyone on the schooner on deck, but they were all dead, their faces covered with black scabs, skin pulled tight, smiling in rigor mortis. Captain Hale was lashed to the wheel, his skull shining through at the back of his head. Chauncey sprawled at his feet, gazing up at him, her tangled locks moving with a whisper of air. A seabird landed on her exposed clavicle and while I looked on helplessly, made a meal of her face.

I awoke breathless, in a sweat, feeling thirsty, thick-headed, and hot. I heard nothing but the sound of wind in the rigging and the rush of water against the hull. I willed myself back to sleep, to dream the same dream again.

"Patrick, it's Chauncey!" Everett Lee's voice, urgent in my ear.

My dream turned to ashes and blew away. I tumbled out

of bed to follow Everett as he limped and thumped down the dark passageway. Yet even as I hurried to tend to her, I knew there was little I could do.

She lay on her father's bed crying like a kitten, her cheeks hot and red. Was this the desired response, the mild form, or was this the killing version? The next few hours would tell.

"More candles, bring more candles. And water, fresh water and soap, is there none to be had aboard this wretched boat?"

Captain Hale was called down from his turn at the wheel. "What do you want of me?"

I looked at him incredulously. "What is it with fathers? Are they all so uncaring? Are daughters the world's most dispensable creatures, or is there some other, more insignificant form of life on this planet?" My voice sounded shrill. It was the voice of a furious woman and I made no effort to curb it.

His dark face reddened, his eyes popped, thunderstruck. He seemed to swell with his fury, but I didn't shrink back. My anger had wrenched free of its stays. *Go ahead, strike me*, I thought. *You unfeeling bastard.*

"What I want from you is for you to sit here with your daughter," I said. "Mr. Thomas can take the watch. Your job, sir, is by her side. Your presence, your fatherly love, is the best medicine we have."

The air was so charged it nearly crackled as we faced each other, red-faced, nostrils flaring. Neither of us spoke. Then without another word Dominic Hale sat on the edge of the bunk and removed his cap, as if to stay awhile.

He had listened to me; he had done what I had asked. Yet, I had no idea if his presence would help. I only hoped it would.

Everett leaned against the doorjamb. "Anything you need in there?"

"Tea," I said, peremptorily. "She needs warm tea with

sugar, if there's any to be had. It's the best thing for a fever brought on by inoculation. All of us should have some tea." I had no idea if warm tea with sugar had any value or not, yet I felt I must maintain my authority. "Bring on the tea!"

We all took our turns sitting with Chauncey—Dominic, Everett, Eli and I—through the long day and night that followed. Uncle Everett kept the stove hot, the kettle boiling, and the tea steeping. He made it his own task and took it very seriously, glad for the responsibility. Pots and pots of tea were spooned into Chauncey's mouth and sipped by the tankard ourselves. It was as if the dried oriental leaves, steeped in brackish water, were a magical potion that would keep us well.

A pustule erupted on her face, to the right of her nose, soon followed by two more on her forehead. I chose not to bleed her or do anything that might adversely affect the workings of her own body. None of us dared voice the question, yet it was on everyone's face, clear as printed letters on a broadsheet. *Was this due to the inoculation, or the disease itself? Was this the weakened pox, or the killing sort?* And one by one we were all experiencing symptoms, the warm flush of fever as the pustules burst open like well aimed bombs, on our faces, our arms.

* * * * *

Daybreak found the captain passed out next to his daughter, who slept deeply, like a fairytale princess under a dark spell. Eli kept the helm while I fed the livestock and Everett made oatmeal and brewed coffee. For the next eight hours the three of us kept the vessel on course and making good speed. We pumped the bilge, trimmed the sails, threw the log line, estimated our position, and rubbed down the horses. Infused with a new strength, a purpose, we were more considerate of one another, as if Chauncey's illness had consolidated us, if only temporarily. There were odd moments when

I realized I was content, if very briefly. Content to be moving, to be going somewhere. To be sailing again.

* * * * *

There is something about a crisis that obliterates both the past and the future, and all you are left with is the moment at hand. Time slows down and seems to pause at the end of each breath. The facades of everyday objects crack and fall away, and what you once admired turns out to be nothing worth having. Tawdry trinkets. Other things—a bent but still serviceable spoon, a sliver of soap—take on new importance, become almost sacred, and the least little task you set yourself to do shimmers with significance.

By sunset Chauncey was much improved, and hungry. In fact, she was ravenous, as was I, as were we all, collected about the table slurping Everett's salt beef, turnip and onion melee with relish. No more pustules erupted, our fevers had waned. Dominic Hale, restored by sleep and transformed by his daughter's recovery, actually smiled. I pronounced the threat of smallpox over and asked the captain to lift the quarantine. He did.

"You can disembark at Saint Kitts," he said, pouring us each a mug of coffee. We had had enough of tea, and were ready for the comforting infusion of the bitter black Arabica bean. "I plan to clear customs there, and look for a buyer for the horses. You'll have no trouble getting passage back to England, or wherever you might want to go. I owe you, MacPherson. I have little coin but I'll give you what I have. I'm indebted to you. You tended my wife and saved my child." His craggy face punctuated by three scabbing sores looked almost humble. I was disarmed.

"But there's nothing ashore for me," I admitted. "Truth be told, I'm through with the navy. Or rather, His Majesty's Navy is through with me."

Linda Collison

"What do you mean?" A glint of suspicion returned to Hale's bloodshot eyes. "I thought you were so eager to rejoin your frigate."

"I am." I drew a breath. "But it's complicated, but I can't —not as surgeon's mate, anyway. Still, the frigate *Richmond* is my home and I have a protector who will sponsor me, if I can but find the ship. I must find it."

"What have you done?"

"I've done no crime, sir. And nothing I'm ashamed of."

He continued to size me up, but pressed me no further.

"The *Richmond* was my life." I felt as if the shirt had been stripped from my back and I stood before him, ready for a flogging. Still, I chose my words carefully, for I needed to continue the ruse. My eyes stung as I thought of Iris Wickham, the Hollister twins, Mr. Frick. "*Richmond's* people are my family."

"What happened?"

How to explain? How to tell the truth, but not the whole truth. "I fell afoul of an officer—my credentials were... questioned. A man I thought was my friend turned out to be my worst enemy. The long and the short of it is my future as ship surgeon's mate has been ruined." Feeling humiliated, I bit my lip hard to keep from crying.

Hale looked away, allowing me to compose myself. He studied his pewter mug, as if reading the grounds. At our feet, under the table, Chauncey played with her doll, who had taken up with an assortment of wooden spoons for company. I could almost make sense of her garbled speech, her little throaty mews.

The captain left and came back with a bottle of rum. Poured a little splash into his coffee, and pushed to bottle across the table toward me. "Mr. MacPherson, can you steer a ship?"

I nodded. "I can."

"Can you keep a course? There are no idlers aboard a schooner, no supernumeraries, no slackers. Every man must stand his watch."

"I can," I was proud to say.

"You were born a gentleman, I'll wager. Yet, every hand aboard my ship must pull his weight. There are all sorts of odd jobs that need done aboard a little trader such as ours, and we all do our share, myself included. We're not staffed as the Navy is, with a man for this and a man for that; but you'll be paid well. Hard money is scarce, but sugar and molasses are valuable in the colonies. A share of it will be yours. If you agree, we can work out the particulars. Eventually, when you're back on your feet, you can buy some shares. There is money to be made, sir."

"You mean sugar?"

"What else?"

"From Martinique?"

"Of course from Martinique—or wherever. We're colonial traders, MacPherson, just trying to make a profit. I've no quarrel with French Creoles, even though our countries are arm wrestling for world dominion. Molasses, sugar, it's in great demand, war's been good for business, and the French Islands have more to sell, at a lower price, than do our British sugar colonies."

"I have to admit, Captain Hale, I am rather ignorant in matters of commerce. I know more about anatomy than economics. "

He slurped at his coffee, now emboldened with rum. "It's not hard to understand MacPherson; in fact it's simple. Supply and demand. Buy cheap and sell dear. Free trade. The French were raising as much cane as they were able, making sugar, making rum for their soldiers stuck in outposts in Canada, Africa, India, the Caribee—a far cheaper nostrum than French wine or brandy. But now that England has the advantage, now that England rules the shipping lanes, all that sugar, all that rum, is piling up in their warehouses, with more being produced every day. They can't ship it out to their markets, so they're drowning in their own liquor!" His fist crashed down on the table in emphasis. "Ha! And good rum it is, too." With that, he handed me the flask. "Have a taste of the best."

I poured a splash of it into my coffee and swirled the mug to mix it. "Rather improves the bean," I admitted, tasting it. Yet, honestly, this business sounded like nothing in which I wanted to be involved.

"You wouldn't believe the amount of money being made in the Northern colonies on French sugar. You would be astounded. New York, Rhode Island, Massachusetts, why I'm just a little fish in a big pond, MacPherson. But I'm making money myself, and if my father were still alive today, he'd be a wealthy man. He was a trader too, mostly local. Fact is, there ain't much land to be had in Rhode Island. Sure as hell ain't any titles. Rhode Island's a refuge of scoundrels, smugglers, Quakers, and rejects of all sorts, and some of them have done well for themselves. Every damn one who's got more than a pot to piss in, earned it from flaunting the Navigation Acts, I'll wager. Those laws weren't made for our advantage. But there's a risk involved, anytime you go to sea. My father went to sea one day, and never came back. And I never knew what happened to him, not for certain. No trace was ever found of his ship."

He stopped his tirade and reflected, tapping his thick forefinger against the rim of his mug. Then looked me straight in the eye, through a stubborn strand of black hair that fallen across his face. "Nothing's guaranteed. And I should warn you that Parliament has given the Navy the authority, as of late, to seize Colonial vessels they suspect to be carrying proscribed goods. They're cracking down, got to pay for this war somehow."

Navigation laws put in place before I was born were favorable for the British sugar growers, such as my father had been, at the expense of the Northern colonies. It was all part of England's mercantile empire, and trading directly with the French was forbidden. Yet, Pocock had captured Martinique for Britain just before the Havana operation began. I had not considered the implications. I knew nothing of commerce.

"I'm told the provisional governor is a New Englander, an army officer, and he's opened Saint Pierre to trade, though who knows how long that will last. And it's still French sugar and molasses that we'll be carrying home. Without the proper invoices a naval frigate hungry for prize could make a prize out of us as soon as we weigh anchor."

I squirmed uncomfortably in my chair.

"That's why I clear customs first, in English Harbor or Basseterre. Trade some candles for a bit of British grown sugar, enough to be legitimate. Then on to Martinique and Guadeloupe and the free port of Statia, that's where the real money is to be made. But the risks increase along with the rewards. The waters are thick with patrol boats, cruisers and privateers on both sides, trolling for vessels as if for fish."

"The profits must be great, to face such risks."

"Of course the profits are great, we don't take such risks for the hell of it. Of course, if you don't want to take part, you don't have to. You're a freeborn British subject, MacPherson, same as the rest of us. Unless Parliament has passed a law denying us our natural rights, which they are wont to do. Rhode Island's very charter is threatened. But it's your choice. You can be one of us or you can remain an unwilling passenger. Which might prove the safer course should we be captured. But no risk, no reward."

I sat staring at my coffee, as tongue-tied as little Chauncey.

"Thank you for your offer, Captain Hale. I'll need some time to consider it."

Chapter Thirty-One

The days were mostly gray and wet as *Andromeda* beat into the sullen sea. Swells broke over the bow, drenching the deck, and a persistent trickle of cold water found its way to my bunk, dripping directly over my ear.

On the occasional days when the sun peeked through the clouds, Hale took the noon sight, plotting our progress on an ancient, coffee stained Admiralty chart. Whoever was at the helm kept time by the sand glass, turning it when the last grains had run through. No one ever bothered to strike the bell.

There was no land in sight, nothing but a vast country of water to be crossed and an ocean of time to endure. I often found myself on deck, wrapped in my great coat, watching the men set or lower a tops'l, reef or shake out a reef as the weather directed. *Andromeda* was a fast little vessel, and with her fore-and-aft rigging, she could point higher into the wind than even a frigate. But the schooner's real advantage was in sailing shorthanded; she required only a few men to sail her. The gaff rigging made going aloft the exception and not the rule for making sail. Being shallow drafted and highly maneuverable—as well as convenient to load—made her an ideal coastal trading vessel, though *Andromeda*'s route gave a new definition to "coastal".

Hale, like a lot of other Yankee captains, regularly travelled back and forth from the New England coast to the Caribbean, competing with bigger companies and larger ships by having less overhead and fewer investors. And schooners like *Andromeda* were quite handy at slipping into a hidden cove to escape nosey revenue cutters, which were becoming more bothersome lately.

On this run, our cargo included barrel staves, candles, the aforementioned herd of sheep, and the two Narragansett Pacers, a breed developed in Rhode Island and popular among the British planters. I had a fondness for horses and visited them often to console them with a handful of oats sweetened with a crumble of brown sugar taken from the galley.

When conditions allowed the helm to be left unattended the five of us took our meals together in the galley, where it was warm and snug, redolent with the smell of scorched coffee and sour-smelling overcoats hanging to dry.

My berth was a coffin-sized alcove in the galley, next to the iron stove and above the compartments where the coffee, sugar, flour, and biscuit were stored. It was little more than a shelf with a lee cloth to keep me from tumbling out, and a moth eaten scrap of flannel that served as a curtain. Inside my berth, there was a narrow shelf for my effects, but too small to accommodate the clothes that were to have been my disguise to get back on board the frigate. I kept the dress, bonnet, and shawl with my spare shirt and breeches rolled up in my haversack. It made a serviceable pillow.

The clang and rattle of pot and ladle in the galley meant that Everett was preparing the next meal or washing up from the previous one. He was often accompanied by Chauncey, who crawled under the table to play with her collection of spoons and other miscellaneous objects that served as toys.

Over the pots of bitter coffee, spliced with generous splashes of rum, were the ongoing and energetic discussions between Captain Hale and Mr. Thomas. They took pleasure in arguing, the way some men take pleasure in cards or horse racing. Economics, philosophy, government, they debated endlessly; and while they agreed in principle on many issues, the devil was in the details. The war was good for business, yes; but the government was greatly in debt, there were armies and navies to pay, and where would the money come from? Occasionally they would bring me into the question, plumbing my opinions for a shred of logic to shore up their own argument. Dominic Hale, well informed and arrogant in his beliefs, usually had the last word.

The Americans seemed to be all of the same class, more or less. They were yeoman farmers, merchants, and craftsmen, the working sort. There were poor men but no peasants; there were wealthy men, but no lords. All had left their titles and pretensions behind when they, or their ancestors, crossed the Atlantic. In America people felt free to reinvent themselves, and seemed to do so as they pleased. This rather appealed to me.

How unlike the Caribbean sugar colonies where only a fortunate few could amass wealth. These were places where men like my father—Englishmen, second sons of barons—men of breeding but without title, could still be grandees on a lesser isle and could increase their slimmer share of inheritance by investing in sugar cane. There they could live like sultans on the labor of their Africans, purchased like draft animals and worked just as hard. Far away from their London town homes, their proper wives, and the expectations of daughters like me, these men fashioned their kingdoms to their liking.

The Northern colonies had not yet been spoiled. Perhaps they were too big, too diverse for a pack of elite gentlemen to corrupt. I learned a lot, just by listening to the saloon table talk. There was something in the air that crackled when Hale and his first mate debated over their endless cups of coffee spiked with rum. But I had no interest in mercantile matters, taxes, and import duties. All I wanted was to get back to the *Richmond*. If the authorities caught us, so much the better. I was an officer of the Royal Navy kept aboard under the quarantine law; surely, I would be exonerated.

And then the truth hit me in the face: I was no longer an officer. No longer a surgeon's mate. Everything I had worked for was gone, poof, just like that. To the British Navy I was a non-entity; to the officers of the *Richmond* I was an inconvenient embarrassment they had washed their hands of. At best, I was the gunner's woman. Not even a lawful wife.

* * * * *

We were now crossing the Great Current, beating into the wind, ploughing through walls of water, adjusting our course to compensate for the drift. It was as if the current had a mind of its own; and for the life of me, I couldn't figure out how there could be within the ocean, rivers of warmer water that flow contrary to the wind and swell? These currents could sweep a ship off its course and carry it along like a piece of rotten timber. It was said this Great Current could take a ship under bare poles all the way to Ireland.

All the while, deep in the hold with the barrel staves and tallows lay the body of Chauncey's mother, patiently waiting for landfall. On deck, the sandglass kept running and running, the grains slipping and tumbling through the tiny passage, never at rest.

Chapter Thirty-Two

The harsh monotony of ship life imposed itself. I watched the others go about their work, learning how to sail a schooner by observation. I yearned to join in, to raise the peak and throat halyards or throw the log line and count the knots as they slid through my hand, but my role was still undefined, for I had neither accepted nor refused Hale's offer.

I tried to sleep away long hours in my bunk, curtain drawn, my head resting on the pillow of my belongings. My future was a gaping hole, a dark and frightening abyss. At night, I sometimes had the feeling I was falling into it and would jerk instantly awake. *Find the Richmond. I must find the Richmond.* This mantra was my handhold on sanity.

Sometimes, alone in my bunk, I dared to imagine my reunion with Brian, the feel of his rough cheek against my skin, his knowing hands, the weight of him upon me as we lay together in his cabin. These imaginings were a balm; a sort of morphine, my private and pleasurable escape. Throughout the day any fleeting imaginary moment that brought his scent or the low hum of his voice, causing my blood to warm me from within. Even in my masculine attire, I felt decidedly female, my secret flower opening like some exotic plant, moist with dew and startling in its beauty.

How to resolve these desires? I vowed I would discover the *Richmond's* whereabouts once I was ashore, surely someone would have word. The waterfront was the place to be, ships coming and going, all the latest news from everywhere. Dressed as a man I had access to all of it; the wharves, the coffee houses, the taverns. There would be packets and sloops, I could post a letter to Brian Dalton, gunner; *HMS Richmond*. It might take months to reach him, but now I had had nothing but time. Time was as vast and monotonous as the ocean we both sailed upon.

* * * * *

Sometimes my thoughts and dreams of Brian went beyond our passion, to the other 23 hours of the day. What would I actually *do* aboard the *Richmond*, if not tend to patients? Roll bandages and pick oakum with the other wives? Help Frank and Henry Hollister with their sick berth duties? Sew buttons on shirts? I supposed I could still be useful to the ship in some fashion.

Inevitably I'd be called into service as a midwife to deliver some unfortunate child into the underworld of the ship's belly, a damp, dark, always rolling world that reeked of human bodies, livestock, piss-buckets and bilge water. Soon enough it would be me giving birth, the ship's bell measuring the half hours of my labor with a mocking ring.

These thoughts terrified me as I recalled the helplessness I felt at Maggie's death in the *Richmond's* fo'c'sle. Yet, even so, I was sure of my love for the gunner and as men must have courage, so must women. I could adjust to any life as long as he was part of it. If only he were here now, even this miserable voyage would be bearable.

I read his letter over a hundred times, I could recite it by heart, and I began to compose a letter to him in my mind, endlessly revising it, embellishing on it, reciting it aloud when I was on deck to empty my bucket in the middle of the night. I imagined my spoken words carried aloft like air-born seeds, traveling on the wind until they reached the frigate that had been my home, finding the man for whom I intended them. This letter—much recited but yet unwritten—kept me focused and gave me direction. It buoyed my hopes and kept me sane.

Chapter Thirty-Three

I was polishing my surgical instruments on the saloon table one afternoon, as was my habit. I wanted them to be sharp and free of corrosion, ever ready in case they were needed. A reminder of my former life, it was also a comforting ritual. Something important to do.

Up on the spar deck I could hear the step-thump, step-thump of Everett walking on his new wooden leg, a prosthesis that Captain Hale had fashioned from a spare baluster.

"A crutch is useless on a ship at sea." Hale had proclaimed, thrusting the peg leg at his brother. The captain's skills were diverse. He was a jack-of-all-trades and I begrudgingly admired him for that.

A flutter of little footsteps on the companionway as Chauncey came below, dragging her rag doll by one of its appendages. The doll was unclothed and its arm was dangling by a thread. She held it up, scowling.

Her silent request touched a tender spot. "It appears your dolly requires my services."

Chauncey nodded. Her complexion was olive toned, but a trail of dark sunspots spilled carelessly across the bridge of her nose. The small scars where the pox had formed were hidden under a broad streak of tar. A little hoyden, she was; allowed to run amuck on deck and aloft, without shoes or a bonnet, mistress of her world.

"Might I have a look at Dolly?"

She offered me the ill-used toy; a doll made of hemp and stuffed with oakum, the face embroidered in crude stitches, a red rag of a turban sewn to her head. I once had a similar doll myself, a blackamoor named Mammy.

Filled with nostalgia for my own lost doll, my own lost girlhood, I reattached the arm with catgut, and reinforced the other joints as the girl looked on.

"Watch carefully how I tie a surgeon's knot, it's a useful knot to know. Can you hand me the scissors please? Now then, you may dress the patient, she is quite well again."

She took back her doll and examined my handiwork, tugging gently on each appendage, a trace of a smile softening her dirty, freckled face.

* * * * *

Late at night when I couldn't sleep, the spar deck was a fine place to be. That night there was no moon but the light from the stars was enough to see. Beneath the water the glow of squid and the phosphorescent sparkle of unseen organisms in our wake, looked like planets and stars in the dark universe beneath us. Chauncey was asleep in her father's cabin, and Hale too. The sails were trimmed perfectly; Eli sat on the steering bench with one hand on the wheel, nodding off. Even the animals were quiet.

The sand ran through the glass and Eli turned it. Four in the morning, ship time. Everett was late for his watch. I volunteered to take the helm.

"Thank you kindly, sir. I find it hard to stay awake on such a fine night as this." The first mate rubbed his face with his hands. "Course is south by southeast, the wind has been on the beam. I'll wake Everett when I go below."

I took the wheel with eager hands, for I had not steered a ship since those long ago nights aboard *Canopus* when Brian let me have the helm and taught me how to keep a ship on its course by compass, wind, and stars. "No hurry, Mr. Thompson."

Andromeda was a joy to handle, all sails perfectly balanced and a fresh wind on the beam, she responded like a blood horse, bred for the race. It was thrilling to be at the wheel of such a vessel, to be in control of the ship while the others slept. My feet spread slightly, my hands on the wheel, I felt a part of her; my flesh and bones and nerves connected to the wood, the lines, the canvas sailing through the night.

The thump of a wooden peg announced Everett's arrival. His greeting was through gritted teeth.

"Your leg pains you?"

His laugh was not that of the optimistic young foot soldier I had come to care for. "My *missing* leg."

"You're walking on it too much," I said. "The stump is not yet healed enough for that."

"But I must," he said roughly. "What am I to do, sit all day and spin? The more I walk on it the less I'll notice the pain."

"You needn't be so stoic. Perhaps I can fashion a softer interface." With a scrap of fabric, a bit of muslin or silk, I could make a little pillow and stuff it with oakum for his stump to rest upon.

I glanced at the sandglass hanging from the binnacle, and then scanned the horizon. Soon the eastern sky would begin to lighten, that hour when the first light of the new day joins with the starlight, making it hard to tell where night ends and day begins. The sky already seemed less dark, or was I just imagining it?

"Everett, what's wrong?"

"Does it matter?"

"Don't be morose. Of course it matters."

"I can't change anything. I should feel lucky to be alive but the fact is, I don't. Truthfully, I'm envious of everyone with two legs. Seeing my brother striding about so easily, not even thinking about it, digs into me. Seeing all of you and your perfect legs. I curse the day we fired that cannon. Did the shot even hit home? Or was it wasted, all for naught?"

"Don't torture yourself."

"If only I'd taken a bit more care—kept my mind on the task. What the hell was I thinking? The flash of some girl's ankle? A drink of rum? If only I could go back to that day and live it over again, live that one moment over again. It's all I want in this life."

Andromeda's bow cut into a cross swell, showering the deck with icy water, causing us to hunker down under our coats and hats.

"What can I do? How can I help you?"

"Can you give me my leg back? Can you do that, Doctor?" His voice was unrecognizable; raw and unpleasant as the seawater running down the back of my neck. I realized I wanted him to be grateful to me for saving him. But Everett Lee had lost his leg, and until the end of his days he would have a stump as a reminder of his moment of inattention, his lapse in judgment.

I thought how our lives can change drastically between one breath and the next; how my life had changed by agreeing to help Everett Lee instead of sneaking back aboard the *Richmond* to be with Brian. Yet, I still had the hope of reunion. Everett would never again have his leg.

"I wish I could give it back," I said. "But I'm not God, only a surgeon's mate. And not very experienced at that."

"You did everything you could, I owe my life to you. Look, Mr. MacPherson, this isn't about you."

"Everett, please. Call me Patrick."

"I don't deserve your friendship, you have troubles enough of your own. You must despise me for ever bringing you aboard this cursed vessel. But my sister-in-law was a lovely, good person. I couldn't bear for Chauncey to be without a mother. Or maybe I couldn't bear to be without a sister-in-law, a kind woman in my life." His sigh sounded more like a sob "I wish to God that cannon had killed me straight away."

I gripped the wheel. "Don't say that!"

"Why not? It's the truth."

His admission pained me. I had assumed he would have been happy to be alive; yet how would I feel if I had lost my leg? What would my future hold?

"I'll take the helm now," he said "It's well into my watch, you've covered for me long enough."

Reluctantly I stepped aside, relinquishing the wheel.

"Everett, you must find courage," I said, placing my hand on his shoulder, the way Brantigan had done the day before the amputation. I expected him to shrug it off, but he didn't.

"It's not so much courage that I lack as it is will."

"I hope you find it, your will." I squeezed his shoulder, as if to deliver it through the damp, salty sleeve of his coat.

"Thanks." But there was no sign of will nor gratitude in his voice.

"Now then, what will you do?" I needed for him to have a plan.

He shrugged and dug in his pocket, bringing out a flask. Took a long pull and offered it to me and I gladly took a swallow myself.

"Very warming," I said.

"Rhode Island rum, from Martinique sugar."

"Well go easy on it, soldier, doctor's orders. I can't bear to see you morose over your bottle; you're too young for that. Have you been reading Marcus Aurelius? You once put great store in his words."

He pocketed the flask. "I seem to have lost the thread of his writings. He lived so long ago. And I'm no Caesar, though brother Dominic fancies he is."

"Then who are you?" I pressed.

"I'm a soldier who went off half-cocked. I could've been a printer, I might've kept our newspaper going; but instead I sold the press to pay off my father's debts. My mother and father knew what it was people wanted to read about; and my father knew everybody. He had his finger on the pulse of Providence. I might have learned. I might have kept that little gazette going instead of joining the army. And for what? To blow my leg away taking a port two thousand miles from my home. I'm a fool, MacPherson. That's what I am, a crippled fool."

"Well you're in good company," I said. "But now what? What do you want from life?"

"What do I want?" He sighed. "I want what you have."

"Everett, you have to move on."

"I don't mean your two strong legs, though I'm envious of them. I'm talking about your friendship."

"My friendship? You mean our friendship?"

"No, not our friendship, Mr. MacPherson—Patrick— though I'm glad you count me as friend. I meant your companion on board *Richmond*."

"Mr. Freeman?" I sniffed. "He turned out to be a false friend indeed. We had a... a great falling out."

"No, not Freeman. I'm talking about the gunner. Mr. Dalton. The two of you were close; I could see that. As close as brothers."

I turned my face to windward and held my tongue. It was so tempting to unburden myself right then and there to Everett, who was buried in his own loss. But I thought of the *Richmond* and how I had lost all authority, all respect once my true identity was brought to light. Every good thing I had done, was undone by the fact I hid a woman's body underneath these masculine clothes. I could never go back to what had been. Perhaps there was no going back, not ever. Maybe it was just the next swell and the next, no land in sight, no point to any of it.

But I sailed on the same sea as the *Richmond*. Water was continuous, it connected everything. On a ship, you can reach any shore if you have enough skill, patience, fortitude, and luck. I imagined a cord, an invisible thread, strong as spider's silk, connecting Brian and I. From his heart to mine, wherever in the wide world we went. And that string would bring us together again, I was certain. Believing was the force that kept me from completely disintegrating.

"Yes, Mr. Dalton and I have a long-standing friendship," I admitted. "You're very observant."

"Then I hope the two of you can be reunited. I'll do anything in my power to get you back to your ship. I owe you that. It's my fault you were separated."

"I came aboard *Andromeda* of my own free well, Everett. Truthfully, part of me was reluctant to go back aboard *Richmond*. But I would appreciate any help I can get to find my ship, my home."

"I'd do anything for you, sir."

"The situation is more complicated than I've let on. There are things... circumstances." I took a deep breath. "Everett, I'm not who I claim to be. I..."

"You don't have to explain anything to me." He held up his hand, almost as if he wanted to stop me from saying what was ready to come out. Maybe he did know or suspected, but could not yet bear my truth being revealed.

"You're an honorable man, you're a good surgeon, and you went out of your way to help Marguerite, because I asked you to. Because of me, you're not aboard the frigate. Look, I want to help you. Somehow."

Around us, the horizon was lightening. Though it was still dark, the night sky was no longer a heavy velvet curtain. It was the beginning of dawn, yet still a good two hours before the sun would rise.

One cannot choose one's family. I certainly had not chosen to be with these sullen, grieving Yankee sugar runners. Yet, I *had* chosen them. I had chosen to come aboard; and, although I had only been among them for less than a fortnight, Everett and the *Andromedans* were all I had.

"Good night, my friend." I reluctantly went below, leaving Everett at the helm with his bitterness for company. I hung my coat near the stove to dry and crawled into my bunk, that warm, leaky womb, suffused with the smells of burned wood, burnt coffee and damp wool. I was alone now with my memories and desires

It was much too warm in the galley. Now that we were in tropical waters, it was almost too warm to sleep. I traced the swirl of a knothole on the bulkhead. It looked like an eye, the eye of a glowering troll, the spirit of the oak tree the ship was made from. It was a tree that had been cut, hewn, and fashioned into a ship—nevermore to know land or its forest home. I tried to tame the little fellow, make friends with him. We had much in common, he and I.

Nearby I could hear the rustlings of the animals, impatient for the feel of land under their hooves. I, too, longed for land—but how exactly was that going to work? My real home had been the crowded, floating kind for several years now.

Tonight I had taken a short turn at the helm—did that mean I had joined them? But a man must survive and so must a woman, and I would rather hand, reef and steer than be a mere passenger, awaiting my fate like one of the sheep.

So far, I had managed to survive. I had survived and reinvented myself, finding love twice in the most unlikely situa-

tions. First as the reluctant young bride of the old Scots doctor, then as a young widow pretending to be male and loved
by a good man who knew me for what I was—and what I had
been.

Yet, Brian was a man my father never would have ap-
proved of—the father I imagined and invented, that is. My
real father, had he still been alive, probably wouldn't have
given a damn. The father of my own making had also passed
away, but I wasn't sure when that had happened? Yet there
he was, dead as Mrs. Hale, packed in salt and waiting in the
hold of my heart. Now was a good time to drop him overboard. I imagined the casket sliding down the plank with a
splash. *Rest in peace, mythical father.* I tried to squeeze a
tear, but there were none to be had. Instead, I felt unbur-
dened and light of heart. I thought of a ship in ballast, sailing
home.

Chapter Thirty-Four

I heard the bosun's call piping hammocks down, my awareness struggling to rise like a cormorant from some dark dream. For a lingering moment, I thought I was in my hammock next to Dudley Freeman, and only after sitting up and knocking my skull against the overhead did I realize I was in my shelf of a bunk in *Andromeda's* galley. The shrill tweet of the bosun's call had been the screech of a tern. I heard it again. A tern, most definitely.

Scrambling out of my berth I discovered a new rhythm, the jerky motion of a cross sea, a collision of swells felt through the bones of the ship. Birds and cross swells meant land was nearby and I hurried up the ladder, not bothering with shoes. The sun was bright and the deck glistened with salt crystals, like a morning's hoar frost, rough underfoot.

On the foredeck, I saw a small silvery fish struggling and I went to inspect. It was a flying fish, an *exocoetus*, washed aboard with a breaking cross swell and now struggling to return. Picking it up by its diaphanous wings I flung it back into the deep. The Roman Pliny had studied and described these fishes; he believed they flew to shore to sleep at night. I remembered thumbing through his *Naturalis Historia*, one of my late husband's treasured encyclopedias. I watched the fish disappear into the blue thinking *Godspeed and may we both sleep on shore tonight.*

"Is that what you do in His Majesty's Navy, Mr. MacPherson?" Hale groused, appearing at that instant from the rear companionway, chart and spyglass tucked under his arm, with Chauncey, looking tousled and in need of a comb, in tow on the hem of his shirt. "Does the purser throw away perfectly good food? Would you throw away a marrow bone or a hog's cheek?"

Another swell broke on our bow, throwing water onto the deck and providing us a brief rainbow. I was not in an argumentive mood. Quite the contrary. "Forgive me, Captain," I said cheerfully. "My sympathy for the poor creature overcame me. I was merely returning it to safety."

Did I imagine a softening of his stony face, a gleam of light in his eye?

"Damned magnanimous of you, MacPherson. Into the jaws of a larger fish, undoubtedly, or some sea bird. The bigger eats the smaller, that's the hard truth of it." He opened the telescope and scanned the horizon. "If my reckoning is correct that is Barbuda ahead, just off the starboard bow."

Chauncey tugged on his coat, reached for the spyglass, and her father obliged her. "There, look there, can you see anything?"

Hand shielding my eyes I squinted and made out a fuzzy smear on the horizon.

"My wife, she could do wonders with those creatures. Dipped in egg batter and fried to a golden..." The effort of speaking about this pleasant reminiscence seemed to take the wind right out of him. He never finished his thought. From below in the galley came a whiff of coffee, the clatter of pots and spoons. Everett, at work.

"In Barbados we ate them too," I ventured. "When I was

young." I wondered who had prepared them. The cook, I supposed, not my mother. So much I didn't know about those first years of my life, would never know. If Hale asked me to elaborate what would I say? The truth, I supposed, with one important modification. I had never invented a fictitious childhood, never had to, for no man had ever asked me anything about my growing up. Men don't pry into other men's lives, I've found. On the other hand, perhaps they don't really care that much. What's past is gone; it's today that matters.

Just then, an entire fleet of fish broke the water, flying in a single shimmering mass, an unlikely flock of birds skimming the crests in one long breathtaking glide. Chauncey gasped, the three of us watching until they disappeared into the water.

"Fantastical creatures," Hale admitted. "The world is filled with marvels."

High above us two frigate birds hung like kites on the warm wind. Soon, very soon, we would be able to smell land, that rich, seductive perfume of vegetation, the sweet burnt tang of boiling cane, I was eager for it.

Chapter Thirty-Five

We approached the crowded Basseterre roads cautiously, ghosting along under mains'l and stays'l. Everett and I stood by on the sheets, Eli at the helm, and Hale at the bow with the anchor ready to splash. No gun salute, no pipe, no scramble of feet across the deck—yet it took hard nerve and a fine bit of seamanship to navigate the sixty-eight foot schooner through the crowded anchorage and safely to rest.

Squinting against the dazzling sun I searched the roadstead, scanning the logjam of hulls and masts, the skiffs and longboats weaving between luggers, merchantmen, and warships. There must've been more than a hundred vessels—but not the one I wanted to see.

Of course, the odds were slim that the *Richmond* would be here in Basseterre when she could be almost anywhere, and was most likely halfway to Portsmouth by now. However, that didn't stop me from wishing. It's a good thing I'm not a gambler because I would likely bet on the poorest of risks based on a lucky feeling. Then again, since I had nothing to lose at that point but my life itself, why not hope extravagantly?

Having found his spot to drop the hook, allowing room to swing between the brigs and barks anchored nearby, Hale signaled to Eli to put the helm down. Mains'l luffing, the schooner slowed to a drift, and when we had lost our way Hale let go the anchor. The rattle of chain through the hawsehole played its happy tune as Everett hauled the main boom to windward to give the vessel a little sternway, setting the hook firmly in the sandy bottom. Another landfall; and, although the ship I was looking for didn't seem to be here, every landfall is a welcome homecoming for prodigal sons who go to sea.

* * * * *

"Captain Hale, would you be so kind as to give me a piece of paper and the use of your inkwell? I must post a letter." Having gathered my few effects, I approached him on the deck with my haversack slung over my shoulder, ready to go ashore. This was an inopportune time for me to be asking, having just arrived, but I was anxious to get my letter off, and see what news of *Richmond* I might learn ashore.

The sails were already neatly furled and the three men were at work building a crude launch with scrap lumber from the hold, to replace the ship's boat the deserting crew had taken in New York. Hale, straddling a raw plank, flipped a strand of dark hair from his eyes and looked up at me, scowling. Yet, he put down his plane and took me to his cabin where he allowed me the use of his desk. This, from Dominic Hale, seemed generous indeed. Rifling through stacks of invoices and ledgers in a great flurry, he ripped a blank page from his logbook and thrust it at me.

"Writing paper is dear, I hope this will do."

"I am ever grateful, Captain," I said rather archly but he either missed my sarcasm or chose to ignore it.

"I suppose you'll also be wanting a sand box and sealing wax."

"Well, yes. If you please."

"Top drawer," He snapped, leaving me to return to his business, his footsteps impatient on the companionway and overhead on deck. I sat in the slat back chair and faced the blank page.

Now that the time had come to put my feelings onto paper, my mind seized like a fouled block. I couldn't recall a single word of what I had been planning to tell him. I stared at the empty sheet for long moments, a fly buzzing at my ear, twirling a coil of my hair that had escaped its queue. I was aware of the heat, the cabin air was oppressive now that we were at anchor and no wind scoop had yet been rigged.

Above me, the querulous talk of the men as they worked, curt comments back and forth, the three of them not quite agreeing on how the launch was to be made. Hale of course, had the last word, though I suspect John Eli knew a little more of carpentry than did the captain. And the fluttering sound of Chauncey's bare feet running across the deck, unattended, alone in her own little world that seemed to orbit ours, like a moon.

Too, I could hear the muffled sounds of sheep bleating, the horses stamping and blowing in their stalls, forward. All sounds I had become accustomed to, this past fortnight.

Ships are alive with sounds, and at sea, I relied on them like a blind man. Especially on moonless nights, below decks my ears learned to pick up the slightest change in the wind or the swell. My sense of hearing and sense of motion had become much keener than on land, and now that we had come to anchor, my head was still filled with the background din of ocean and wind. It was a sort of a swishing roar upon which the voices of my shipmates and the shuffling and nickering of farm animals impatient to disembark were punctuated. Eyes closed, I could reconstruct the entire vessel and its surroundings in vivid detail, through sound and motion alone.

I remembered how aboard the *Richmond* I could distinguish the footfalls of Dudley and Brian and Iris Wickham, and how in the darkness the shipboard sounds gave a dimension to the flatness of the black night. The ear, or the mind, could detect whether the sounds came from above or below, from fore or aft, or from right next to my ear, like Brian's hoarse whisper. The memory of his low murmurs of endearment brought a squeezing pain to my chest. Sounds held the key to unlock the words inside me. Still, I hesitated. The paper seemed much too small. My heart clambered and thumped as if it knew what to say if only my mind and hand would cooperate.

Sneaking a peak inside the logbook, thumbing the water stained pages, Hale's handwriting was as bold as the man himself. Though he wrote small, and from margin to margin so as not to waste precious space, the letters and figures were as clear as his voice and seemed to jump off the page at me. *...and I expect to make landfall tomorrow if this wind holds. Believe the danger of smallpox is past. The young Mr. MacPherson wants to rejoin his frigate but I'll not go a-cruising to chase it. He may disembark at St. Kitts, if he chooses. He is not altogether forthright with me about his circumstances, but I owe him for his services as he did his best. Horses are well enough but needing exercise...*

I shut the book and picked up the quill, twirling it between my thumb and fingers. How to begin? *Dear Mr. Dalton? My dear Brian?* Should I apologize or just explain why I hadn't come to the frigate as planned? Do I dare hope for a reunion? At last, I plunged the quill into the ink, blotted quickly, and in a mad dash let, the words tumble forth as they would.

November 24, 1762
Basseterre, St. Kitts

My Dearest Brian,

I could not join you aboard Richmond that night in New York, because I was called to see a sick woman, a relation of Private Lee (the young soldier

*whose leg I amputated.) I planned on joining you af-
ter looking in on her, but the woman had an ad-
vanced case of smallpox; indeed, she died soon after.
I might have been foolish enough to join you anyway,
had the captain not quarantined the little trading
vessel and forbid me to disembark. The Richmond
sailed, and I was beside myself having been left behind, and so I have stayed with the Yankee trader (a
Rhode Island schooner named Andromeda), still in
hopes of meeting up with you. Also, it presents a better option for me than do the streets of New York. I
inoculated myself and the rest of the party against
smallpox, and that appears to have been successful. I
miss you so very much and I pray we may meet
again and that you still think well of me. I am still in
disguise, as it best suits me under the present circumstances. You have my heart, while I have only re-
grets.*

Your princess ever,

Patricia

Reading it over, I was dismayed. The handwriting looked
childish and ill-planned for I had begun writing too large,
had to cross write and even then ended up mashing the last
few lines together to fit them on the page. Yet it seemed
rather too brief compared to everything that had happened
and the roil of emotions I felt inside. But there was no possible way to express all that had happened in the past few
weeks and why I had responded to Everett's request rather
than come straightaway to the frigate.

I stared at it, watching the ink dry, rereading it several
times. Inadequate, yet heartfelt. Now it must be folded,
sealed, and sent as quickly as possible, in hopes of finding
him.

Before leaving, I took a good look around Hale's sparse
cabin, his overcoat, cap, and gloves hanging on hooks, all

very orderly. A shelf held a row of books with worn, stained bindings. The bed was made up, covered with a patchwork quilt. Such colorful and economic creations were far more practical than the fancy but useless needlework I was taught in boarding school, but never mastered.

Had Mrs. Hale made the quilt? Had she shared this cabin with her husband, before she took sick and was moved to the adjoining one? Just then her spirit seemed to waft through the room, a cool breeze, as if she had forgotten something and had come back to retrieve it. I caught a slight whiff of frangipani, and then like a ghost, it was gone. The cabin was once more stifling and sad.

Chauncey's Mammy, whose arm I had recently repaired, peeped over the edge of the child's hammock strung in the corner. Her embroidered grin fraying, one black button eye dangling from its socket, she was as battered as the rest of us aboard this vessel.

* * * * *

Captain Hale had waved down a boat and gone ashore to find a buyer for the horses, leaving the other two to put the finishing touches on the tender. Both pacers were in poor spirits from their long confinement below decks and he was anxious to get them to shore. It had been more than three weeks since they had been taken aboard in Rhode Island and their strength had deteriorated. Still, a pair of Narragansett Pacers should fetch a good price here; the English planters were mad about horses, the faster and more expensive, the better. I should know; my father having come to ruin at the track.

The captain also wanted to have clearance papers from a British port. Although the recent British takeovers of Martinique, Guadalupe, and Havana had opened the doors for legal colonial trading, certain expected stamps and signatures would make his dealings with New England customs much smoother. Given the right papers—and a little silver—the agent would be much too busy to actually inspect *Andromeda*'s hold to verify the cargo.

Having packed up my few belongings, I was eager to go to shore to see what news I could learn of the *Richmond*. Eli and Everett were preparing to launch the crude little skiff fashioned from scrap lumber in the hold and caulked with oakum and pitch. With Hale gone, they worked quietly, communicating with grunts and grimaces. I left them to their work.

Chauncey had climbed out on the bowsprit and was looking at the island with her father's telescope. Seeing her in that rather precarious spot reminded me of my skylarking days, or rather nights, aboard the merchantman *Canopus*.

"Ahoy the tops! May I join you, little Miss Hale?"

She studiously ignored me. Taking her silence for a yes, I pulled myself up onto the bowsprit and sat down next to her. She said nothing, just kept looking through the glass as if I weren't there.

Over the customs house, the Union Jack flapped in the breeze. To the north was Brimstone Hill, hidden behind cloud. This was the army's high ground where my husband Aeneas MacPherson was buried, dead nearly two years now from yellow fever. Aeneas had wanted a child and I had not. We weren't married long before he died, and I had unfortunately not become pregnant. It was funny to think that I had been married at seventeen and widowed at eighteen. In fact, I felt twice widowed, having been separated from Brian so abruptly.

Now who—or what—was I? A widow of nineteen, pretending to be a man? Pretending to be a surgeon? Not exactly pretending, I *was* a surgeon, a good one, though I practiced under a dead man's name and credentials. Sacked by the Navy—hence unemployed—I was now in company with a family of smugglers; yet I held onto the hope of rejoining the man I love, so that I might keep his cabin and bear his children. My situation was absurd. Yet, here was this child of five who had just lost her mother, and I felt very tender toward her. Like an aunt—or an uncle, under the circumstances, I suppose. For the first time since I had donned a man's costume, my charade bothered me. I wanted Chauncey to know who I really was and what we had in common. I wanted to hold her on my lap and wrap my arms around her in commiseration.

"See that big green mountain, Chauncey? That's Mt. Misery. It's an old volcano. Do you know what a volcano is?"

Her little fingers clutched the wooden telescope as if she feared I might take it from her. Yet still she said nothing and I felt utterly foolish, gabbling on like a goose. Maybe what I said was so obvious she didn't bother to comment. Perhaps she's been here before, many times, and knows more about Saint Kitts and Basseterre than I do. Then again, this could be her first voyage. There was so much about these people I didn't know, and had not bothered to ask.

I had been her age when my father sent me to England, to that dreadful boarding school in Salisbury. Looking at Hale's daughter was like looking back fourteen years and seeing myself. I had to remind myself this wasn't so. Still, I fought the desire to share my secret, to tell her I wasn't a man at all but a girl, just like her. But surely, that would only confuse her. I wasn't a good example; I must keep my secret.

"See there, Chauncey? Just below the little skirt of clouds, those are the cane fields. See them, divided by the ghauts, that's what they call those deep ravines in the side of the mountain," I babbled on. "Monkeys live in the trees that grow in the ghauts, trees the Negroes tend to have a bit of fruit. Have you ever seen a monkey Chauncey? They climb really well, you know. They're quite clever, almost as clever as you."

Frustrated by her aloofness and determined to get a response, I scratched at my armpits and made ridiculous monkey noises until the girl could not help but laugh. Chauncey's laugh, such a rare, joyous sound and all for me. Her laughter, and the sight of her little white teeth, was a treasure. If only I had cut her frenulum, to release her tongue. If only someone would work with her, teach her to speak. Was she forever destined to be neglected?

And now for the tearing away. "Well now, Miss Chauncey I'm going ashore now to look for my ship. If I find word of her, I'll be parting company with you. You'll be careful, up here on the bowsprit, won't you? Promise me you won't be careless and fall."

She said something in her garbled way of speaking, I think it was "Good luck, sir," then returned her attention to the telescope leaving me with a fresh little nick on my heart like that on a tomcat's ear. How she had managed to worm her way into my feelings in such a short time, I didn't know. With tears pressing at the corners of my eyes and stinging my nose, I raised my hand and hailed a boat to take me to shore.

Chapter Thirty-Six

"Have you seen His Majesty's frigate, *Richmond*?"

The boatman shook his head. He was a broad shouldered youth with golden brown skin and the blended features of a mulatto.

"No, sir. I've not seen the *Richmond*. Seen lots of other frigates in the roadstead and one in the careenage now, but no *Richmond*."

"Then drop me off near the post office."

He steered deftly past the stern of our closest neighbor; a British merchantman rimmed with weed, and then let out the sheet to take advantage of the wind. "If you're in need of some pleasure sir, I know the best houses in town. Anything you like and a price for any purse."

"No pleasure for me," I said, forcing a laugh. "Not today at any rate. But if you should come across the *Richmond* that would give me great pleasure and I would compensate you well for your efforts."

Ashore, the wharf seemed to sway beneath me and my head swam as my sea legs adjusted to *terra firma*. I felt entirely out of my element. Nothing held me, I realized; I could go and do as I pleased. Free of the morose men and the grieving, unkempt girl, I need not return to *Andromeda* if I didn't want to. The island was small but the traffic through here was considerable. Indeed, I had brought my effects along, few though they were, stuffed tightly into the bulging haversack—that, and a handful of coins in my pocket. I was an abandoned ship, running under bare poles.

At the post office, I learned that *Richmond* had not been here since before the siege of Havana. I inquired if there had been any news of smallpox in the Northern Colonies and was told that there was word of outbreaks in Paris, Stockholm and Prague this past year but none reported from North America, and none locally.

I watched the clerk toss my letter into a dirty canvas sack, feeling a strange emptiness in my breast pocket where I had carried it. How long it would take to reach him was anyone's guess. I inquired whether he had a recent newspaper from London or New York, and was told there were none available. "If they are on this island at all, you'll find them in the coffee houses sir, or the taverns."

Now back out into the streets feeling extremely fragile, as if an accidental nudge from someone's elbow would shatter me.

"Are you lost, sir?" A young lad asked me. He was dressed rather shabbily, a tradesman's apprentice, most likely; or some officer's servant who had been given a day of liberty. Then again, he could be a footpad for all I knew.

"I'm not lost, just getting my bearings," I said, squinting against the sun. "Do you know of a ship, a frigate, the *Richmond*?"

"I've not heard of her; but a convoy of British merchantmen came in just this morning. If you need a message delivered or an errand run, I'd be happy to do so."

I had neither—no more messages, no errands. I was curiously free, with nothing to do. Dismissing the boy, I walked aimlessly searching the faces of strangers. I walked on, baking in my waistcoat, past warehouses and counting houses. I turned onto another street with chandleries, dry goods stores, taverns, and pothouses. At last, I chanced upon the Red Bullock, the tavern where I had supped when I was last here in Basseterre. It was the very establishment where last January I had come across some of the warrants of the Richmond, before signing on myself. I had come full circle. Except this time the frigate was not anchored in the Basseterre roads.

It's curious how one's memory is flawed, for the tavern looked smaller and shabbier than I remembered it. It was crammed between two larger, more prosperous looking buildings that I didn't remember at all. Had they been there before? I could not recall. Against the building's stone foundation in the narrow stripe of midday shade, lay a spotted bitch nursing a litter of whelps. As I approached the door she cocked an ear and gave me a yearning look as only a dog can do. I made a mental note to bring her a bit of gristle or a bone from my plate.

Inside, a low roar of noise met my ears. It was pleasantly dark in here and a few degrees cooler than the streets at high noon. The smell of burning cigars, those fragrant fat rolls of tobacco leaves so reminiscent of these West Indies, clouded the air. I stood just inside the door, waiting for my eyes to adjust, listening to the clink of pewter, the raucous talk and guffaw of masculine conversation. It was as comforting, welcoming, as I imagined coming home to Christmas dinner would be, the happy jesting of a large family of brothers.

There was a threesome of men on the far side of the room, and one of them beckoning me. For a moment, I thought perhaps they knew me and were *Richmonds*. I made my way through the crowded room to join them, but found them to be strangers. Perhaps they had mistaken me for someone else.

"Good day, sir. You look as if you've lost your bearings, and are overcome with this horrid heat. We've an empty chair here, won't you join us in refreshment?"

"Honored, sir."

"I'm Henry Doyle, second lieutenant of the frigate *Mercury*. Midshipmen Higgins and Teague," he said, indicating his two young companions.

"Pleased to meet you and thanks for asking me to join you. I'm Patrick MacPherson, surgeon's mate."

"Do sit, MacPherson. You look like you're parched."

Indeed, I was.

"What ship do you serve?"

"The frigate *Richmond*. Do you know her?"

Doyle shook his head. "But I know of her. Is she here in Basseterre?"

"Well that's my problem. I'm trying to rejoin her."

"Rejoin her? How did you become separated?"

I scrambled to come up with a version of the truth to tell them, for the whole truth was rather fantastic and even if I wanted to tell them, it would take too long and they wouldn't believe it anyway. "I fell to a fever during the siege of Havana and was sent to a hospital ship to recover." As soon as I said it I realized I had erred, for such vessels were rare and I could not for the life of me remember the name of a single hospital ship, other than the one I once had served, which had sunk in these waters. "I'm lucky to be alive," I added, hoping they wouldn't ask me the name of the ship.

"Was it the yellow fever?" The lieutenant looked slightly alarmed.

"Yes, but I'm quite well now. I've regained my strength, and I am eager to rejoin my frigate. She sailed for New York early November. You've not heard of her whereabouts?"

"No. We've only just arrived ourselves. But she's well spoken of," he said, which coming from an officer of another frigate, was praise to my ears.

"*Richmond*? Oh, we've heard of her all right. And the *Centaur,* the *Intrepid,* the *Defiance,* the *Alarm, Hampton Court,*" admitted Doyle with a touch of envy in his voice. "It's my pleasure to stand you a drink, I'm in awe, sir. You'll dine with us too, won't you?" He waved down the yellow turbaned serving girl and ordered another plate for me, and more beer all around.

It was clear these three officers were newly arrived in the tropics, and had not yet spent much time at sea. Their faces glowed with new sunburn; their foreheads and upper lips were dewy with perspiration. They had not yet worn out their cuffs and stocks; they seemed fresh and eager for action. Though they were probably about my own age, I felt so much older than they looked. They seemed solicitous of me and in awe of my experience as they barraged me with so many questions about the siege, most of which I couldn't answer. My memories of it were vivid, yet strangely incoherent, a pastiche of sensations. The thundering of cannon, the nerve-wracking whistle of mortar, the screams of grown men, the arms, legs, and entrails covered with flies and rotting in the heat, the annoying whine of mosquitoes and the stink of bloody diarrhea in a shallow latrine. But these young fellows wanted to hear stories of strategy and heroics. Of these, I had no knowledge, no recollection.

I had only ever known a minute part of the whole operation. I was blind to the bigger event that was now being called the Siege of Havana. My knowledge of the long and brutal engagement was limited to my own duties, the duties of a surgeon's mate sent ashore behind the gun crews to assist Albemarle's troops. I had been intent on surviving, on helping the wounded and those falling to disease, anxious for the order to return to the ship. I had fallen ill myself and was captured, and my memory of that was patchy and dreamlike. It was the gunner who rescued me from the Spanish stronghold when the walls of the Morro Castle at last crumbled under the assault of our ships and our sappers. How odd that these young officers just off the boat had a better overall knowledge of the engagement than I did. I had my own personal experiences but they knew it from a more distant perspective. It was already part of history. The siege they spoke of was not quite the same as the one I had taken part in, and I couldn't quite reconcile the two in my head.

Doyle, I realized, was talking to me and I was nodding my head with feigned interest.

"...a brilliant move by Pocock, though Albemarle nearly ruined it, we hear, by dragging his feet. Had it not been for the navy's assistance on land, the siege might have failed."

"Don't forget the timely arrival of the North American troops," I said, thinking of Everett Lee.

I listened as they filled me in on what they had heard about the long battle of Havana and our eventual victory. What was already part of the official record? According to them, we now had possession of three million pounds of Spanish gold and silver, and a quarter of the Spanish navy— twelve ships of the line and three of their frigates. I felt a searing in my chest remembering the sweet little prize we had taken off the coast of Florida, a prize I would never see a pence of now.

"I only hope the grand high diplomats don't give back all of our hard won territory in their negotiations," said the lieutenant. "They say thousands of our own died during the siege from battle wounds and tropical disease. They say thousands more are still ill and may yet die."

So, the final toll was not yet in.

"Your efforts and sacrifice have given us the advantage, we've got the bastards where we want 'em."

I marveled at his confidence. "Do you really think so?"

"Ha! We've the best Navy the world has ever seen!"

"Is there any word of peace?" I asked.

"Peace? Nothing in it for me," the officer laughed. "I hope

we stay at war for a long time, or at least until I'm quite rich from capturing enemy merchants and privateers." The others agreed, and drank to that.

"But peace is on its way, they say," conceded Doyle. "Preliminary articles have been signed, at least that's the rumor. There's talk of taking Manila, over in the Pacific, grab it while we can before the final treaty is signed. Perhaps we already have taken it. I heard a sloop arrived just this morning, from those waters."

I wondered if that's where *Richmond* was bound, to the other side of the earth.

"When the treaty is signed we shall all be resigned to working revenue cutters, chasing down smugglers, I suppose."

"So you've no news of *Richmond's* whereabouts?" I said, to change the subject from illicit trade. "I'm eager to rejoin her."

"No doubt. You must have a good piece of prize money coming!"

I smiled at the sad irony of that. "I'd love to catch up with her before she pays off."

"Maybe she's patrolling off Guadeloupe, or taking orders to Admiral Rodney, who sits sulking in the governor's mansion overlooking the St. Pierre roads. The war is ending too soon for him."

"Rodney?"

"Yes, your Pocock stole all his thunder and half of his ships in his assault on Havana. Oh how I wish I had been with you on that one! Damn, what a pot of gold that was, Pocock will be rich beyond his wildest dreams. But I'm sure you'll get back to your frigate eventually, MacPherson." He flashed me his cocksure smile. "The Admiralty's all-seeing eye is like God's own. They know of your whereabouts, you won't be forgotten. Stay with the hospital ship and await your orders, that's my advice. Enjoy your rest, you've earned it."

"Thanks, Lieutenant. But if you do come across *Richmond*, will you deliver a message to the gunner for me?"

"My pleasure. But surely, but a posted letter would have more chance of reaching him. We may never cross paths."

"I have posted a letter just this morning but it might take a year to catch up with him. If fortune brings you in contact with my frigate, please tell my good friend Brian Dalton that a bad set of circumstances keep me from rejoining my ship. Tell him..." My voice broke and I took a long pull of warm beer. "Tell him I'm quite recovered. That I... That he is... That I am trying to get back to the ship. "

"I'll pass that along. Should we come across your frigate."

"Those words are for the gunner alone. If you should happen upon him."

Lieutenant Doyle squirmed a bit at my heartfelt words, probably thought I was a bugger, weakened by a deadly tropical fever. I was likely a disappointment to them; they were looking for heroes to emulate. Yet, the officer pulled out a slim notebook from his breast pocket and with a stubby graphite pencil wrote down *Patrick MacPherson, surgeon's mate seeking Brian Dalton, gunner, Richmond*. This gladdened me in an inexplicable way.

Just then, the dark skinned girl in the bright yellow turban served up our meal, a steaming pot of callaloo, with a ladle and four trenches. The young men eyed her appreciatively and although she surely felt their stares, she was unperturbed, carrying herself with the languid grace so common to the dark skinned women of these isles.

"What is this?" Midshipman Teague asked, tentatively poking his spoon into the pot.

"Callaloo," said I.

"Calla-who?"

"Callaloo. Also called pepperpot. Very popular here in the tropics. Is this your first time in the Caribbean?"

"Actually, yes. We just arrived a few days ago from Portsmouth. This is our first liberty. The heat is ungodly, I suppose we'll get used to it."

"What's in it?" The other midshipman asked, looking askance at his plate. Englishmen are so conservative in their eating habits, and sailors are the worst.

I spooned a sip of the fragrant broth. "Depends on what they have in the larder. A little of this and a little of that. Peppers, onions and herbs, mostly. And meat if they have it."

"What sort of meat?" Higgins ventured his spoon into the dark, steaming waters.

I shrugged. "Goat, most likely."

"Goat?"

"Goat."

"Well it's a change from salt beef, that's for certain." He slurped a spoonful of broth. "Not bad."

We tucked into our dinner, the young men breaking out in even more perspiration from the spices used in the stew. They all pulled out handkerchiefs and mopped their red foreheads. I envied them their fine kerchiefs, made of snowy white lawn, the midshipmen's still fresh and creased. I thought of my own handkerchief, stained in spite of bleaching, ragged edged. I longed for a new one, a set of three, and a new shirt and stockings too. And shoes, most of all I yearned for a new pair of shoes! An impossible dream since I could not even afford to have my old ones re-soled. They were so outdated, an old man's shoes. Oh, but what of the dress and bonnet? I had nearly forgotten them, stuffed into the haversack along with my surgical instruments. All of my belongings hanging on the back of my chair. I should be thinking of ladies attire, should I not? Ah, but what was the use? My gunner was not here and I had no need to wear a dress for any other man.

The talking ceased as we cleaned our trenchers and re-filled them, and cleaned our tankards and refilled them too. I remembered to set aside a bit of meat for the dog, surreptitiously wrapping it in my own sorry handkerchief and sticking it in my pocket.

I was pleasantly full from the callaloo, my head swam with the effects of the warm beer. I could have sat there in the dark, happy atmosphere of male braggadocio and cigar smoke until supper, but I saw a blurry John Eli waving to me from just inside the tavern door.

"Oh, there's my friend with news for me. It's been a pleasure, gentlemen. Good luck on your cruise." Not wanting to muddle my story by introducing the Yankee to the warrants from the *Mercury*, I quickly excused myself, dug in my greasy pocket for a small coin for the serving girl, and nearly knocked over the chair in my clumsy exit.

I stumbled out after Eli into the bright afternoon.

"Are those your men from the *Richmond*? Have you found your ship?"

"No. No word of her."

The sunlight was now more golden than hot white, and cast shadows onto the crushed coral street. This was the best time of day in the tropics, from now until darkness fell.

"They're from the *Mercury*, they haven't seen my frigate and know nothing of its whereabouts—or maybe they do, but they aren't at liberty to say. They think I'm still in good standing with the Navy, they don't know I'm on a Yankee trading schooner."

He smiled. "Is that so undesirable?"

"I don't know," I admitted, my words running together. "It's a long story. There are some things you don't know about me, Mr. Eli."

His laugh was sympathetic and he clapped his arm around my shoulder, steadying me. "I'm sure, and there are some things you don't know about me either, MacPherson. Let's bare our souls sometime over a couple of pints of ale and a bottle of rum. However, right now we could sure use your help unloading the pacers. Can you swim, sir?"

"Can I swim? Ha!" My voice was too loud. "Like a stone."

He laughed and slapped my back. "We'll put you on the boom tackle then. You can haul, can't you?"

What to say? I didn't have to, of course. I didn't owe Dominic Hale a damn thing; in fact, he owed me! But what else was I to do? Sit around Basseterre taverns, waiting for word of my ship? I had not enough money to do that for very long. These misfits were all I had. Besides, I wanted to see the horses safely ashore, for I had grown rather fond of them.

"I can haul, Mr. Eli, I most certainly can."

"Glad to hear it! But first, we must find young mister Lee. Basseterre seems to have swallowed him up."

Chapter Thirty-Seven

After much searching, we found Everett upstairs at Miss Callie's Tea Parlor, which wasn't a teahouse at all, but a brothel. It appears he had spent the afternoon enjoying the company of Calixte, a beautiful dark-skinned woman old enough to be his mother. I was shocked and would have lit into him right away but Eli just laughed and said Everett was a red-blooded soldier turned sailor who, having lost half a leg, had to make sure his other limbs were in good order.

I held my tongue until we were well clear of the establishment but told him he must now be dosed with mercury, and I knew many of men who had ruined their health over a prostitute. But Eli gave him the high sign and a slap on the back. He asked if she was worth the money, and Everett smiled and said, "Oh, yes." I have to admit he, walked with a spring in his step and nary a limp on his peg. Although I had grown to prefer a man's world, and a man's dress, I could not endorse this exchange of money for sexual favors. Better to shut my mouth than to rail at him like some officious, effeminate uncle. Maybe he wouldn't be so morose and ill tempered now that he had proved himself a fully functioning man.

* * * * *

When we got back to the schooner Hale was fit to be tied. "I've got a buyer and you all go off a-gallivanting, leaving me stranded. This isn't the army Everett, this is a Rhode Island merchantman and no one gets his liberty until the goods are delivered," he thundered.

"I'm sorry," he said, though he wasn't at all. "You've found a buyer?"

"They're valuable creatures, I could sell them anywhere. I'd love to see them in Martinique, on my father-in-law's plantation. But yes, I've got a buyer here in Basseterre who'll give me top dollar, in gold and silver."

"How do we get them ashore?" I asked.

"We swim them."

"Swim them?"

"Over to the beach at Frigate Bay, the new owner and his hands are waiting. We'll weigh anchor, move in as close to shore as we can."

"And then?"

"The same way you load guns onto a warship, more or less—with canvas slings and a cargo boom. Only we don't have a boat to transfer them to, so we'll lower them into the water and they'll swim to shore."

"What if they don't swim to the beach?" I asked.

"They'll swim to the beach; they ain't stupid. For insurance, we'll tie them to the skiff and row along with them. That keeps them together as well."

"What would you have me do?"

"Help me work the cargo boom. Eli will be in the skiff and Everett in the water. Everett's my swimmer."

"Can Everett swim?"

Hale shrugged. "He assures me that even with one leg he's better in the water than I could ever hope to be." This was indeed Everett's day to shine.

"Now, let's get cracking before it gets dark."

* * * * *

The mare came up first, her fine head tossing, eyes rolling, hooves pawing the air in a desperate attempt to gain purchase on thin air. Below decks, the stallion neighed to his helpless companion and kicked at the timbers confining him. Meanwhile Everett unstrapped his wooden peg and stripped naked. Grabbing hold of the spare halyard, he swung himself over the side with a little yelp of glee. Even with one leg, he was a good swimmer, more at ease in the water than on land. He talked to the horse as we lowered her into the water beside him, looping a rope around her neck and fastening it to a hook on the side of the tender. He then dove down and released the leather sling around her belly so that the stallion could be hauled out.

With both horses in the water, Hale got in the boat. I tossed him Everett's breeches and shirt, and they all made for the shore, leaving Chauncey and I on the schooner. Everett stayed in the water with the horses and within a few minutes, they had reached the beach. The horses clambered up onto the pebbly beach, salt water flying as they shuddered and tossed their beautiful dark manes. Even weak from the long passage they were magnificent creatures and I was sad to see them go. The buyer was waiting for them there on the beach, he and a servant led the horses away, their legs wobbly on the sand. My heart ached to see them go, and I felt foolish for feeling such a strong emotion about horses that had never been my own.

Everett drug himself out of the water, ungainly on land as a sea lion. Hale gave him a hand to stand up, wrapping his arm around the younger man's slim white shoulders, a sort of brotherly embrace. Unable to keep his balance in the sand on one leg, Everett leaned against Dominic whose stout frame kept him from falling.

Behind me there was a tug on my coat. It was Chauncey wanting to see what was going on. I lifted her up and stood her on the rail, my arms wrapped about her so she wouldn't fall. My nose against the back of her neck, I breathed in her smell. Though she was unkempt and in great need of a bath, her hair a sticky tangle, she smelled like the bloom of an iris.

"Don't worry, Chauncey, they haven't forgotten you, they'll be back soon. Papa and Uncle Everett and Mr. Eli, they're just seeing the horses safely to shore."

* * * * *

That night we dined together on deck. Hale had bought a cockerel and some onions from a bumboat, which Everett managed to turn into a pretty fair stew. Chauncey fell asleep on her father's lap, clutching a greasy chicken bone in her fist.

"Mr. MacPherson, if you'd like to get off on English soil, this would be your last chance to do so. Our next stop is Saint Pierre." Hale pronounced *Saint* as the French do.

"But Martinique is British now."

"I'm well aware of that little brother," snapped Hale. "But only in name. Saint Pierre is a miniature Paris and the French privateers still rule the backwaters and hidey-holes. There's no longer the British blockade to run, but that has only encouraged the filibusters. The port is less than two days away, but it's a hazardous passage, I'll not kid you."

"Why do you take such risks?" I asked.

"Because the rewards are well worth it, MacPherson. Men, ordinary men in Newport, in Boston and New York have gotten richer than Croesus taking such risks, and Mr.

Eli and I plan to be among them—or go down trying. Nothing ventured, nothing gained, as Chaucer penned."

"Stay with us, Patrick," said Everett, calling me by my given name. "At least until you find the whereabouts of your frigate."

Eli too, wanted me to stay. "Might as well make yourself a little money for your troubles. We're not such a bad lot."

"My offer still stands," Hale said, glancing up from his plate. "If hauling halyards and unloading sheep ain't beneath you."

To him it was a simple question. My hesitation wasn't that it was beneath my station. It was that Hale was a harsh man, a tyrant who traded with the enemy. Yet, I would rather be afloat and employed than be to be alone ashore, with no prospects for making a living. At least I knew these fellows. The devil you know, and all that.

"You're free to go if you don't want to be one of us. If you want to quit us here, I'll pay you what I can for your services. What is your fee, MacPherson?" Hale set down his fork and knife and turned his big hands palm up, spreading his fingers wide. It was a rare gesture for him, almost a supplication.

I had no idea what I would charge for tending the dying woman, a nurse's work really, except for the bleeding. And the inoculations, what did one charge for such a thing? I had no idea but whatever amount Hale could pay me would not be enough to live on for more than a few days. It would not be enough to buy me passage to England, and even if it were, should I go to England alone? To Portsmouth? What would I do if the frigate wasn't there, or had already left? What if Brian had already found himself a more compliant woman to share his cabin, certainly there was no shortage of pretty girls eager to warm his bed and share his fate.

Having eaten every shred of meat, I picked up the thigh-bone and bit into it to suck out the marrow.

Hale's eyes grabbed mine and locked on. "MacPherson, you have my gratitude. For tending to my wife in her last hours, for saving my daughter and the rest of us with the inoculations." His dark brows furrowed, he shook his head. "But I'm a merchant captain, I've got investors to answer to and this is a schooner, not a man o' war. I can't afford to have a dedicated surgeon aboard, who does naught but bleed, and dose, and polish his instruments. Nor can I afford to feed and house a passenger. What I need is a man who can be of some practical use, who can hand, reef, and steer. Do you understand?"

I nodded, snapping the bone between my teeth.

"Well then? Is this our last meal together? Do you sign on for the remainder of the voyage, or do I see you to shore?"

To the west, the sky was awash in red. Overhead, was the ungainly silhouette of a pelican flapping its way inland to roost for the night. The time had come for me to make a decision. I tossed the broken chicken bone over the rail and wiped my greasy fingers with my handkerchief. Then I finished off my rum, savoring the burn in my gorge all the way down.

"Captain Hale, I find myself at loose ends and with empty pockets, at the moment. I've much to learn about the workings of a schooner but I'm not above pulling my weight and I'm willing to learn. In addition, if I may be perfectly frank sir, I've grown rather fond of Everett's cooking. Nothing like that to be found on shore, I'm quite certain."

A rueful smile formed on the face of my former patient, a snort of amusement erupted from Eli, and Dominic Hale's fist pounding the table, causing the plates to jump. "Is that just banter or a commitment, MacPherson?"

"My word, sir." I swallowed hard for I was not without misgivings. "I accept your offer of employment. For the duration of the voyage, at least."

"Here, here," said Everett raising his cup. There were handshakes all round, another tot of Hale's rum and I was a full-fledged *Andromedan*.

Chapter Thirty-Eight

Having made our easting, we turned south, toward Martinique. Now we saw no other vessels, just the wide blue sea and a bowl of Delft blue overhead. We had left behind the pelicans and terns, but high above two frigate birds hovered on the steady wind, watchful sentries standing guard for us.

As Hale had warned, this was a chancy run, especially for little merchant ships like ours. Out here, any vessel we saw might be a threat. We kept well away from land, for French and Spanish privateers lurked in the hundreds of isles, coves and inlets of Guadeloupe and Dominica, hidden by mangroves and protected by treacherous reefs. Britain's warships too, had been authorized to stop us if they suspected we were carrying French sugar—which we would be, on the return trip. *Face it, Patricia; you are a smuggler now.*

That night I stood my first full watch as a crewmember. Hale teamed me up with John Eli; one of us at the helm and one of us keeping a lookout through the hours of eight until midnight, then again from four until eight in the morning. Although I had my misgivings about my commitment to Captain Hale, I loved being at the helm and in control of the ship, especially at night. Overhead, the constellation of Andromeda glittered, while in our wake phosphorescence shimmered like stardust. The wind in the sails and against my face was exhilarating.

You get to know your shipmates a little better standing watch with them. John, normally a rather taciturn man, told me about growing up on a farm and striking out on his own because there wasn't enough acreage to support he and his five brothers and sisters. He had attended school, was well versed in the classics, and had a penchant for Virgil. He recited passages from the Dryden's translation of the Aeneid when it was his turn at the helm. "Helps to keep me awake," he laughed. *"Endure the hardships of your present state, live, and reserve yourselves for better fate.* Everything you could want is in the Aeneid."

"Everett swears by *The Meditations*," I said.

Eli shrugged. "Marcus Aurelius has some good philosophies, sure; but he'll not keep me awake through a middle watch. For that you need a bigger cast and a little more passion and unpredictability, which is what Virgil and Homer serve up so well. Can't you just fancy all those arrogant, bickering gods up there? They back us up or they try to take us down, we're their pawns and how they play us! I do enjoy the drama of it, don't you? Who is your favorite author, Doctor? What books have changed your life?"

These middling Yankee smugglers certainly were a bookish lot. Were all of them so well read? "Galen's treatises, I suppose," I said. "Especially the one on blood-letting."

"Yes, but for pleasure? Whose works excite your imagination?"

"I like Defoe," I said, though I hadn't read for pleasure for some time now. Growing up I had thrilled to *Moll Flanders* and *Robinson Crusoe*, both of which had been banned at school, as were novels of any kind. They were too frivolous, or perhaps too dangerous, for young ladies to waste their time on. That was the rationale. Yet, novels circulated widely amongst my schoolmates and were far more memorable than the required *Pilgrim's Progress, English Grammar*, and *A Gentlewoman's French Primer*.

"Did you know Defoe was the son of a butcher?" Eli said. "He studied for the ministry, but flunked out and became a merchant instead. That was before he became a famous writer. Just goes to show you a man can do anything he puts his mind to, no matter the circumstances of his birth."

"But what if he's born a she?"

"What?"

"Never mind. My thoughts aren't so logical after midnight. Rather like a woman's, I suppose."

"Bah! Sleep deprivation, that's all. Nothing a few winks won't cure. Say Doc, did you know your man Defoe served time in prison for subversion?"

I shook my head. Did most young men know these things? The list of what I didn't know was impossibly long; how would I ever catch up?

"Are you married?" I asked, out of the blue. Curious. I'd never heard him mention wife or children, but then most men didn't talk about their private lives.

"Who me? No sir, not yet. But, after another run or two I hope to have made enough money to quit the sea and buy a house. If I continue to invest in Hale's little company, maybe in a couple of years..." His voice trailed off and he shrugged. "What about you, Mr. MacPherson? Oh, but you're too young to be married. You can't be more than one and twenty. Don't settle down too early, that's my advice."

A shrewd guess on his part. Yet, if he only knew I had already been married, widowed—and spoken for again. It's quite different for women, who bloom too soon and fade too quickly. However, as a man I was not yet in my prime.

"Well I can't support a wife right now, that's sure. Maybe I'll follow your lead, Mr. Eli. Put aside my bleeding cup for the import business. Sounds like there's more money to be made in sugar than in surgery."

"Only if we don't allow the customs man to bleed us. Oh, don't worry sir. It's not as if we're criminals. We're just ignoring inconvenient and arcane laws that we had no hand in making. Besides, what's the worse that could happen?"

I shrugged. "Prison?"

He chuckled. "Not likely. But should we wind up behind bars we can do like Defoe did and turn to writing."

I laughed out loud. "Then I may waste away in prison for I'm too quick with my tongue and too slow with my pen."

"Well, don't forget your surgical trade. You've always got that to fall back on." The first mate turned serious again. "I don't believe I ever expressed my gratitude to you, Mr. MacPherson, for inoculating me and the others against smallpox. And all you did for the captain's wife. Poor Mrs. Hale, she was too far gone when you came aboard."

I took his thanks to heart, glad he had recognized my efforts. "I appreciate that, sir."

He patted my shoulder affectionately. "Though you're a sailor for the moment, I do advise you to keep your instruments sharp, sir. You never know when your skills might come in handy. Once a surgeon, always a surgeon."

* * * * *

With daybreak came the clanging and banging of pots and spoons and the smell of coffee mingling with the stench of sheep, growing ever more rank. Chauncey's incomprehensible chatter bubbling up from below as she talked with Mammy doll and her odd little family of wooden spoons, who no doubt understood her completely. On deck, Hale was at the helm.

"Look there," he said. In the distance, just off the larboard bow was Mount Pelée: velvety folds of greenery draped at her feet, a shrug of soft mist enveloping her shoulders.

Turn of glass, change of watch, my belly full with Everett's gluey porridge, made palatable with a spoonful of Martinique sugar. My head rang with Dryden's rhyming verse recited in John Eli's Yankee accent. Captain Hale was at the helm now, and Everett stumping grumpily across the deck on his wooden leg. All's well and I was ready to turn in for a long morning nap.

* * * * *

"Ship ho!" Eli called down from the ratlines. "Hull up and headin' our way."

"Damnation," Hale swore. "Brother, take the helm," he said to Everett, striding to the ratlines to have a look for himself.

She was a two masted ship, a hermaphrodite brig, combining square sails and fore-and-aft sails for versatility and speed on all points of sail. She was not flying colors, but then neither were we. She could be a merchantman or a privateer. She could be British, French, Dutch, Danish, Spanish—anyone's guess. Ships could change hands quickly in these waters, sometimes captured and recaptured the same day. Nevertheless, one thing seemed certain, and that was she was coming our way.

"Go below and catch a quick wink, MacPherson. I want you fresh, you and Eli. This could get exciting."

* * * * *

I went below to my bunk in the galley but was unable to shut my eyes, much less sleep. My berth was too stuffy and hot now that we were in tropical waters. I lay sweltering in my stinking sweat-soaked shirt, feeling my stomach bubble nervously, listening to a pot in the galley bang against another pot with the motion of the ship. A nap was not to be had. Alone in the galley, I took the opportunity to bathe myself in a pail of cool water with a sliver of soap. If I stood the chance of being taken prisoner, for some strange reason I wanted to be clean.

When I returned to the deck the hermaphrodite was noticeably closer and definitely coming for us. She had the wind to her advantage. Hale looked unconcerned, and was even showing some attention to his daughter, fumbling with his big fingers to tie her bonnet. "You need to keep this on, you'll bake your brain, you hear me?"

Soon he called us all to the binnacle. "Here's the plan, men. We'll assume the worst, that it's a French privateer intent on capturing us. We keep pressing on, but don't be tempted to fall off our course to make better speed. With her square sails, she'll have the advantage if we let the wind get abaft the beam. Besides, the closer we can get to a harbor, any harbor, the better. Martinique is occupied by the British, so if they're French privateers they'd be crazy to risk boarding us so close to a commercial port. If they're British—Navy or privateers—they'll allow me to proceed to bury my wife."

"Maybe they're just traders, as we are," I suggested, hopefully.

Hale shook his head, perturbed by my ignorance. "Unlikely, Mr. MacPherson. Because of the course she sails, she plans to intercept us, and that can mean no good. I doubt a fellow merchantman is looking to share a cup of coffee with us this morning, or to engage us in a hand of cards."

"What do we do? Other than run?" asked Everett.

"We ready the guns so we don't look like a shipload of frightened hens. Make sure you've got shot, powder cartridges, slow match, and buckets of water, you know the drill. If we can get close enough to Saint Pierre there should be enough British guns afloat in the roadstead to discourage our pursuers."

"If they fire, will we answer?"

"Hell, yes we'll answer, and loudly!"

They were mad, the pair of them. And John Eli, so verbose last night on the middle watch spouting Dryden, offered nothing now, just standing there la-di-da, like he didn't have a thought in his head.

"May I say something? Doesn't the fact that they're bigger than we are with more than twice the arms and men to fire them, doesn't that give you pause?

"Hell yes it gives me pause, MacPherson; but it doesn't stop me cold. Firing these six pounders has discouraged boarders more than once. We must make them ask themselves if taking our little schooner is really worth the damage we can do in return. Now let's fly this beauty, let's give 'em a race they won't forget." Hale's voice sounded boyishly eager, as if he were enjoying himself. My mouth was dry and my palms were wet as I strained to hear Hales next command. He conned *Andromeda* with great finesse, calling to us every minute or so to sheet in or out, riding every little gust, taking advantage of every swell. I tried to resist looking over my shoulder, for it did no good to see the brigantine growing slowly larger as it inched closer, closing the gap. She was a rakish looking rig, bigger than *Andromeda*, with more muscle.

"They're French, alright," called Eli from his lookout on the ratlines, fifteen feet above the deck. "A French privateer, by their ensign. And now they're running out their leeward guns. Six of 'em. Twelve pounders, I'd say."

"Go below, Chance," Hale said to his daughter. "Go below and stay there until I tell you. Leave your dolly here with me; I've a special assignment for her. John, you and Everett will stand by on the starboard gun."

We continued on, not talking, only the swish of water, the

spray of swells cut by our bow to relieve the tense silence. Hale went below with Chauncey's ragdoll, I assumed to give it to her for comfort. He returned a few minutes later and took his place at the helm. The sheep seemed to sense danger for they began to bawl, the whole herd at once. It was a good thing the horses had already been sold, for if firing commenced they'd probably break down their stalls in blind terror.

Now we could hear the creak of their spars, the swish of water against their hull. A voice hailed us through a speaking horn and although I couldn't make out the words, the meaning was clear. The hair on my arms stiffened and I felt a portent tingling down my spine. They were almost abreast of us, and upwind. Any moment now.

Seconds later it came, a warning shot, and my stomach lurched at the boom.

"MacPherson, take the helm," Hale barked. "Maintain course and speed." I took the ship's wheel in my sweaty hands, glancing uneasily over my shoulder as Hale leaped to the sternpost and ran up the New England merchant flag, already hanked on.

"Return their fire," Hale called out, and with a pop, I heard him fire the swivel gun on the stern. Our pathetic little six-pounder and stern chaser were no match at all against their guns; yet Hale would not be so easily subdued. He would risk our lives, it appeared. I prayed for a rush of bravado to see me through.

Everett and Eli answered with a shot of chain to the fore rigging, tearing off a piece of the outer jib, a well-placed and lucky shot. A cheer burst from my own throat, more of an animal-like bellow. The sound of it sent warmth to my shaking legs and released my pent up fear. Looking at Everett standing firmly on his wooden leg as he sponged the hot gun, his face shining with sweat, his eyes fully intent on the task, I felt emboldened. My job was to keep the course and speed, keep the sails taut, the wind on my cheek.

Though we had surprised them by firing back and had ripped one of their sails, it was like hitting a wild beast with a pebble, it only served to anger them. Knowing what was coming I clenched the wheel and hunched my shoulders as a shot whistled by, followed by a great boom that felt like a huge fist striking my chest. I knew they weren't firing to sink the ship, but to kill or maim the men sailing her. The ship was valuable, the men were not, but if I were hit, I'd rather be killed straightaway, for I had seen what chain shot and grape shot can do to a man. I kept the course, staring at a dark spot on the slope of Mount Pelée, while two more cannons fired, blasting off our jackyard and destroying our tops'ls. The stinking black smoke drifted across our deck, stinging my eyes.

"Helm down!" Hale boomed, perhaps thinking of little Chauncey, about to become an orphan. "Heave to!" Then with a curse, he struck his colors and raised the white cloth of surrender.

Eli and Everett scrambled to the sheets and I turned *Andromeda* into the wind, slowing her, reining her in. Within minutes the boarders were climbing nimbly over the side, and drawing their sabers and pistols.

* * * * *

The French are so polite, even when they are robbing you blind. The first officer bid us good day and introduced himself as Lieutenant Guyon of the brig *Caprice*.

"By the letter of marque granted me by the King of France, I am seizing this vessel." Lieutenant Guyon sounded as gracious as if he were inviting us to dinner.

His English was technically perfect, his French tongue gracing it with a smoother, more mellifluous sound than any native speaker could. I believe I might have stared, for the privateer cut a striking figure in his tight silk breeches, his ruffled shirt made of a fine white lawn. I envied that shirt; the hand and the cut of it, the way it suited the tropical heat and complemented the wearer's good looks. Unlike my pale skin, which had become ruined by the sun, the French lieutenant's olive complexion had benefited from the rays.

"This is piracy," protested Hale. "The treaty has been signed, have you not heard?"

The officer laughed, with a flash of white teeth. "A good effort, Captain. However, my sources say otherwise. And so we continue our efforts for France." He touched the gilded hilt of the saber that hung at his side, a loving caress. "Now then, shall we become better acquainted? Who are you, what is this vessel, and where are you bound?"

"Dominic Hale, shipmaster, and factor. You're aboard *Andromeda*. A Rhode Island schooner bound for Martinique.

"Yankee smugglers, I suspected as much. And what are you carrying, Captain? Permit me sir, to see your manifest, *s'il vous plaît*." Yet there was no "if you please" about his request. With six armed men to enforce his whims, Hale was pressed to produce it.

"What I'm carrying is a load of grief which my manifest can't account for," Hale countered, handing over a ledger.

"Grief?" Guyon sniffed the air with his prominent, blade-like nose. "Your grief smells like livestock to me. I hardly need to look at the manifest." He turned his head and put his hand to his ear. "Sheep, I would say. Hear them bleat, poor things. No doubt, they're terrified by all the boom boom of cannon, a waste of powder and shot. Now then, Captain Hall, where is the rest of your crew?"

"It's Hale, not Hall. These three men are what's left of my crew."

"You, sir." The lieutenant addressed me with a polite nod of the head. "You're dressed like a gentleman, not a sailor. With whom do I have the pleasure of speaking?"

It's true; my clothes though dirty and worn were a cut above those of my shipmates, yet the Captain and first mate were far from being ordinary sailors. They were men of a new order, self-made in America, their homespun work clothes and unpolished speech belying both their intellect and their means.

"My name is MacPherson. Patrick MacPherson. And yes, I was born a gentleman but..." I groped for the right words. "Recent circumstances have reduced me to earning my living."

"Then you're a *matelot*? " He scrutinizing me from head to toe in one long glance and I found myself blushing.

"Well yes, in a fashion. Actually, I'm a surgeon," I blurted out. "That is, I came aboard as a surgeon."

"A surgeon aboard a schooner? Curious." Then, "Who else is aboard?"

"My dead wife," said Hale.

At that, the man's dark eyes widened.

"*Ma femme. Qui est morte*," Hale repeated, in French. Perhaps to emphasize the fact, and perhaps to show he could speak the language. "Mr. MacPherson here, was good enough to come aboard in New York at my request to attend her. But it was already too late. Nothing could be done for her." His voice thickened. "She died. I should've run up the yellow flag rather than the white one. We've been under quarantine so you might want to think twice before taking this schooner for a prize. The air below is likely still tainted."

The Frenchman was not so easily discouraged. "Yet you all are quite alive and well it seems."

"Thanks to the doctor here, who inoculated us. And the good Lord who saw fit to spare us."

The lieutenant looked to me for confirmation and I nodded. "Lieutenant Guyon, have you not heard of the recent outbreak of smallpox in New York?"

He shrugged. "Smallpox is nothing new. Down in these climes it's tropical fevers that give us pause."

"In any case," Hale interjected, "My wife's body is below, packed in salt. We're taking her to be buried in her homeland."

"Her homeland? And where is that?"

"Martinique. *Habitation Billette,* in the shadow of Mount Pelée. If you look through your telescope, just there," he pointed, "You can see my *beau-père's* cane fields, and the darker green of the coffee trees, above."

The officer did not look toward Pelée at all, but kept his keen eyes fixed upon us. "Perhaps you are telling me the truth, Captain; and perhaps you are not. Rest assured, I will find out. Meanwhile, we'll take your vessel and all that's in it, for a little excursion. A little *de tour.*" He lifted the edge of his tricorn, whether in respect or merely to cool his head, I couldn't tell. "I am very sorry about the loss of your wife, but you are not French, Mr. Hall. And neither is this vessel."

"The name's Hale, not Hall. Dominic Hale. And my wife is—was—French. Creole, that is. Born and raised on Martinique. Perhaps the name *de la Touche* means something to you, Lieutenant?"

"De la Touche?" Again, the dismissive shrug, the condescending smile. "But of course. Everyone knows the governor. What of it?"

"He's related to my wife. His wife and mine are cousins. Surely, you're familiar with the Billette Plantation? *Habitation Billette?* Guillaume Billette is my *beau-père.* He'll be watching for our arrival. Maybe he can see us now, through his telescope."

"So you think I should release you because you say your wife was some relation to the deposed governor of Martinique? A man who practically handed the keys to the city to your Rodney?" Guyon laughed and stepped into the shade of the mains'l. "Beauharnais was much more respected than de la Touche. If you said your wife was a Beauharnais, now that would be a different story altogether. A horse of a different color." He smiled and shook his head. "But then, if you said your wife was a Beauharnais I would have trouble believing it."

Hale scowled. "I warn you there will be unpleasant consequences for you if you take this vessel."

"Captain, please don't threaten me. We French privateers aren't such uncouth pirates as are your privateers. We have superiors to answer to. It will be up to our captain to decide whether to honor your rather dubious connections with the recently deposed governor—or not. "

"Why don't we go below and you can see my wife's coffin for yourself? Unless you don't want to risk breathing our contagion."

Guyon sniffed the air. "All I smell is sheep."

At that moment, Chauncey came up onto the deck crying, rubbing her eyes as if she had just woken up from a nap. Under her arm was her doll, the one I had recently repaired. Hale scooped her up in his powerful arms and whispered to her, "Don't be afraid. Chin up, there. Hold tight to your dolly, Chance."

"And who is the young miss? Your daughter?"

"My motherless daughter. Who is longing to be reunited with her *grand-père* Billette."

Guyon chose three of his men to search the vessel and they were off with a clatter, down the aft companionway. We could hear them below, rummaging about, banging open cabin doors with the butt ends of their rifles, laughing and making lewd comments about the sheep. Hale's face grew very red. I looked at Everett who returned my glance with one of despair. When the crew returned to the spar deck, they reported there was indeed a casket below—along with a herd of sheep and a hold filled with barrel staves and candles.

"*Alors*, here is what we shall do, Captain Hall. You and your company shall be guests aboard our vessel, and I shall supply a crew to sail your funeral barge. We'll render a visit to our captain to validate your story about your deceased wife's ties to the Martinique, and to see what he wishes to do with *Andromeda*. Meanwhile, we'll relieve you of a few of the sheep."

He looked to his men who were lean and hungry looking, as if they had not eaten a good meal in some time. "*Gigot d'agneau ce soir*?"

Hale fumed.

Chapter Thirty-Nine

Once aboard the privateer, we were immediately separated and confined under guard. The ship set sail downwind, toward Dominica, to some clandestine privateer hide away.

Guyon, believing me to be a gentleman in spite of my present position, took me to the great cabin and offered me a seat and a glass of brandy. "From the House of Martell," he said, tapping the cask. "On the banks of the beautiful Charente."

"Is that where you're from?" I asked. "La Charente?" A woman's question, I realized, as soon as the words left my mouth.

"Yes, the town of Cognac. And not from Saint Malo or Dunkirk, as so many of Englishmen assume. We think we know our enemies, but we are quite often mistaken, don't you agree?" His smile was engaging, but with an edge that made me wary.

"That's true. People are always making false assumptions. But why did you leave Cognac?"

He gave me that self-assured yet seductive smile and raised his glass. "I shall indulge you by answering your question. I left because there was nothing in the chaises of Martell for me. My silk pockets and silver spoon were empty. Too many older brothers and conniving brothers-in-law. I was the sixth born, what was I to do?

"One day I went downriver on a gabarre to Rochefort. I tried to join the navy, but they wouldn't have me. I had no experience, no title, no money, or influence. So, I looked to join a privateer, and found Captain Ranwez. He took me on his brig, he saw my desire and my potential, and he had faith in me. Now, four years later, I am his second in command." His eyes, I noticed, were the color of brandy, with the same glints of amber "The captain means more to me than does my own father or brothers. Is there someone who has shaped your life in that manner? Someone you would do anything for?"

That sounded like a trap I wanted to avoid. I shook my head. "No longer."

"Ah, but there once was. I knew it. Something about you reminds me of me, Mr. MacPherson. Like you, I was born a gentleman but there was nothing in it for me. Now the sea is my home, and whatever vessel I happen to command. Ships are like women that way, you know."

Oh, he was a handsome devil.

"You're rather young to be a lieutenant," I observed.

"And you are rather young to be a surgeon." Guyon parried. Swirling the brandy, he stuck his nose into the glass, nostrils flaring as he breathed in the vapors. "I took command of my first prize when I was seventeen. I barely knew stem from stern, but I knew how to command. I knew how to use the men to their best advantage, and we brought the little schooner safely into port. He took a mouthful of the golden brown spirit, and regarded me shrewdly over the rim of the glass.

I in turn, looked around at my surroundings. The great cabin had an air of shabby gentility; the antique desk of inlaid wood and gold gilt was splendid but badly water stained, the green velvet curtains faded and threadbare. The chair I sat in was one that had been in fashion a hundred years ago; it's brocade worn smooth and shiny. I turned my attention to the glass of brandy, sniffing it as Guyon had, consciously mimicking him, tasting it slowly, rolling the smooth fire around in my mouth, feeling the lovely smokiness fill my mouth and nose before swallowing.

"What do you think of the Martel?"

I nodded with feigned discernment. "Quite good, actually. A little young yet, like us. But I'm sure it will age to perfection."

"Touché, Doctor." His eyes narrowed and he leaned forward intently. "But enough about me. I want to hear about you. Come, let us be frank."

I raised my glass again and went through the ritual, buying time. "I was born a gentleman, as you so astutely guessed; but I have no income at all, no inheritance. I too, must make my living."

"Yes, but where do you call home and what circumstances threw you in with a sorry lot of New England smugglers?"

How to respond? His Majesty's frigate *Richmond* was my home, yet do I tell him that? Or leave that part of my life out. But what if one of the others tells him I served aboard *Richmond?* Maybe I should simply say I was born in Barbados and raised in England. No wonder they split us up—to question us separately to see if our stories conflicted. Yet I must take advantage of this opportunity of being held captive in the great cabin, interrogated by the striking Lieutenant Guyon over a fine brandy.

I faced him directly and met his eyes with mine. My real eyes, my woman eyes, allowing my soul to shine through; as if I were flirting with him, *faire de l'œil* as they say in French. The warmth rose, flushing my face, could he see this? Guyon was a very attractive man who knew how to manipulate his prisoner. Maybe I should tell him the truth about me; confess to being a woman in disguise and appeal to his masculinity, or his mercy. Yet that could be dangerous as well, for it would remove the respectability of being a gentleman, which Guyon had believed me to be. Being a female didn't guarantee me anything. Besides, where would that leave the *Andromedans*? We were in this together. As Patrick MacPherson, gentleman in reduced circumstances, I believed I had the most clout for myself and for my shipmates.

"I was born on the Hatterby estate in Barbados," I said with a little upper-class sniff, running my forefinger around the rim of the glass. "My grandfather was Baron Avery of Whiteparish, but my father wasn't the first son. Neither the title nor the estate passed on to me. Poor little Patrick," I said, shaking my head and affecting a pout, to make light of myself

"And so you somehow became a doctor?"

I didn't bother differentiating between physicians and surgeons, yet phrased my response with a large measure of truth, so as not to get caught in my own web of deceit. That seemed to be the best course.

"I studied medicine and surgery under one of the best physicians in all of Britain, my uncle, Aeneas MacPherson."

"And?" His fingers drummed the desktop.

"And through his influence I got a position as surgeon's mate in the Royal Navy."

"Yet you're aboard a colonial merchant vessel. A fine little schooner, but a far cry from one of King George's warships."

I told him briefly how I had come aboard the vessel as a favor to Everett Lee, and had been quarantined because of the smallpox.

"And so you're a supernumerary? Just along for the ride?"

I allowed a jaded smile. "I don't have the luxury of being

an idler. No, I'm a surgeon who stands a watch and does whatever else is asked of me."

Guyon got up to replenish our brandy.

"And would you consider yourself a good surgeon?"

"One of the best, Lieutenant."

He nodded soberly. "Then perhaps we can come to an arrangement, you and I. If peace talks are underway between England and France as is rumored, let us follow suit with a compromise of our own."

"Who is the patient?"

He smiled. "You'll find out shortly, I must first consult with our captain. We're on our way to see him now; but meanwhile, we have an hour or two to kill. Do you play backgammon, Doctor? Shall we pass the time engaging our little armies of stone?"

Men and their games. I smiled indulgently, as if I were the captor and he the captive, settling in, crossing my legs and stretching my arm casually over the back of the chair. "Let's have at it, Lieutenant."

His warm eyes fixed upon me. "My pleasure, Doctor." Without breaking eye contact, he pulled a board out of a drawer in his desk and placed it between us. Tossing me the pouch of black checkers, he then began to set up the white ones on his side of the board.

"We are like the little checkers, are we not? Arranged by the hand of fate, we go to war for our kings so they can rule more land, so they can control the seas. We are just so many little black and white checkers to be raced around the board and born away, *n'est pas*?"

"And who will win? Black or White?" I asked.

"It doesn't really matter, who wins. It's all about the game, and there will be another game after this one, and another after that. Frankly, I rather like playing war, Doctor. My affairs, my life, depend on it."

I set up my own men, wondering if he was somehow trying to bait me—or was he just a jaded privateer, weary of a long war that had not been profitable for him.

"Let us see who has the advantage of the first move. Be my guest, Doctor."

Shaking the one ivory die in my horn cup, I rolled out a two. Guyon rolled a four, and so had the first play.

"So much in this world depends on chance, *non?*" He moved his pieces, smiling happily at this small success.

"But luck changes," I said. "Of that you can be sure."

The afternoon wore on, the rattle and roll of dice muffled by the ringing in my head cause by the brandy. Concentrating on his strategy, Guyon chewed his beautiful bottom lip. I took chances, my pile of black stones growing. Then the boat slowed and a rap came at the cabin door.

"Please excuse me, Doctor."

He left me under the watchful eye of one of his guards and went up on deck where the squeak of blocks told me a boat was being lowered. There were voices and the splash of oars, followed by an occasional little jolt and sensation of dragging as the keel nudged a sandbar. We were being towed through a narrow, shallow channel, perhaps to some secluded hiding spot, for which these islands are famous. Through the stern lights, I saw overhanging mangrove branches and coconut fronds. Soon Guyon sent for me.

"It's been a pleasure Doctor, and I do hope we meet again someday. Under different circumstances and in different disguises." With a knowing smile, he disappeared below and I was transferred from the brigantine to a smaller vessel, a lugger moored in shallow water at the head of the sheltered cove.

* * * * *

Inside the lugger's aft cabin, I was brought to face the captain, who had heard Guyon's report. It was late in the afternoon now; golden sunlight streamed through the stern gallery where a large black cat napped. Captain Ranwez sat behind the desk, his wigless head cradled in his hands. His once handsome features were creased and sagging from the weight of age, and pinched too, with pain. The man was in agony; I needed no interpreter for that. His face spoke it well. The grey stubble on his chin hadn't felt a razor for at least two days. He wore no stock and his rumpled shirt was open at the neck, indecorous for a French officer. The soft nest of curls below the hollow of his throat glistened with perspiration. The man was wrapped up in his pain like a blanket, nearly incapacitated by it.

"You're in pain," I remarked.

He grimaced and touched his left cheek. *"Il s'agit d'un mauvais dent."*

"A bad tooth is understood in any language. My sympathies."

"My lieutenant has told me the honorable thing for me to do would be to release your schooner so that you may go to Martinique to bury the Creole woman. Right at this moment I'm not feeling very honorable, Doctor. I'm feeling rather, how do you say it... spiteful. Obstinate." The very effort of talking seemed to take a toll and he closed his eyes as if to gather his strength to continue.

"I would be much more inclined to be honorable, however, if you would reciprocate."

"What do you propose?"

"What do I propose? Pull this goddamn tooth out of my throbbing jaw, that's what I propose. Be a gentleman and relieve me of my misery and I shall be a gentleman and release you and your beautiful little schooner so that you can go bury Madame Hall in the hallowed ground of her parish. An eye for an eye and a tooth for a ship, how's that?"

"And my shipmates?"

"Yes, yes, the pack of you," he snapped. "Now let's have it done before I just go blow my head off and let my men do what they will with you and the ship."

"I'll need my instruments. And a medicine chest, if you have one."

"You shall have them." He ordered one of his men to fetch my supplies and three others to stand guard while I worked—I suppose to make sure I didn't slit his throat with my scalpel.

"This is one of the worst cases I've ever seen," I said, peering into his stinking mouth. "You're at risk for blood poisoning. The second molar seems to be the culprit. I'll remove it, of course. But first, you would benefit from a poultice." I knew if the procedure were too quick, it might cheapen the price. I didn't want the captain to reconsider his offer.

"Well then, get to it immediately."

"But surely you have a surgeon of your own aboard? A well-manned fleet such as yours."

"I've had to dismiss my last two surgeons for being immoderate with their bottle. What is it with your profession, Monsieur? So many of you are drunkards."

"Captain," I smiled, "May I suggest it's unwise to offend the man who is preparing to work inside your mouth with sharp instruments?"

He returned my smile with a weak one of his own. "*Vous avez raison.* It was just an observation."

"Surely there must be a few sober surgeons on Martinique."

He shrugged and sighed. "But your price is more affordable to me. Besides, you are here now and they are hours away. The roads are terrible and by now, they are all deep in their drink. Not to mention the whole island is crawling with red coats. They watch for us like cats for mice."

When my haversack arrived, the guard pulled out my few effects, including the gown and bonnet, along with my surgical kit.

"What is this costume?" The captain demanded.

"The dead woman's clothes," I lied. "I wouldn't touch them if I were you. I should have thrown them overboard; they're likely infested with smallpox." I shrugged. "But I thought they might be of value."

The guard hastily stuffed them back into the haversack, which he passed to me as quickly as he could, looking perfectly aghast. I retrieved my surgical kit, inspecting it to make certain all the instruments were there. The toothkey, I noticed, showed a speck of corrosion though I had just polished it a few days ago.

It must come out easily, without undue pain. Preferably in one piece. It wouldn't be good if I had to go digging with the scalpel and tenaculum. Our freedom depended on a successful extraction.

"Some spirits, sir? To dull the nerves?"

He shook his head. "That's been seen to. I've enough of Guyon's brandy on board to numb a mule, yet it hasn't helped a bit. You may proceed, sir."

I rolled up my sleeves and his guards moved in for a closer look.

The lugger's medicine chest held little of value. I found some oil of cinnamon and soaked a cotton pledget with it. This would not only cleanse the gum but would shrink the swelling and dull the sensation. It also sweetened the foul stench coming from the oozing pus. While the cinnamon did its work, I prepared a tincture of hyssop to follow the extraction, to sooth the empty socket and reduce any bleeding. The men watched with morbid curiosity. Next, I readied my instruments, picking each one up and holding it to the light for inspection, more for dramatic effect than anything else. A thick roll of gauze doused with a few drops of cinnamon oil to keep his mouth from clamping down, should he reflexively try to bite me. Now I was ready.

"I'll need one good fellow to hold the captain's head, from behind like this, to support his neck and to counter my force." A stout lad raised his hand and I gave him the honor. "Hold firmly now; *comprenez-vous*? Gently but firmly."

The boy moved into position and the captain opened his jaws once again. I removed the pledget and dropped it into my silver bleeding bowl, placed the roll of gauze in the opposite corner of his mouth. Took another good look at the offending tooth, probed it with my finger to determine how much pressure would be needed. At my touch, he flinched and tears welled in the corners of his eyes. No matter that Captain Ranwez was the enemy and held me captive; at that moment I felt pity for him and wanted to relieve his pain. Picking up the toothkey, I slid it over the offending molar and tightened it, causing the patient to say something, probably a curse. But good placement was essential, as was a firm grip, physical strength, and speed. So much of my work depended on these—and luck, which was worth as much as all of the above. I was confident in my skill, speed, and strength, so I prayed for luck.

"Ready sir?"

Mouth wide, he grunted his assent.

I gripped the key in both hands and pulled with all my might. The captain gasped and groaned, yet I felt the tooth give way and held it up, rotten roots dangling and dripping blood, for all to see before tossing it into the pan. *Fait accompli.* I hoped no one noticed that my knees were shaking.

Chapter Forty

Captain Ranwez made good on his word. The privateers left us in the middle of the Dominica Channel where we made our way to the Saint Pierre roadstead and anchored by the light of a rising moon.

Below decks we found Mrs. Hale's coffin was undisturbed, as were ship stores and our personal effects. But Guyon's men had taken the sheep, every last one, as well as the barrel staves and candles—a heavy financial loss for Hale and the other investors, but not as bad as if they had taken the boat as well. Captain Hale's stash of coins from the sale of the pacers was safe where he had planted them, inside the ample body of Chauncey's rag doll.

"Where was your frigate today when we needed her, eh MacPherson?" He goaded. "Not to be found, no sir. We had to save ourselves and once again your surgical skills have served us well."

Indeed, and I was glad he acknowledged my role.

"Now then, Doc, since you're so handy with a needle and catgut why don't you help Mr. Eli repair our tops'l?"

* * * * *

Later, while my shipmates were taking inventory of their personal belongings, I went forward and climbed out on the bowsprit to be alone with my thoughts. So much had happened in such a short time, I longed for a pair of strong arms to comfort me. Instead, I felt a light tap on my shoulder, a child's hand.

"Good evening Chauncey," I said, wiping my eyes on my sleeve before looking over my shoulder to give her a smile. "You're still awake?" Her eyes too, were bright with tears. I moved outboard, making room for her beside me on the spar. "Are you in need of a good stout shoulder?" I stretched out my arm and she took hold of it, pulling herself closer. We sat in silence wiping furtively at our cheeks.

"Are you my uncle too?" She said at last, and somehow I understood her perfectly.

"You may call me Uncle, it would be an honor. Uncle Pat, I am." My first promotion aboard *Andromeda*.

* * * * *

We supped on ship biscuit, hard cheese, and beer, begrudging the Frenchmen their leg of lamb at our expense. It had been a harrowing day and tomorrow Hale must go to shore and arrange for the burial. We were a morose lot, yet ashore there was much revelry on this Saturday evening. We could hear the gaiety of the British soldiers and sailors along the waterfront, the animated voices in the boats going to and from shore. Who knew how long the occupation would last? This game was nearly over; Martinique was a playing card, a chip, soon to be cashed in. As Lieutenant Guyon had said, we are checkers to be born away, let the new game begin.

Anchored in the middle of the roadstead like a sleeping swan, gun ports closed and sails neatly furled, was Rear Admiral Rodney's new flagship *Foudroyant*, a French prize assigned to him after his *Marlborough* had been given to Rear Admiral Pocock for the Havana mission. The 80 gun ship of the line looked to us like a floating castle. I thought of the hundreds of men, and dozens of women, who called her home and what they were all doing tonight. Did their gunner have a wife, and were they already in their snug little cabin, or out on the town this fine Saturday night.

Here on *Andromeda* we tapped a new cask of rum.

"Ha! That's one thing the French bastards didn't help themselves to; but only because they're drowning in it here."

"Is it true what you said, Captain? About your wife being related to the Governor?"

"Possibly," he said, scraping the mold off a wedge of cheese with the side of his knife. "Half the island is related. I'll have to ask the Old Billette; he claims all sorts of connections."

Behind the waterfront gaiety, we could hear the throb of drums, barely discernable, like a heartbeat. Somewhere the Africans were celebrating a feast day or a marriage, the French planters being more inclined than the British to encourage matrimony among their people. No one used the word "slaves" in polite society, preferring words that are more palatable. In the French islands they were called *les noir*, or even *les sujets*—subjects—as if each planter ruled his own little kingdom of loyal serfs. And what of the mulattoes? To which world did they belong?

Recalling Mrs. Hale's features, I suspected she had been of mixed blood, and Hale had probably met her right here in Saint Pierre. Chauncey was a child of two worlds, of Martinique and Rhode Island, and in which world would she be happiest, where would she thrive? Ah, why did I concern myself with a child who was not my own?

One by one, we stumbled off to bed, Hale sleeping on deck to make sure the anchor was set.

* * * * *

I awoke to the pealing of Saint Pierre's church bells and the sound of voices overhead. The captain had just come back from shore with news. We had been given permission to tie up at the docks to unload his wife's casket; a boat was standing by to row us in. With a great flurry of activity Everett, John, and I set up bow and spring lines and raised the anchor.

Before we went ashore I saw to it that Chauncey washed her face and hands and I trimmed her fingernails, then took a comb to her dark and tangled mop. While the others were shaving, I got out my scalpel and, with the promise of sugar as a reward, I neatly severed the thick fold of skin that bound her tongue. She was a little surprised, in fact, she nearly bit me; but it was done in a wink, and I gave her a whole cone of sugar, from the galley supplies. The incision would heal quickly, as all mucosal wounds tend to do. By tomorrow, she will have forgotten all about it. She would still need training to speak more clearly, but at least the physical limitation had been corrected, and with far less difficulty than untangling her hair.

"Now then, be a good girl and go put on your clean dress. And don't forget your bonnet and shoes; you must be a proper young lady today when you go ashore. Hurry now, Papa is waiting."

* * * * *

The five of us accompanied the coffin to shore where a horse and wagon waited. We followed the cart to the churchyard, our procession growing longer with townspeople as we walked through the streets. The word had spread to old friends and neighbors, most of them mulattoes, and the poorer sort of whites. There would be no vigil at the plantation house on the windward side of the island where her father lived, The roads, such as they were, were steep and poor, rutted and overgrown with vegetation. Why take the casket all the way to the plantation for a night, only to haul it all the way back to town for burial? I suspected there was another reason.

Marguerite had been Billette's natural daughter, good enough to be received into the hallowed ground of the Catholic churchyard, yet not legitimate—not good enough to be welcomed into her father's parlor as a true daughter. We *Andromedans* stood with the large crowd in the cemetery, a motley collection of artisans, tradesmen, schoolmasters, and merchants, most of them mulattoes. Only a few planters attended, a little clot of them, at the back with Monsieur Billette himself. They knew how it was. They probably had fathered such accidents themselves. It was an embarrassing little fact of life.

* * * * *

Back aboard ship, that afternoon Hale broke the news to us. We would weigh anchor now and sail to the other side of the island, to a cove near Marigot, where we would take on molasses he purchased with the silver from the sale of the horses. Tonight we'd start back for Rhode Island, if the weather allowed.

"Alright, let's prepare to cast off."

"But wait, where's Chauncey?" I looked to Everett, but he looked away, biting his lip.

Then Hale dropped the bomb. "Chauncey won't be coming with us."

I was stunned. "You can't be serious!" I burst. "You'd leave her here on Martinique?"

For once, the captain spoke softly. He looked out across the water, toward town. "She needs a woman's touch. With her mother dead and the situation being what it is. My own mother is dead, and I have no sisters."

"But who will take care of her better than you? Surely not Billette—he barely recognizes her as his own grandchild."

"The nuns, Doctor. Better than I. How can I possibly raise a daughter aboard a ship?"

"You'd actually put her away in a convent?" I looked to Everett and John, to get their support, but they busied themselves with the davits, preparing to bring aboard the boat.

"You make it sound like it was a prison sentence instead of the honor it is. And it took some influence on old Billette's part to get her in—not to mention money. He's got a heart, but he can't very well take her in himself. The Sisters will do her good. I'm not of that religion myself; my own father was a Quaker, though I've strayed far from that. But her mother was raised in that church. She won't have to take vows or wear a habit. It's just a good, safe place—and what the hell am I explaining myself to you for!" he thundered.

"But she's just lost her mother and now she's to lose her father too?"

"Do you have a better suggestion?" He said, his voice had found its usual strength. "Do you want to put on a petticoat and be her nursemaid? Why is it that young men who ain't yet fathers are full of advice about how to be a good one."

"I'm sorry if I've overstepped my bounds. I've just become fond of the girl and I worry for her welfare," I said lamely.

Hale scratched his head. "Look MacPherson. Patrick. I appreciate your concern for Chauncey; but she's going wild growing up aboard ship, you've seen it yourself. My wife and I had been talking about it before she took sick. About living ashore and raising Chauncey proper, instead of letting her gallivant in the rigging, not to mention the chance of drowning, of getting captured. A few more runs and I'll be in a better position. I'll hire a shipmaster. I'll build a house. In a few years, I'll send for her, when she's old enough to look after herself. Until then, I'll rest a hell of a lot easier knowing she's safe in the convent. It's all settled, I..." His throat caught and he turned it into a cough, but his eyes were glistening and red and he turned away, pretending to inspect one of the halyards, looking for a fray.

"Now then, we've got sugar to load. The land breeze has come up, let's weigh anchor and make sail. The factor and his porters will be waiting."

Chapter Forty-One

Homeward bound with a hold half filled with Martinique molasses, which would fetch a good price in New England where the distilleries couldn't get enough of it. We weren't carrying as much as we might have, had the privateers not taken the sheep and the staves, but we should make enough to break even.

It was too quiet aboard, with the horses and sheep gone, and Chauncey not among us. Although we continued our discussion of politics and philosophy around the saloon table or on deck, we were all aware of her absence. Everett took too much comfort in his rum, I thought, and told him so.

"I'm not cut out for the sea," he said. "The galley slave's life is not for me. As soon as I get my back pay, I'm buying a printing press. I'm starting a newspaper. I'll spend my time in the coffee houses of Providence gathering the gossip. I'll post sardonic essays under the pen name M. Aurelius, emperor at large."

"Our mother had a way with words," Dominic admitted. "And your father had the gift of gab. Maybe you inherited a little of both. Either way, your writing has got to be better than your cooking."

"A newspaper and a cup of good Arabica at the Water Street Tavern sounds pretty good right now," added the first mate. "As does a full night's sleep in a dry bed. A little female companionship would be nice too, as long as I'm dreaming."

* * * * *

Three days out, horrid weather battered us continually, drenching us with cloudbursts. We had doused the tops'ls and were crashing through choppy seas. It was difficult to keep a course. I went below for a cup of coffee. Standing against the still warm stove, I heard a clatter in the storage locker. Thinking something was improperly stowed and had been shaken loose by the rough passage, I knelt down and opened the locker to secure the offending article. There, to my great surprise, I spied a grimy face peering out at me— Chauncey, a forlorn little stowaway, drinking the dregs of our coffee and gnawing on a biscuit!

My heart leapt with surprise and joy, I laughed out loud. "Why, Chauncey Hale!" To my delight, she threw her arms around my neck and squeezed tight.

"But how did you manage to get aboard without us knowing it?"

When she spoke, her mangled words were easy enough for me to understand. "Somebody helped me."

"Who? Who helped you?"

Her dark eyes fell. "It's a secret. I promised not to tell. Uncle Pat, tell Daddy not to be angry with me."

Now it was I who was mute, unable to speak past the hot lump in my throat.

* * * * *

The wind had picked up to nearly gale force. Having doused the tops'ls and the jib, we ploughed through steepening seas under a reefed main, fores'l, and fore stays'l, making little headway but keeping our course. We were coming up the Florida straits, studded with low-lying islands, and submerged reefs. Hale himself had the helm.

"Captain, I must speak to you." Beneath my sodden overcoat, I shivered, my teeth chattering.

"What? Are we about to collide? Is the ship taking on water?"

"No, she sails well enough."

He wiped the spray from his eyes and pulled his hat down further. We hadn't seen such miserable weather the entire voyage.

"I think you should hear this," I persisted.

"Out with it, then."

"We've a stow-away, sir."

"Damn it, this is no time for games, MacPherson. Don't tell me you've brought aboard a goddamn monkey, or a puppy, or some other nuisance. We haven't seen the worst of this, look at those clouds."

"Yes, I know." I hunched my shoulders against the wet wind. "I went below for my coat and... well... it's your daughter, sir."

"What about her?" He bellowed.

"Chauncey's aboard; she managed to stow herself away. She must've followed you back from the convent. I found her hidden away in the galley."

Hale's face darkened, nearly purple, and then paled. He squinted as he examined my face. "Did you have a hand in this?"

"No," I shot back. "I did not; but I must say I'm glad she's here and I hope you won't be too hard on her, Captain. She's only a child, a child who so recently lost her mother. I think she..."

"She is my daughter, MacPherson," Hale interrupted. "In case you've forgotten," he thundered against the wind. "And she has disobeyed me. But I ain't the ogre you seem to think." He chewed his lip for a moment. "Is she all right?"

"Hungry and frightened. But yes, quite alright."

"Ha! Well, I'm a son of a bitch. Imagine that!" The look on his face was one of relief, and pride in her defiance, her resourcefulness, and will.

I wanted to tell Hale that I too, was female. That she would be all right here on *Andromeda*, with her family. But that talk was for later, in a warm galley over coffee and rum. Right now, we had a ship to keep on course and off of lee shores.

* * * * *

It promised to be a long night of stormy weather, a night of continual sail handling, of reefing or handing, then raising and trimming, a night of careful helmsmanship. A shivery night, drenched to the skin with an eye out for uncharted reefs, for privateers and revenue cutters. The wind was fickle, veering first, then backing, as if unable to make up its mind which way it wanted to blow. Each gust became stronger, threatening to knock us down.

Hale, at the helm, roared "Ease sheets" and I hurried to the bitts willingly, with a little burst of joy in my heart as I slid across the wet deck in my slippery second hand shoes. I don't believe I could ever sail on a ship and remain aloof from its labor. No longer a reluctant passenger, I felt truly one of the company now—one of the *Andromedans*.

The hemp line burned my bare hands. Feeling the sheet pull against the power of the wind, I felt another pull on the invisible cord connecting the *Richmond's* gunner and I across miles of water. The world was enormous but it was mostly water, and water connected everything. Surely, it would bring Brian and I together again. Meanwhile I took comfort knowing that Chauncey was below decks making a mess of Everett's galley, playing with Mammy and her odd little family of wooden spoons.

Hold course and weather the storm; that was all we could do just now. With any luck, tomorrow would find us a little closer to home.

DON'T MISS ALL OF THE EXCITING BOOKS IN THE FIGHTING SAIL SERIES BY

ALARIC BOND

His Majesty's Ship

A powerful ship, a questionable crew, and a mission that must succeed.

In the spring of 1795 HMS Vigilant, a 64 gun ship-of-the-line, is about to leave Spithead as senior escort to a small, seemingly innocent, convoy. The crew is a jumble of trained seamen, volunteers, and the sweepings of the press; yet, somehow, the officers have to mold them into an effective fighting unit before the French discover the convoy's true significance.

Jackass Frigate

How do you maintain discipline on a ship when someone murders your first lieutenant—and a part of you agrees with their action?

For Captain Banks the harsh winter weather of 1796 and threat of a French invasion are not his only problems. He has an untried ship, a tyrant for a First Lieutenant, a crew that contains at least one murderer, and he is about to sail into one of the biggest naval battles in British history—the Battle of Cape St. Vincent.

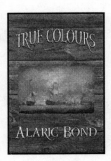

True Colours

While Great Britain's major home fleets are immobilised by a vicious mutiny, Adam Duncan, commander of the North Sea Squadron, has to maintain a constant watch over the Dutch coast, where a powerful invasion force is ready to take advantage of Britannia's weakest moment.

With ship-to-ship duels and fleet engagements, shipwrecks, storms and groundings, True Colours maintains a relentless pace that culminates in one of the most devastating sea battles of the French Revolutionary War—the Battle of Camperdown.

All Fireship Press books are available directly through our website, amazon.com, via leading bookstores from coast-to-coast, and from all major distributors in the U.S., Canada, the UK, and Europe.

CPSIA information can be obtained at www.ICGtesting.com
Printed in the USA
LVOW041845230112

265193LV00004B/63/P